TRVE CVLT

MICHAEL BETTENDORF

Cover Art by Echo Echo
Interior Illustrations by Matt Blairstone with M. Bettendorf
Edited by Alex Woodroe

Content warnings are available at the end of this book. Please consult this list for any particular subject matter you may be sensitive to.

Published by Tenebrous Press.
Visit our website at www.tenebrouspress.com.

Production of this novel was made possible in part by a grant from the Regional Arts & Culture Council. Visit https://racc.org/ for more information.

First Printing, September 2024.

The characters and events portrayed in this work are fictitious. Any similarity to real persons, living or dead, is coincidental and not intended by the author.

Print ISBN: 978-1-959790-23-5
eBook ISBN: 978-1-959790-24-2

Cover art by Echo Echo

Interior illustrations by Matt Blairstone with Michael Bettendorf.

Edited by Alex Woodroe.

Formatting by Lori Michelle.

All creators in this publication have signed an AI-free agreement. To the best of our knowledge, this publication is free from machine-generated content.

Selected Works from Tenebrous Press:

From the Belly
a novel by Emmett Nahil

Mouth
a novella by Joshua Hull

Lumberjack
a novella by Anthony Engebretson

Posthaste Manor
a novel by Jolie Toomajan & Carson Winter

The Black Lord
a novella by Colin Hinckley

Dehiscent
a novella by Ashley Deng

House of Rot
a novella by Danger Slater

Agony's Lodestone
a novella by Laura Keating

Soft Targets
a novella by Carson Winter

Crom Cruach
a novella by Valkyrie Loughcrewe

Lure
a novella by Tim McGregor

One Hand to Hold, One Hand to Carve
a novella by M.Shaw

More titles at www.TenebrousPress.com

For Nicole—for all the times you've heard *The Mantle*

AUTHOR'S NOTE:

Several years ago, I wrote a note to myself to "write a black metal book" but had nothing beyond that in mind. I had another note about "Cult Road" which is an urban legend of a road that may or may not exist in my hometown. We looked, of course. Not sure if anyone ever truly found it. Then one summer my buddies Trevor, Steve, and I went looking for it. We loaded into Steve's pick up and drove around the outskirts of town where a supposed cult was said to have met. Carried torches. Sacrificed animals. Did the whole druid-robe thing. We never found them, but we did find an abandoned farmhouse. It was terrifying. Even in the summer heat in broad daylight, that house was abysmally dark. Suffocating. Completely desolate.

Skip nearly twenty years to the week before StokerCon 2023, when Alex told me to have a pitch ready for her and Matt when we finally got to meet. She said something along the lines of, "make it weird, be experimental." It was the final piece. I finally knew what the black metal book had to be about. Where it would be set. Why I had to write it.

Black metal has a storied past, full of white nationalism, violence, anti-organized religion, Satanism, and the occult. It's also inherently silly, in my opinion. A genre full of weirdos who often take themselves so incredibly seriously. This book does not condone, nor support, the opinions of Nazis. Neither do I. I purposefully didn't put that shit in here because with the rise of white nationalism in the U.S., I'm tired of them. Black metal deserves better. You all deserve better. They don't deserve the attention.

YOU'VE BEEN HERE before. This pit. This blackened headspace where all of your memories are blurry. They're jumbled and soft-edged and don't fit together like they should, but instead, they melt into one another until they become a collage of mental ichor that resembles everything you know and yet nothing at all. Maybe that's all life is. A dance between everything and nothing.

It's hard to tell how long you've been awake. There are no windows in this room, a term you use loosely. It's more of a closet. It's pitch dark, and judging by the fire webbing across your skull, you believe that's for the best. Your teeth are gritty, and your tongue feels heavy and bloated, weighed down by whisky breath and poor decisions.

You feel around for anything within arm's reach. Something to align your senses and give you any hint where you are. To your left, a box of bottles clinks together. Soft cloth—robes—hang above you. Candles, some smooth, some disfigured, wicks crispy, lay spilled all over the floor. Despite the fog of a brutal hangover, you're beginning to piece it together. A wedding reception, not just another night of getting fucked up because there was nothing else to do.

Your stomach writhes in cruel response.

The deafening chord from an organ vibrates into the small, enclosed room. Soon, there's chanting. You burp. Bile snakes its way up your throat, coating your esophagus in venom. You choke it down. Oh fuck, you know nothing good is going to come from this.

Both the hymn and the pressure in your gut crescendo.

You stand—instinctual, but too quickly—and you know it's now or never.

You run to find a bathroom—
go to pg 3

You take a deep breath and wait it
out—go to pg 4

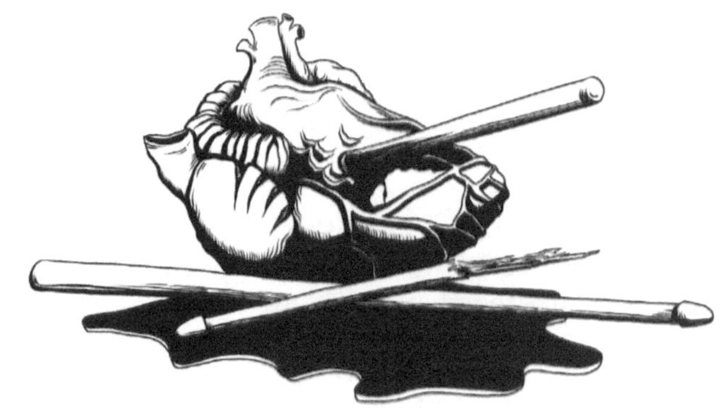

IN A LIGHTHEADED DAZE, you stumble into the wall. A candle flattens into a waxy smudge beneath your feet, reminding you of animal fat. You've grossly underestimated how drunk you still are and overcompensate while trying to regain your balance. There are hushed whispers outside the room, audible despite the organ music. Feet shuffle outside the door while your legs become tangled in a robe, obliterating your balance once again.

The door opens, and you squint in the brilliant morning light bleeding into the sanctuary as you fall to your hands and knees.

There are gasps.

The organ stops abruptly, giving you center stage as you shower the pastor in puke.

Someone in the background can be heard saying, "Holy shit."

"Hi, dad," you say.

You take the robe at your feet and use it first to wipe your mouth, then to sop up the vomit filling the sanctuary with vile fumes. Guttural screams bellow behind a wall of drums, tinny and harsh, from your pocket. You grip the phone through your clothes trying to stop the incoming call. Fumbling through the entanglement of robes, you yank the phone from your pocket and answer. Austin's voice bursts through the speaker, "What the fuck is up? I've got killer fucking news."

Everyone knows there's fuckall to do in your quiet Midwestern town but go to church or cause chaos, and you've managed to do both at the same time.

GREAT JOB!—GO TO PG 5

YOU DON'T WANT to puke, but you absolutely do not want to go out there. Not right now. So you take a deep breath and do your best to recenter yourself. Black Sabbath's *Black Sabbath* plays through your mind for solace, but it's no use.

You drop to your knees, feeling around the darkness. You consider taking off your shoes and doing what needs to be done, but it doesn't come to that. Your fingertips graze a wooden bowl behind you, wedged into the corner. The song continues to play in your mind. The distorted riffs pound at your booze-addled brain. Your stomach. Sweat drenches your forehead and slicks your back. You feel it—*Oh, noooo*—and fill the offering plate with sour sludge.

There's a hushed silence outside of the makeshift vestry as the organ music stops. Slowly, the realization of where you are becomes perfectly clear.

You wipe your mouth and blow your nose on one of the robes. All that's left to do is ride out the rest of the service and sneak home. You feel around for one of the bottles and uncap the screw-on lid. A little bit of the hair of the dog while you wait.

You swish and spit the first couple of gulps, but then you take a long pull from the blood of Christ. The door opens. The light pouring in around the pastor is offensive. He looks at you—at the offering plate at your feet, vile fumes rising to meet his upturned nose, and mutters a disappointed, "Jesus Christ." He takes the bottle from your hand. "Go take a walk."

You think about apologizing, but all that comes out is, "Hey, dad."

Oof.—Go to pg 8

YOUR DAD PLACES a hand underneath your armpit and helps you to your feet, while he motions for some assistance with the mess on the floor. He's apologizing to the congregation for the inconvenience, but all you hear is *for my fuckup child. The inconvenience. The problem. The thorn in my side. The lost sheep.*

Your dad isn't the corporal punishment type of parent. He backhands you with words. The ones spoken with subtle contempt, and the worst—those that aren't spoken at all.

You think about asking him if he's proud of you, even though you know the answer in this moment. But at least you'd hear the words. The acknowledgement.

Shrugging off your dad's embrace, you glance back and lock eyes with your mother whose hardened steel eyes scream, despite her indignant silence. Parishioners hem and haw, forming their own blathering choir. The last thing you hear as you take a rear door out of the sanctuary is *can you imagine?*

You can't count how many times you've heard that phrase muttered about you—around you—but never to you. Never with you. To learn who you are. The piercings. Your musical tastes. The closet full of black shirts. The tattoos.

Can you imagine?

You don't have to because you aren't imaginary.

***

It's weird that Austin called you. The last time you hung out, things got out of hand over some bullshit. It was always bullshit with Austin. Usually, it was over a disagreement about a band that he took personally. Like any difference in opinion was an attack on his personality. Everything he believed was true. Objective. There was no alternative.

You walk outside and weave through minivans until you reach your own—a mid-90s Chevy Lumina APV the color of your grandma's lipstick—purchased not to tote around future kids, but your drum set.

Your set hasn't been touched in over a year.

The small rectangular front screen on your phone reads: *3 Missed Calls*. All from Austin. You wonder what he wants, because you know he isn't calling to apologize. There's a couple of bottles of water rolling around the floor. You drain one. Then the other.

You text your friend Ryan even though you're out of monthly texts and you're going to be charged extra for it. Talking on the phone just doesn't appeal to you right now. All you say is, *I'm coming over.*

The aftermarket six-disc changer cycles to disc three, aligning with the year 1993. The year Cynic released *Focus*. The album that Austin called pretentious. The one he threw across his basement like a frisbee when you tried to play it for Ryan.

***

Ryan sits and smokes on the front steps of his red-brick duplex. He taps ash from his cigarette and drinks from a coffee mug.

"Want some?" he asks.

Your mouth is clammy and your breath is a fire hazard.

"Yeah," you say. "Thanks."

Ryan stubs his cigarette out on the bottom step and flicks the butt into a rusting Folgers can. He leads you inside. Someone you don't recognize is asleep on the futon. Ryan's tabby lurks behind his 5150 half-stack and stares. Ryan pulls a mug from the cupboard. It reads: *Fuck That's Hot* in bold yellow font that slowly bleeds red as he pours hot coffee into the mug.

"Rough night?" he asks.

You laugh.

"You stay for the whole reception? You wandered away. Figured you went home."

"I woke up in a closet *during* the morning service. Fucking puked communion wine and whisky all over my dad."

"Holy shit."

"Yeah," you say. "Why didn't Austin show?"

Ryan pours another cup of coffee and motions toward the front door, "Let's talk."

***

"So he wants me back in the band?" you ask.

"He needs you. Toni's going on her honeymoon and we don't have a drummer. At least not one that can keep up."

"Then wait till she gets back," you say.

"That's the thing. Waste Doctrine is swinging through town for some fucking reason and we're going to open for them. Could be our shot at impressing a signed band. Maybe they'll let us in on this leg of the tour. That's why Austin bailed on the wedding. He's been planning for the show. Putting some really weird shit together."

"How so?"

Ryan takes a long drag off a cigarette, "I'll show you. Let's go."

CONTINUE—GO TO PG 12

YOU SNEAK OUT of the sanctuary through a door behind the pulpit. The congregation's collective whispering turns into a choir of nosy gossip as your dad fights to regain control of his flock. You wade through the back of the church past classrooms of kids who don't know any better. You can't blame them. Not yet anyway.

You make it to the parking lot full of minivans and SUVs when your phone starts blaring tinny blast beats. The screen reads *Austin* and you hesitate to pick up.

Things got heated the last time you hung out. It always tended to happen with Austin. One drink too many and all of a sudden, any disagreement was taken personally. God forbid you didn't like an album he was into, or worse—liked one he didn't.

Your ringtone continues to scream. By the time you reach your van—purchased to stash your drums—the signal drops momentarily before the song starts over as you slide your key into the door. You answer, not to talk to Austin, but to quiet the noise. At least that's what you tell yourself.

"Hello?"

"Where the fuck are you? I'm at your place," Austin says. "We need to talk."

"At church," you say, but you continue before he can give you shit. "Not like that. I blacked out in the sanctuary at Toni's wedding last night. Which, by the way, you fucking bailed on."

You knew Austin was invited and you knew he had shit-else to do, so why wasn't he there?

"Toni's folks shelled out for an open bar," you say.

"Whatever, good for her," he says. "I had shit to do."

You rummage around the floor for a water bottle while Austin hypes some opportunity.

"All right," you say. "So spill. What was so important you had to miss her wedding?"

Excitement alters Austin's typically monotone tenor. It's a rare enthusiasm you aren't used to hearing and it sounds almost distorted through your phone.

"Waste Doctrine is going to play a show here. Fucking here," he says. "And we're going to open for them."

"Didn't think I was in the band anymore," you say. "Something about me being a *poser bitch*."

"Forget that, we're cool."

Toni replaced you forever ago and you may be hungover, but you're smart enough to know she'll be honeymooning, so you ask, "When's the show?"

"Next week."

Ah, there it is. Confirmation for what you already knew—Austin needs you. You know he'll never say it, but hearing the tone of his voice shift from elation to near-desperation, his mood hanging on the precipice of your response, is enough for you.

"This could be big," he says.

And you agree.

Maybe you can finally leave this town. Tour with a signed band. Impress a label. You're well aware that metal bands rarely break even. Deep down, it isn't about the money though, is it? It's about getting out of your hometown. Making something of yourself. Crushing the bones of dissatisfaction beneath your heel. Doing something other than work at a call center because Associate's degrees just don't cut it these days. *This* . . . could be the catalyst you've been waiting for.

You're beat down. You need this. This push. This drive to shove all of the aspirations—the ones your parents tried to instill, not the ones you carefully cultivated over time—into the ground to be buried here where they will rot.

Then, a thought surfaces to the forefront of your mind. You're a bit shocked Austin wants any part of this—the spectacle—because it's antithetical to his authentic sensibilities. And you think something is up. You don't vocalize this. Not yet. It's too early for that.

Instead, you say, "Okay, I'm heading back to my place."

***

Your place is, of course, your parents' place too. A fact you and your parents resent, though for completely different reasons which go unspoken until someone decides to lob the proverbial verbal grenade. More often than not, it's you who does this. Sometimes you need an explosion to be seen.

You park and step out of your van.

Austin's music blares. You hear specific notes through the closed doors of his vehicle. It's as if the soundwaves are trying to escape Austin's presence. You imagine each blast beat, each *thud* of the kick drum, filling his car, perhaps with pressure, and if he doesn't open the door soon, it will burst. The frame will buckle. The glass will shatter. His body will be shredded. Mangled—

The music stops, and now your thoughts are too loud. You say, "hello" as he steps out of his car in order to quiet them.

"Damn, you look like shit," he says.

You give him the finger, and motion for him to follow you inside of your parent's upper-middle class home. It isn't the parsonage. You moved out of that 1920s dump when you were seven, the age you began to think something was wrong with the world, though you were too young to conceptualize why. It was just a feeling then. Your mom said that the wrongness you felt were the evils of the world, but good men like your father were bringing slow, positive change. Even then, you weren't sure that was accurate, but again, your age and still-developing brain couldn't quite make heads or tails of what you were told. But change required action. That much made sense to you. And so the parsonage was donated to a single-parent family in need. A member of the congregation whose tithings were never grand, but always consistent, and delivered with an obligatory smile of gratitude for all of that positive change your father and the church provided them.

"I'm going to clean up," you say, kicking your shoes off at the door.

Austin leaves his well-worn skater shoes on. Small wedges of dirt fall from the bottoms of his shoes, leaving a trail behind him. You know your parents will bitch about it. They'll probably blame you, too.

TELL AUSTIN TO SWEEP IT UP—GO TO PG 16

SWEEP IT UP YOURSELF—CONTINUE READING

You open the coat closet and grab the plastic hand broom/dustpan combo from the floor. It hides behind your father's snow boots. The edge of the dustpan is lined with a thin piece of metal, no wider than your pinkie fingernail. It runs down the entire length of the dustpan. You consider how flimsy it is, like aluminum foil or most of your interpersonal relationships. It could snap at any moment. Sound familiar? You sweep, and empty the dustpan into the kitchen trash can. When you return to the coat closet, Austin has already walked downstairs and made himself at home. The TV is on, but it's nothing but shitty Sunday programming. You hear the faint rattle of your hi-hats as he likely bumped the stand while sitting on your drum throne. *Your* drum throne. Remember that. Remember how Austin takes what he wants without regarding others?

There's a slight pang in your stomach. Booze perhaps? No. You know it's disdain. It's almost always disdain.

You walk to the top of the stairs and yell down, down, down, "I'm going to clean up. The PS2 is input two if you want to play anything."

But you know he won't. You know he's going to try to play your drums.

CONTINUE—GO TO PG 17

RYAN STEPS INSIDE and leaves you on the stoop with your cigarette, coffee, and thoughts to occupy yourself. You're curious what Austin could be up to. He's always up to something. He's got nothing but time, it seems like.

A wisp of a thought enters the forefront of your mind—a real doozy—just as Ryan steps out of the door, keys jingling in his fingers. You grasp at the thought as Ryan turns the key, latching the deadbolt, but it's like trying to catch smoke. The thought dissipates before it can solidify.

Ryan taps you on the shoulder. "Let's roll. I'll drive."

Oh, thank fuck.

You're not hammered any longer, but you're queasy. Easily the worst part of a hangover, and you've gone and added a cup of coffee to the brine.

Ryan's car chirps as he unlocks it with the fob.

You ooze into the passenger seat of his low-riding Pontiac.

Cynic's "Veil of Maya" emanates through crackling speakers when Ryan starts the car.

"Better not let Austin hear it. He might chuck it out the window," you say.

Ryan backs out of the driveway. "He'll get over it. Sorry he was such an asshole about it. You know how he is."

"An asshole."

"Yeah," Ryan says. "But it's whatever. He's the one missing out. It's a good album."

"Do you think it's because he doesn't play? I know you don't have to be a musician to like an album or whatever, but—" Your thoughts are tangled in a revolving door of qualifying statements. A loop of justification and excuses. "I guess, I mean if he played an instrument, he may appreciate the album more."

Ryan pulls out of the neighborhood and onto what counts as a main drag in your small Midwestern town. It's one of the only four-lane roads in town, and if you follow it in either direction it will take you far, far away from this place.

"Maybe," Ryan says. "It isn't that Austin doesn't appreciate good music. It's that he has to decide what counts as good music first. That, and he has to be the one to deliver it, like he's some prophet or something."

This is what you've been thinking all along. That Austin sees himself as some sort of divine messenger. Perhaps *prophet* is too elevating of a word. *Pastor* might be more accurate in this instance, and the similarities between Austin and your father do not escape you. Austin needs to be the one to deliver the good news. If he isn't the one being worshipped, he has to decide who is.

As Ryan continues to drive west toward the outskirts of town, you already have an inclination of what Austin has planned. You know what's there. Cult Road is out there.

* * *

Ryan barely slows as he takes a hard turn off of the highway and onto the gravel road. His car fishtails ever so slightly, kicking gravel and clouds of dust into the air. Your stomach flutters at this momentary loss of control. It only takes a second for the tires to find their grip, and tear into the uneven surface of the road. It's not Cult Road proper, but rather, it's one of the many rural gravel roads which snake around this edge of town that will supposedly lead you there. You aren't sure anyone has ever truly been to Cult Road.

"Do you believe that any of the occult stuff actually goes on out here?" you ask.

"What—the shrouded figures or animal sacrifices?"

"Sure," you say, adjusting in your seat. "But—" You stop yourself from blurting out what you really want to say. That Austin is a liar.

At first Ryan seems lost in the riffs coming through the rattling car door speakers, but he's with it. He answers for you, "Or that Austin saw it."

"Yeah. I mean, we haven't talked in a while, but last time we hung out, he was saying all this weird shit about finding Cult Road and stumbling upon a ritual. Black magic shit. I don't buy it.

"He's been saying this for a while now and it's gone to his head.

Basically, turned spying on these people into his own ritual. Voyeur stuff. He probably didn't see anything though," Ryan says. "He might think he did, but he didn't. No one has, because none of that shit is real. I mean, I'm not saying people don't fuck around out here in robes, starting fires, and killing farm cats, but the rituals and all that other *stuff* is bullshit. Meth-head shit."

The word *stuff* fights with the guttural screams and pounding drums for your focus. You know what Ryan means by the other stuff—Austin's bullshit. The floating bodies. The skinned animals walking around like nothing was wrong—like they weren't in pain. The otherworldly voices speaking in strange tongues to Austin.

"The only true part of that story was that he was completely fucked-up on something. There's your explanation," Ryan says.

Part of you wishes Austin was right, because it might mean some of the shit your dad says is real. That maybe there is truth to his ardent, spiritual servitude, and there is some sort of good in this world we can be a part of.

"Help me keep an eye out." Ryan turns the music down. He always does this when he's thinking and driving. "Should be coming up on the right."

You've lost track of the mile markers, but you know the CD restarted around the time you turned off of the highway, and track four has just begun. Only one house has been visible so far from the road, but it was a few miles back.

Up ahead, a line of trees forms a windbreak, indicating the presence of some kind of structure. "This it?" you ask.

"I think so."

Ryan slows and turns into a gravel driveway, overgrown with weeds. He pulls his car into the yard, and parks alongside the trees.

The oppressive Nebraska sun beats down on you, causing your clothes to stick to your body like plastic wrap. You're still wearing a rented outfit from Toni's wedding, and it dawns on you that you will be charged a late return fee. The things you do for friends. At least you were there for her, which is more than you can say about Ausin. You gaze at the farmhouse and hope whatever it is he's put together was worth missing the wedding for.

The front porch is in a state of disrepair. You're thirsty just looking at the dry, warped wooden boards, which have turned ash-gray over time. The steps creak the moment you put any weight onto them.

You pull the storm door open, and the spring groans in response. As you place your hand on the doorknob to the interior door, you turn to see Ryan leaning on the hood of his car, smoking a cigarette. "You coming?"

"I'll be in in a sec," he says. "I think it's best if you see it for yourself for the first time."

NAH, YOU AREN'T IN THE RIGHT HEADSPACE FOR SURPRISES—GO TO PG 29

ENTER THE ABANDONED FARMHOUSE BY YOURSELF—GO TO PG 31

"CAN YOU CLEAN THAT?" you ask. It's a simple request if there ever was one, but as the words crawl up your throat and leave your mouth, you almost regret it. Almost, is the keyword here, because you are not in high school anymore. You've been better at sticking up for yourself. Besides, it's a simple request. It's not like you asked the guy for money.

"Yeah, whatever," he says with annoyed nonchalance. It's his typical attitude. As if doing anything for anybody beyond himself is a galactic-sized inconvenience.

You ask yourself how he will ever make it in the real world, and you feel the slightest bit of disdain in your stomach because that is the exact thing your parents ask about you. You can practically hear the phrase uttered in your father's voice. *Real world.* Like it's in air-quotes. It's a simple matter of responsibility and—oh god, what are you thinking? Is this what it's like to grow up?

"There's a dustpan in the hall closet," you say. "I'm going to go clean up. TV's still downstairs. PS2 is input two. Games where they always are."

It's odd having to give those instructions. It's not like you two have been estranged. Then again, it has been some time since Austin's hung out over here.

"Cool, got it," he says.

CONTINUE—GO TO PG 17

THE WATER FEELS INCREDIBLE as it rains down and strips last night's grime from your body. In fact, you think this might be the most pleasant shower you've ever had. Hangover showers always feel like this.

Austin is playing your drums by the time you're through, and it's so godawful. You can't figure out how someone who's been in a band this long can't even keep a 4/4 beat. Even the most uncoordinated of people should be able to do so by osmosis given how many hours of band practice he's been a part of. You'd think simply by listening to as much music as Austin does, he'd be able to stay on time for a few bars.

Of course, you know he doesn't try. Not truly anyway. He tried drums for a month and quit. He'd tried guitar for a month and quit. He tried bass, thinking it'd be easier than guitar, and quit after two weeks, hands and fingers sore from trying to manhandle the thick strings.

Austin has no patience; you and Ryan agree.

He's not a great vocalist by any stretch, and if you had to guess, his improper technique is going to cause irreparable damage to his vocal cords.

But, to give credit where credit is due—Austin's lyrics have always been where the magic is. Visceral, touching on the cerebral, even if a bit ostentatious, it's where Austin's creativity shines brightest. Perhaps darkest. He revels in grim and often taboo ideology. His words tackling themes of blasphemy and death and pointed and poignant politics with a level of intention that you've never seen come out in any other aspect of Austin's demeanor.

It might be the only reason you've hung around him as long as you have.

You dry yourself off and throw on some clothes.

The carpet is soft underneath your feet, but there is nothing but hard feelings saturating your mind as you reach the bottom of the stairs, and walk into a cloud of smoke.

"What the fuck, dude?"

He can't hear you, not because of the off-time thumps of your bass drum, but because he doesn't care. The little shit. You walk—no—you *lunge* at him, and pull the cigarette from his mouth. Austin doesn't stop whacking your set with your brand-new sticks. You choke your left-side crash cymbal and use it to stub the cigarette.

Austin blows the last drag into the air. You imagine squeezing his lungs, the soft tissue crinkling and shriveling like a wet grocery sack between your fingers.

You consider carpet bombing the basement with air freshener, but it won't matter. It'll cover up the smell some, but either way your parents will know, so why bother trying to hide it. You can blame Austin. They won't care. You can take the blame. They won't care. They'll lob the verbal grenade in any case.

You check the time on your phone. Just before noon. Your dad has wrapped up his sermon for the contemporary service, and the church band is about to play one more song, dosing the congregation with enough endorphins to feel good for the remainder of the day before they head to work on Monday, grumpy and unchanged. The God-high—a euphoria that comes and goes like the breeze, or doing dusters.

"C'mon, let's get out of here before my parents get back."

"What are they going to do? You're not in high school anymore," he says.

"I know, but you know how they are. C'mon, let's go for a drive or something. Tell me about the gig and all that." You make sure not to sound too commanding, but rather like it was his idea all along.

The afternoon heat is oppressive. Sweat forms at the nape of your neck, and slicks the small of your back as the sun reminds you of your all-black attire.

"Who's driving?" Austin asks.

A handful of change rests among the lint in your pockets from the last time you wore these jeans, leftover from buying CDs. You don't really want to drive, but you don't really want to be Austin's passenger either, but life is about making decisions, remember? And this is an easy one. Option A or option B. It really is quite simple.

Your keys hang loose at your side, clipped to your belt loop with a gas station carabiner. Go ahead, pull them from your jeans and put the pedal to the metal. What are you waiting for?

Reaching into your pocket, you've made the decision to leave it up to chance, which isn't making a decision at all now, is it? You rest the quarter on the edge of your index finger and ready your thumb.

"Heads, I drive. Tails, you drive," you say, and send the quarter flying into the air with a metallic *ping*. It dances and shimmers in the Sunday afternoon sunlight. It cascades into your palm, the coin warm against your skin. Without looking, you slap it onto your other hand, revealing the result.

FLIP A COIN.

HEADS, YOU DRIVE—GO TO PG 20

TAILS, AUSTIN DRIVES—TO GO PG 25

"GUESS I'M DRIVING." You slip the quarter into your pocket and unclip the carabiner of keys dangling from your belt loop. You slide the van key into the lock cylinder, the uneven ridges engaging with the series of springs and pins. There's the slightest resistance, like a serrated knife tearing through meat.

Austin impatiently pulls on the passenger side door handle.

You slip into the driver's seat and unlock the passenger side door for him. He gets into the van and an immediate heaviness seems to invade the space. Every action seems to carry some inherent weight with it. From the way his shoes clunk against one other, kicking dirt onto the floor mats as they press into the floor, to how aggressively he buckles his seatbelt—everything he does is so, so loud. Forceful.

Cynic's "Sentiment" fades in as you start the van. You turn the volume a few ticks lower instead of changing the CD, but you find yourself immediately talking over the music, as if to hide it. A simple attempt of obfuscation. "You'll have to tell where I'm going."

But you know he hears the song. And you know he'll say something. It's a matter of when he'll decide to lambast you about your musical tastes. A series of images reels through your mind of the disc soaring through the basement. *Pretentious bullshit.*

"Just take the highway west out of town. I'll tell you where to go when we get closer," he says, settling into the seat.

Of course that's where he's taking you—Cult Road.

You've heard the rumors of hooded figures carrying torches, sacrificing animals in classic ritualistic cliché. All the stories you've heard were painted in broad strokes, usually coming from someone who sounded like they just discovered 1970s esoteric films, blabbing after a few bong rips, already a few beers deep. Colorful cult stories, although they've been almost entirely filtered through second-hand accounts. Intriguing, nonetheless, but all panache. In other words, bullshit.

Austin claims he's witnessed the cult performing rituals. Levitating bodies. All that.

"All right, this ought to be interesting." You back out of the driveway and weave your way out of your neighborhood, past row after row of cookie cutter homes. From above, you imagine the neighborhood would resemble a patchwork quilt. Perfectly square patches of meticulously manicured lawns, vibrant green despite the summer drought, stitched together with concrete. A quilt of upper-middle-class complacency.

It's as if Austin can sense your mental unrest, because he says, "We're going to change this town forever. We're going to fuck up the music scene, too. Everywhere. It's going to be a complete paradigm shift. Old school roots that will grow and choke out all the fucking bullshit music out there. All of that poser-metal shit is going to be finished."

The control of his words and the authority in his voice make your skin flush. Every hair on your neck stands on end. This is the Austin you remember. The Austin you've missed.

The passion. The vigor. The drive to do something—to be something. The almost-militant attitude sparks something in you, too. Strange, but it's almost like forgiveness. It washes over the smoldering coals of resentment you've been harboring, and douses them. It isn't instantaneous, of course, but your neurons are firing, painting pictures in the form of memories—good times—and you remember how much fun Austin is to be around. How fun he can be. His potential. And maybe that's what you're here to do. Not to leave this town and abandon everything and everyone in it, but rather pull him from his pit of apathy, and guide him in the direction of his potential. To take him with you. The thought fuels you with an almost righteous rush. Added purpose. Some messiah-complex.

Yes. That must be it, and you reply with a resounding, "Fuck yeah!"

Austin reaches for the stereo. "Turn this up. Their bass progression is fucking wild on this record."

You don't know where this is coming from, but you don't spoil the moment. Instead, you let him turn the volume to an uncomfortably loud level, and drive.

***

The sky is robin's egg blue and stretches endlessly across the rural farmland, unbroken by only a few man made structures. It is a completely cloudless day, not even a wisp of white adorns the sky, and the wind makes its presence known by jostling your van with the occasional tree-shaker. The belt of trees on the horizon seems like an illusion, never changing in size or appearing any closer as you drive toward them.

"Turn right at the next mile marker," Austin says. He's lit a stray cigarette he'd found while rummaging through your glove compartment. "Then you'll keep going for a bit. I'll tell you when to turn."

"Has the rest of the band been out here yet?"

"Kinda," he says. "Ryan and I have been out here a time or two. Mostly just fucking around. No one has been out here since Waste Doctrine reached out though. But that's how I got the idea to have the gig here. They said they'd be heading through town and have a day off between shows. Said if we had a venue, we could open. Feel like this is going to be insanely more impressive than someone's basement or the fucking Knights of Columbus."

"It's cool they found us," you say, immediately catching the slip-up. *Us.* You don't correct yourself though. The tracks on PureVolume were mixed by you. All but two of them have you behind the kit, too. You and Danny were the ones who pushed to set up the PureVolume account against Austin's wishes because you recognized the importance of getting your music out there, no matter the method. The world was changing. It wasn't just music magazines and word of mouth anymore—it was word of mouth *on the internet.*

Apparently, Austin's changed too.

"Yeah," is all he says. Austin flicks his spent cigarette butt through the crack in the window. "There's going to be a low-maintenance road here in a sec. Don't take it, but the house is another mile past it, off to the right."

And sure enough, a weathered two-story farmhouse stands nestled and enclosed by a windbreak of hackberry trees. The tires slide ever so slightly underneath the top layer of loose gravel as you slow to turn into the overgrown driveway. There doesn't appear to be a proper place to park, so you pull off to the side into the yard and leave your van in the smallest sliver of shade provided by the windbreak. You kill the engine and step out into the god-awful heat. Something keeps you from locking your van. It doesn't matter that there isn't anyone out here to steal it. It's the thought of not wasting any time unlocking it if there is.

Austin stands in front of the porch, arms outstretched, "Home-sweet-fucking-home."

You stand beside him and can nearly feel him vibrate with contagious energy. A surge of creativity flows through you as you envision how this place will look come the night of the gig.

Austin points between the second-story dormer windows. "I think I'm going to spray-paint *Welcome, Waste Doctrine* up there. What do you think?"

"In red," you say. "I doubt they've ever played in a place like this."

"You have no idea—I'm just getting started. This is going to be like nothing anyone has ever seen. Not around here anyway. And look," Austin grabs your shoulder, guiding you in a panoramic motion to the expanse of prairie surrounding you. "There's nothing out here. The sound is going to carry for miles. Complete chaos resounding throughout the night. C'mon, let me show you what I've got in store for this place. Do you want to check out the inside or outside first?"

Looking at the house head on is like staring at smoke. Your vision blurs no matter how hard you try to focus on the details of the exterior as if walking through a dream. Shadows morph into specters in your peripherals. The empty spaces in the second story windows are interrupted as if occupied, but not by anything you can confidently identify as real. A presence you can't quite see, but one you can feel in your gut.

And the burdensome noises filling your ears drones on. Microphone static. A persistent hum that's progressively growing louder the more you try to concentrate on something else. Anything else. It's there, drilling into your eardrums, beckoning you toward the side of the house.

You've always had an eye for peculiarities. Walk up to the front door—go to pg 52

Even your tinnitus can't prevent you from hearing the most minute details. Walk the perimeter—go to pg 56

"LOOKS LIKE YOU'RE driving," you say, slipping the quarter back into your pocket. You expect Austin to protest, but he only shrugs and walks toward his car, the horn chirping as he presses a button on his key fob.

"Hop in."

Austin's Corolla smells like an ashtray, despite the forest of Little Tree Air Fresheners hanging from his rearview mirror. You scoop the pile of CDs from the passenger seat before sliding in.

"Just toss them in the back," he says.

Another dozen CD cases rest at your feet. Deathspell Omega, Burzum, Enslaved, Immortal. You spot a few death metal albums too. Obituary's *Cause of Death*, Morbid Angel's *Altars of Madness*, Death's *Leprosy*. Nearly everything is older than you are. A few unmarked Memorex CD-Rs are scattered among them, blank as Austin's expression as he starts the car.

You're immediately hit by pounding drums and washed-out guitars. The vocalist's screams pierce the distortion and you recognize that it's Bathory, but can't remember which album it is.

"Sounds like it was recorded off a toaster," you say.

"All the good ones were."

Austin doesn't turn the volume down, but instead rolls the windows down to alleviate some of the noise inside of the car. You know it isn't because of that, but because several of your neighbors are outside watering their perfectly manicured lawns and tending to flowerbeds and washing their family-sized SUVs and he lives for their reactions. The scowls of disapproval. Their noses scrunched, as if their flowers suddenly smell of rot.

You love it too.

It's not just the defiance. The against-the-grain culture you've adopted. You love it because it feels as if you're privy to something these people will never be able to see. The irony of their judgment of appearances, despite the fact they live for the exact same thing.

Every. Single. Day.

They get out of bed next to spouses they've fallen out of love with in a house that's too big, so they fill it with children they resent and shit they don't need. Green lawns and SWAT-sized SUVs are the markers of success around here. Palatial homes which serve no purpose. It's a false life—a game of keeping up. Your generation raised and told you're supposed to want this life, yet you're the fuck-up-weirdo because you don't. You can be content with what you have. How is it your problem that others can't be?

You learned a long time ago that it isn't about living a life that brings you happiness—it's about falling in line with everyone else's unhappiness.

Your happiness looks different—and they hate that.

Autin lowers the volume once he turns out of your neighborhood. "I love seeing them squirm. They will never understand it."

"None of them bother to try," you say.

"Well you know that if music isn't on the radio, it isn't music at all. And if it isn't sold at Wal-Mart, it isn't worth having."

"Heaven forbid their tastes are challenged."

"Exactly," Austin says. "That is exactly what our gig is going to do. We're going to challenge this town and reward anyone who's willing to listen. You just wait and fucking see."

Austin pulls onto the highway heading west out of town. His Corolla's four-banger engine whines as he steps on the gas.

You aren't surprised you're going this way—toward Cult Road. The elusive and mysterious root of several urban legends. Hooded figures and sacrifices and ritual burnings. It's all bullshit. Probably, anyway.

You've driven out here before, but it's always the same— cornfields and gravel roads and anti-abortion billboards. None of this is surprising to you. What *does* throw you off is when Austin turns the volume so low you can hear the gurgle in your stomach and the slightest exhalation as he apologizes to you.

"For being a dickhead the past while," he says. "And missing Toni's wedding. I know what it looks like, but I made it up to her."

"She knew you were going to miss it?"

"Well yeah. When I didn't RSVP, she was all over my ass at practice."

It didn't really dawn on you that she and Austin would have worked it out. You'd always been the even-keeled one to alleviate any tension among the band and your friend group in general. It stings a bit—you realizing they've been able to keep things afloat without you around.

Perhaps it's to cut yourself some slack, but you remind yourself that Austin's always been wishy-washy. And it would not have been a surprise for Austin to bail without a word. No RSVP. No conversation. Just simply not showing up without explanation.

"She didn't mention it," you say.

"I asked her not to," Austin says. "I wanted to apologize to you myself. And she had enough shit on her plate. I wasn't going to ask a bride to do anything extra."

People really can change.

You just never thought Austin would. At least not without your help.

"Speaking of practice though," he says, finished with his bout of vulnerability, "grab one of the blanks down there."

"Which one?"

"Doesn't matter. They're the same."

Austin ejects the CD from the stereo.

You grab one of the blank CDs off the floor and swap it with the Bathory album. The stereo whirs as it consumes the blank. As it begins to play, you hear white noise. Drumsticks clattering. The buzz of snares. Whispers are layered within. Subtle feedback, like a guitar is being plugged into an amplifier. Demons chittering. Crying. The sounds of suffering. You place the Bathory album into its case as the song picks up. Trebly guitars play over pounding double kicks and blast beats. Then, a shriek pierces through and Austin's voice takes over.

"We did this in one take," he says.

You remember him wanting to do this for a long time—recording an album in a single live take. It's not a new concept, but it's one that falls in line with his obsession with authenticity. Your music—the band—in its truest sense. Raw. Energetic. Imperfect—but true.

"Everyone is really on point," you say.

"About halfway through the set my dad opened the garage door and there's this awful groaning in the background. The way the mics picked it up makes it sound like steel cables breaking. It fucking rips. This is what I sent to Waste Doctrine when I found out they were coming through town."

You are the only black metal band in town. Deep down you know this, but there would be no reason to point that out unless you're looking for a fight, and you are not looking for a fight. Not now. Not when things are finally being smoothed over with Austin. Instead, you say, "What a way to impress them."

"That's only part of it," he says, pulling off the gravel road and onto an overgrown driveway. Austin pulls into the yard and parks under the shade of a windbreak of trees.

The humidity drains your energy the moment you step out of the car. Sweat already begins to slick your back.

"This is going to kick ass." Austin walks around to you, and guides your vision to the expanse farmland surrounding you. "There is nothing out here. It's going to be just us and anyone who's willing to join us in our decrepit sanctuary."

The ramshackle house stands before you, a dim blight against the otherwise bright and picturesque summer afternoon.

"Come on," Austin says. "Let me show you our church."

The house appears to have been pulled from a black and white photo, creating a striking contrast against the bright blue sky while you stare into the second story dormer windows. A shadow flits by, and then the window slams shut, as if the house winked. A strong breeze rustles the grass surrounding the house, a choir of whispers.

YOUR CURIOSITY PULLS YOU TOWARD THE PORCH—GO TO PG 52

THE PRAIRIE SONG IS ALLURING AND THE URGE TO WANDER THROUGH IT IS STRONG—GO TO PG 56

DESPITE THE HEAT, a chilling surge rushes down your spine. You release your grip on the doorknob, and step away from the front door. As you do, the storm door slams shut, the aluminum clanking against the doorframe.

Big empty houses are not your thing. *Sad*, big empty houses. You clear the porch stairs in one step, and join Ryan.

"Can I bum one. I need a cigarette before I go in there," you say. You don't *need* a cigarette. You've never needed one, you tell yourself.

"Yeah, sure," he says, tapping his pack of Camels against the palm of his other hand.

You pull one from the half-empty pack and tell him you'll buy another on your way back into town, but he waves his hand like it's no big deal.

He hands you his Bic without needing to be asked. The spark wheel grinds beneath your thumb, but it's characteristically windy today, and the breeze continually puts out the flame. You cup your hand around the lighter to protect it like some washed-up Prometheus, but it's no use, and the gods take back their flame with another breath.

"So much for a fucking windbreak." Frustrated, you hand the Bic back to Ryan.

"Here," he says, leaning in to light your cigarette with his.

You drag, and think it'd be a pretty nice day if not for the heat.

Ryan leans forward and stubs his cigarette out on his license plate. He leaves the butt on the hood of his car as if he's saving it to throw away. A half-hearted attempt at environmental consciousness. But the wind steals it, sending it to the ground without a care. You consider the dirt, the place you know we'll all end up someday, ground to dust over time like a spent cigarette.

"All right," Ryan says. "Time for the tour. You sure you don't want to take a look by yourself?"

You pinch the half-smoked cigarette to put it out, and tuck it behind your ear for later. The second story window seems to stare at you. It's not a figure or anybody inside, but it's the feeling that the house itself is holding you in its gaze as its presence looms in the field. "Nah, it's cool," you say. "Let's go."

You meant *go* as in: get in the car, and leave this place, but the steps creak underneath Ryan's weight, and he's holding the storm door open, motioning, *after you.*

CONTINUE—GO TO PG 34

THE DOORKNOB IS cold to the touch, despite the overbearing heat and stifling humidity. Old, rusty springs grind as you twist, and it takes a bit of effort to open the swollen wooden door. You trip into the vacant, dead house and catch yourself before falling into the stairs in front of you.

You're unsurprised by the mess surrounding you: broken furniture, cigarette butts, the cracks webbing across the walls like cobwebs, but this isn't what you expected from Austin's supposed *big plans*. In your eyes, it's just an old party house.

Only your eyes, though.

Because to your ears, this is much, much more. It's the antithesis of a party house—lifeless. The complete and utter silence about this place is unsettling, and though you can't be certain, you aren't sure if your footsteps are making any noise at all. The hardwood floors don't creak. Don't moan, or whine. It's as if the house is consuming the sounds. Absorbing them. And what of that energy? Where does it go and how is it spent? Because if it exists, the energy has to go somewhere.

The only thing you hear is your heartbeat thumping at an increasing tempo inside of you until it reaches double-kick intensity. You stand at the foot of the stairs, gripping the handrails on either side of the steps to anchor yourself to the earth. You close your eyes, but it doesn't keep you from watching some version of yourself detach from your body and float.

The first thought that pops into your progressively disconnected brain is how funny you look down there, arms splayed like Christ, fastened to your invisible cross.

You're pulled down—mind, body, and spirit—as soundwaves

are sent bursting through the ether like cannon fire as the front door opens.

"Whoa, you okay?" Ryan asks, helping you sit on the steps.

You nod in response, trying to get a grip on your nerves.

Shifting from weightlessness back to density—reality—is disorienting, and you feel as if something important was interrupted. Like some strange transformation was interfered with when Ryan entered the house and you aren't sure how to restart the process. Or if you even want to.

"What happened?" Ryan asks.

The answer is simple: you began to astral project, except the words come out all wrong, and instead you say, "Beats the fuck out of me." Other excuses float—just like you did—to the surface: *you're probably dehydrated from last night. Don't have any food in you. Sometimes you get lightheaded.* You know, bullshit.

Though Ryan usually has a good nose for bullshit, he runs to his car and returns with a plastic bottle of water.

"It's been in my car, but it should help," he says.

"Thanks." The thin, cheap plastic crinkles in your hand as you uncap the bottle. The water is warm and tastes just like the bottle smells. Any heightened sense of self has trickled into an unsatisfying little pool of brain stew. *Fuck me*, you think, and wonder if that is what transcendence feels like.

***

The stairs bisect the first floor, separating what appears to be a dining or living space from the kitchen. You sit on the stairs while Ryan points in the various directions where the stage is going to be set up. "Austin thinks this side is probably the best space for it," he says, pointing to the living room side. "Less shit in the way."

All the appliances have been stripped from this place, and the alcove where the refrigerator must have stood would be a perfect nook for merch. You find yourself vocalizing this thought as Austin walks through the door. He responds before you can consider how impossibly quiet his arrival was.

"Fuck no," Austin says. "We aren't having any fucking merch. This is black metal. True fucking black metal. The scene kids can drive to Omaha and hit up Hot Topic for their goddamn baby-T youth-large shirts. With any luck those poser motherfuckers won't even show up."

Are you hearing this? —you can't believe this shit. He doesn't speak for you. Only *you* speak for *you*.

BITE YOUR TONGUE, DON'T LET HIM GET UNDER YOUR SKIN—GO TO PG 39

DON'T TAKE HIS SHIT, SPEAK UP— GO TO PG 41

IT'S HARD TO tell how much of the disarray is Austin's doing, and how much of it is the natural progression of a withering, abandoned house left to the elements, and you'd imagine—generations of teenagers fucking the place up.

"This is where the stage would be," Ryan says, pointing to the area opposite the kitchen. "That is if we play down here. Austin mentioned it could be cool to play upstairs."

"No way I'm lugging my shit upstairs," you say. "I'm already going to have to get it out of my basement."

"I'm sure your parents would love that."

You know he didn't mean it that way. You know, the *I-can't-believe-you-still-live-with-your-parents* way. Ryan offered for you to stay at his place, but you refused. You told him it was to save money, but there's plenty more to it. Rent. The abysmally tiny square footage of his duplex. Your conflicting schedules, which would mean poor sleep, and on, and on—but mostly because everyone has told you that rooming with your friends tends to kill relationships, and it's best to room with strangers. So far they haven't been proven wrong. Just ask your parents. Then again, the more you dwell on this thought, the more you believe your parents have always been strangers to you too.

Your brain clicks back into a place resembling reality.

"Yeah," you laugh. "They bitch because I live at home, but tell me everything I do is wrong. *Directionless*, I think, is the word my dad uses."

You try not to whine about your parents too often, especially around Ryan. If your parents would be considered too involved, too critical, and too judgmental, Ryan's parents would be considered completely absent. Uninterested. Dead to him.

"If things turn out like Austin's hoping, you may find that direction," Ryan says.

"Let's hope," you say, and continue looking around the first floor. It's a pretty basic floor plan. An architecturally symmetrical farmhouse from the 1920s, if you had to guess. The dining room—the stage—is across from the kitchen, separated by about eight feet of open space, which eventually leads to the stairs to the second floor.

You try to picture how all of your gear would be set up, let alone Waste Doctrine's.

"What if we set up in the kitchen, and Waste Doctrine set up in the dining room? Would eliminate set-up time, and then no one would have to lug their shit from the second floor, or from their van. That or, Waste Doctrine could use our gear?"

"I like the two-stage idea," Ryan says. "Not sure what Austin will think of it, but could be cool."

You look at the space and consider your kit. "I may have to play a condensed kit anyway. That space is going to fill up quickly," you say. "What about Danny? What does he think about all of this?"

Even in the piss-poor lighting, you catch the look on Ryan's face when you mention your bass player. Did Ryan forget about your fucking bassist?

"Who knows what the fuck Danny's thinking about?" Ryan asks. "Come on, let's get out of here."

You know exactly what Danny is thinking about, or rather—who. The reason you two went shot-for-shot with one another last night.

As you and Ryan leave the Cult Road House, you see Austin's car parked among the browning yard, overgrown with weeds, but there's no sight of him. The trunk is open, but you can't make out what's inside.

CONTINUE—GO TO PG 36

A PAIR OF WORKBOOTS lies next to some bolt cutters inside of the trunk. From the looks of them, the bolt cutters are brand new. Boots too, if you had to guess. Manual labor and Austin were like water and oil.

You look around, but don't see him anywhere.

"Probably around back," Ryan says. "Could go look for him if you want."

"Nah, let's go see what Danny is up to.

I'll call him," you say, climbing into the car. The flesh on your face tightens like shrink wrap around your cheekbones, like your skin is suddenly too small for the rest of your body.

"Fuck this heat. I need a beer," Ryan says and starts the car.

Your stomach churns at the thought. What you need is a shower and a clean set of clothes.

The A/C kicks in, but the fans churn and struggle to keep up, blasting you with warm air. It'll take ten minutes before the remaining gasp of freon cools the car, but by then you know it won't make a bit of difference. Ryan rolls the windows down and stops at the end of the driveway. Before pulling onto the gravel road, you look in the side-mirror. Austin appears next to the house, almost out of thin air. After staring at you—yes, *you*; you can feel it—he descends into the storm cellar as if descending into a grave.

***

The cigarette lighter *pops*.

Staring into the hot coils, you pull the half-smoked Camel from behind your ear and press it into the orange eye staring back at you. You imagine it winking at you, its iris glowing like hellfire as you reignite your bad habit.

You offer the still-glowing lighter to Ryan, an unlit cigarette already dangling from his lips. He mumbles *thanks* and leans your direction, not taking his hands off the steering wheel.

"What the fuck was he doing back there? In the storm cellar," you clarify.

"Dunno. He wouldn't show me," he says. "*Not yet*, is what he keeps telling me, like it's some big fucking secret. Whoo-hoo a shitty basement. He probably found booze or some dead animals. I just want to play the gig and move on."

"Move on?"

Ryan exhales. The cigarette rests between his middle and forefingers on his right hand. Ash dusts the thigh of his jeans, leaving a gray smudge across his tight, black jeans. Then he drags, long—nearly a sigh—as if preparing for a speech he wasn't ready to give yet, and speaks. "Yeah. I'm thinking about going back to school. Probably shouldn't have waited this long to do it, but I think it's time."

"Think you'll hate it as much this time around?"

You're trying your best to veil your skepticism. The doubt. It isn't meant to sound unsupportive, but the words have already left your lips and sucker-punched Ryan's eardrums. He didn't deserve that.

"What's that supposed to mean?"

"Nothing, man. Just. You know . . . " You're scrambling. "Last time didn't pan out all that well is all."

"Last time we drank till three a.m. every night and didn't go to class."

You went to class, but you don't say so. You followed through with *the plan*. Two years at community college while you wrote music and kept up with the band. Earned your Associate's Degree. It's not your fault two-year degrees didn't land you a job out of town. It's all about the four-year programs now. That or the military. That's what the school preached. The counselors. Your parents too. But you didn't listen.

"That doesn't matter though," Ryan says, turning back onto the highway into town. "I'm a different person now. I'm more—"

"Responsible?" you ask in a razor-sharp tone.

"Don't be an asshole," he says. "I was going to say *focused*. Got my shit together enough I think I can make it really work this time."

"You thinking of staying in town? The audio production program is pretty legit. Pretty sure it's the only one in the state. The university would be great for performance though. We could even room together or something."

The words come out so fast, pathetically so, like a plea.

"Rooming would be cool, yeah," he says. The pause in his voice, like a skipping record, says there's a catch. A *but* coming. The other shoe dropping. "But I'm not just thinking of leaving town. I want to leave the fucking state. There's a solid program in Colorado. A couple in Minnesota. I even sent an audition tape to Berklee."

You wonder if he's good enough. You don't say it, but Ryan picks up on it—graciously. "I mean, I know I'm not Berklee-good, but I've been practicing a lot since you left the band. Like, a lot-a-lot. The band doesn't really hang out that often these days. I've been playing a lot more technical stuff. Sinking all my time into learning theory and technique. Don't get me wrong, I love black metal, but there's more to music than it. You of all people can appreciate that, but please don't mention it to Austin," he says. "For real. I don't want to deal with that shit right now and neither do you. Trust me. Just play the gig and move on. We could still be roommates if I move out of state, you know? There's nothing keeping you here."

Cynic's album restarts as Ryan pulls into his driveway. He might be right. Even if Waste Doctrine is impressed, Toni's honeymoon is going to end, and her place on the drum throne will be waiting.

"I'll think about it," you say. "I'm going to go home for a bit and call Danny. Swing by later to practice. My parents won't be around."

CONTINUE—GO TO PG 47

YOU WANT TO tell Austin to go fuck himself, but you consider this might be your only ticket out of this place. Best not to let him get under your skin. At least not yet. Not here. Take your frustration out on your drum set. Focus this energy on practicing. Besides, you don't need to impress Austin; you need to impress Waste Doctrine.

"As long as we have a decent turnout, I don't care," you say. "Merch or no merch." You hold onto a thought: *it doesn't matter who shows up as long as people do show up.*

A classic church thought.

Line the pews to spread the good news.

It won't convince everyone, but enough of them will stick around, and that's what any good church needs, isn't it? Numbers? Perhaps that is too cynical, even for you. Followers. *That's* what a church needs, but even then, it boils down to numbers, doesn't it?

Austin doesn't want numbers though—he wants devotees. Believers. Listeners who ascribe to what is true. He makes his thoughts crystal-ball-clear, reiterating, "There won't be any fucking merch."

You don't acknowledge this. No. That would give the impression that Austin's the leader and you buy into his self-ordained authority.

Your silence speaks volumes though, and Austin appears agitated, like he was hoping for a fight. Like a heavy pendulum he cannot control, his mood swings from combative to something else. Not calmness, but angst. Anxiety. At one point you used to be able to gauge what was going on in that head of his, but not so much anymore. All you know is that whatever it is Austin's feeling, he's feeling intensely, and he lights a joint.

He takes a massive hit—gargantuan—a true Jethro-Tull-Locomotive-Breath type of drag, and holds the smoke for what feels like an eternity. You almost call him Ian Anderson because he'd hate it. The tights. The flute. But you let it go.

It's sweltering in the poorly insulated farmhouse. Ryan peels his shirt from his chest, and tugs it back and forth for airflow. It's the perfect excuse to leave.

"I'm roasting. Let's get out of here," you say.

"Yeah, we'll catch up with you later," Ryan says, putting some space between you and Austin. "We still need to fill Danny in on everything anyway."

Oh yeah, your bassist. How could you have forgotten about Danny? Your other half in the band. Your rhythm buddy. He was at the wedding reception, and the reason you got completely and utterly wrecked. The way you two were going shot-for-shot, trying to keep up with one another, you'd think you two had a death wish.

Maybe Danny does. You know how hard it was for him last night, watching the person he loved most in this world get hitched. Nobody on this planet knows except for you. Not the band. Not Toni. Not the man both Toni and Danny love. And especially not Austin.

Austin's reduced the joint to a roach already and flicks it to the floor. "Whatever dudes. I've got shit to do around here."

"When should we practice?" you ask. "We can at my place, but—"

"You'll have to talk to your *roommates* first. We know."

"Fuck off," you say, pushing your way through the smoke and animosity, and out to the porch. You don't bother catching the storm door on your way out. It crashes shut, drowning out Austin's obnoxious laugh and defensive, accusatory *what? What?* He knows goddamn well what.

CONTINUE—GO TO PG 44

RYAN GIVES YOU the subtlest, most ghost-note of a look—*don't*—but there's a fire in you, sparked by Austin's incessant, hypocritical bullshit, and fueled by the lingering alcohol in ravaging your gut. "You can't be fucking serious. We've got an opportunity to impress a signed band, and you're actively hoping people don't show up to the gig? What the fuck is wrong with you, dude? Who gives a shit who shows up as long as people show up?"

"I give a shit," Austin says. He's inched up to you. Everything about him is stale. His breath is like exhaust. His clothes are dingy, bordering on sour. You know he doesn't sleep when he gets like this. Insomnia instigated by a whirlwind of ideas.

And you. You're no different, standing here in your hangover attire.

"Well, I want to leave this goddamn town. And if that means scene kids show up to the gig and pay for merch, then so be it. And if you ever want to leave your dad's basement, maybe you shouldn't give a shit either."

"Like you're one to talk. Like you're not a fucking basement dweller."

You've been absentmindedly ascending the stairs as Austin moves toward you, and by the time he's done berating you, you've reached the top. All it'd take is one push, and you'd watch every dumb thought be knocked loose from his head, one step at a time.

"Just fucking back off." Ryan interrupts your train of thought. "Both of you."

"Asshole," Austin says, turning around.

You don't follow, and instead wander around the second floor. The humidity is stifling, and has turned the air thick and musty. Petrified husks of dead mice punctuate your path, adding to the overall decay of the place. There's chattering below, but you can't make out any of their conversation. It's almost as if the woodgrain is talking to you, trying to tell you secrets—no, not secrets—directions.

The energy about this place is wrong. It's as if you're walking on sacred ground. But your anger shifts to curiosity. Wisps guide you to the master bedroom, and just like the main floor, this room has been stripped of its furniture—except for an ancient looking rocking chair that's wedged into a corner of the room. Wicker spirals into an ornate pattern across the back. It's covered in decorative loops that curlicue around the arms and rigid back. It looks like something an old church lady would love. The perfect place to sit and knit, or rock a screaming infant.

It's positioned near the second-story window, but it doesn't face the window. You're smart enough to know it has probably been moved a hundred times since someone last sat in it, and yet you picture something darker here. Something bordering sinister. The image of a tired, toothless, and broken matron sitting in the chair facing the wall, rocking slowly, speaking in tongues to herself during the dead hours of the night.

Sunlight tears through the window, illuminating a beam of dust motes which focuses on something glinting on the chair. You walk further into the room and note the gilded pages of the book resting on the seat of the chair. A Bible, you assume. Because of course it is.

As you walk toward it the chair begins to rock, the wood beneath creaking. Shrieking. The shrill scream pierces your tinnitus-ridden ears, raising every hair on your neck, and sends your psyche plummeting down, down, down—and suddenly, you feel weak and alone.

However, the feeling doesn't keep you from backing out of the room, not breaking eye-contact with the chair which continues to rock, despite the stale dead air filling the room.

You find Ryan sitting on the bottom step.

"Let's get out of here," you say. "We can meet at my place later to practice."

"You sure your *roommates* won't care?" Austin asks.

"Fuck off," you say, and walk to Ryan's car.

CONTINUE—GO TO PG 47

RYAN FOLLOWS YOU out and places a hand on your shoulder. He wants to make an excuse. You can sense it as he opens his mouth, his tongue clicking against his teeth before letting out a breath and ultimately saying nothing. What is there to say? Austin's an asshole. All three of you know this. It doesn't change anything.

And you know nothing will.

The thought ricochets against your skull and solidifies into what you know as the truth—*nothing is going to change. Austin is not going to change.*

It's a hard thought to swallow, but you've been chewing on it for so long and finally, you gulp it down, gristle and all. It's the only way out of this. Digest his bullshit. Get rid of the waste later. You just have to grin and bear it until you can make it out of here. It's the same approach you take with your dad. When you think of it that way, it's not so bad. Just a means to an end. Being a pastor's child paved the way for your drum lessons.

Putting up with Austin long enough to get some recognition is all you need. Maybe you don't need him as much as you thought. There are plenty of vocalists out there. Austin and the band are simply a conduit.

"Come on," Ryan says, pulling you from the pit of your mind and back to reality. "Let's get out of here."

The air conditioner struggles as his car comes to life. Ryan cracks the windows as if to let the car exhale the stale air. He ejects *Focus* from the stereo. "Would you put this back?" he asks, his finger wedged into the central hole of the disc.

You grab the tome of music and slide the CD back into its place behind its matching booklet. "What next?" you ask.

He lights a cigarette and lets it hang lazily between his lips, smoke rolling from the sides of his mouth. "This one," he says, tapping an untitled and unmarked silver Memorex CD-R.

You slide the disc from the page. Sunlight reflects off of its surface, briefly creating odd shapes across the smoke-stained ceiling upholstery.

The stereo swallows it, gulping it down with a slight whirring noise.

Ryan pulls out of the yard and onto the overgrown driveway. He stops at the end of the drive and looks for oncoming vehicles.

You're focused on the CD. You listen, but only hear what sounds like white noise: drumsticks clacking against one another, a slight buzzing similar to a guitar being plugged into an amp, and something you can only describe as weight? Maybe a thickness. A heaviness. Perhaps it's just the hum of tension.

You squint, as if that will help you place the sounds in your mind. You tilt your head and lean toward the speaker. As you do, a sudden onslaught of trebly guitars and hollow double-bass boxes your eardrums. Horses galloping, trampling skulls through Hell. You almost ask, *who is this?* But then you hear Austin's shrieking voice emanate through the speakers, cutting through the distortion and deep into your mind. There's a muffled chanting beneath Austin's screams. As you listen, the chanting becomes more obscured, and it's as if the vocal track is layered with one of your father's sermons. Only twisted. Spoken with a slanted cadence.

"We recorded this in one take in Austin's garage right before Toni got engaged," Ryan says. "He was hellbent on the idea."

"It's a cool concept," you say. "Fits his obsession with *authenticity.*"

"It was enough to impress Waste Doctrine," Ryan says.

Your mind fills the unspoken space, *with no help from you, so be grateful*—but those are Austin's words, not Ryan's. You shake them away. Still, it's a lot to contemplate—you and your place within the band. Not just now, but always.

Have you always been the outsider?

And now what? The prodigal drummer, returning for your rightful place on the throne.

It dawns on you that this is all temporary. It didn't cross your mind that Toni will come back, and Toni will take her place back in the band. You are being used. For what? A single night to impress Waste Doctrine? Or does that even matter to the band? No one else seems to see how big this could be for you—not just here, but as a way beyond. Your ticket to touring. Writing a record. Making a name for yourselves for more than a single night in this fucking town.

You're just the placeholder, but that's okay, because rumor has it Waste Doctrine's drummer is calling it quits. Maybe it's a good thing this is all temporary.

"You're quiet." Ryan turns onto the highway leading back into town.

"I'm just wiped," you say. "The heat and all of Austin's bullshit."

"Let him cool off and give him some space. He's gotta prep the house. Once that shit is out of his system he'll come around. In the meantime, we should call Danny and practice. Make this shit go as smooth as possible."

"Yeah. Mind if I borrow the CD? I'll learn the songs better if I can listen through my headphones. I might be able to isolate the drums."

"Sure, I'll burn you a copy, and call Danny. Meet at your place around five."

"Make it six," you say, and slip into your van.

The six-disc changer rotates to disc four, corresponding with 1994. The year Darkthrone released *Transilvanian Hunger*. Austin would be so proud.

CONTINUE—GO TO PG 47

YOU HALF EXPECT your parents to be home when you unlock the door, waiting patiently and painting-still in the front room—*the family room*—the place where most of the intergenerational arguments occur. Your family's verbal boxing ring.

But they aren't there among the decade-old family portraits, the ones taken before you started wearing nothing but black band T's, before you broke your mother's heart and disappointed your father.

Then again, why would anything you do anymore warrant their concern or cause them to break from their Sunday routine? It's you or God, you suppose, and they only believe in one of you these days.

You kick off your shoes and walk upstairs to strip off last night's stale clothes and hop into the shower. Despite the summer heat, the house is frigid, and the warm water lulls you into a comforting trance, and thoughts of Cult Road and the unnerving house begin to permeate your mind. Questions of reality and reliability float to the surface. Unreality and unreliability. How much of that shit was real, and did Austin and Ryan experience or notice anything similar? How long has Austin known about that place? Maybe that's what Austin's been on about this whole time— not the house itself, but the confusion and creeping dread the abandoned farmhouse seems to be built on. Brains tend to do weird things when they're confronted with the unfamiliar.

It's the last thing you need—to be alone and left inside your own head, so you knock loose the fragmented hunks of existential dread and imagine them swirling the drain with the soap suds rinsing off your body. They circle. The built-up ring of soap bubbles chokes the drain. Pipes gurgle as you turn the water off. The steam quickly dissipates, and the sudden shock of the air conditioning bites at your flesh.

You dry off and dress.

There's leftover pizza waiting for you in the fridge, and though you've pushed through the slog of your hangover mentally, you've puked everything up and then some, and are completely starved. You devour the first two pieces, and decide to brew a pot of coffee while you tackle a third slice. And for a moment, you feel normal.

You decide to give Danny a call while the Mr. Coffee and your stomach finish burbling.

The call goes to voicemail. At the wedding, he mentioned he was planning on taking today off from his second job. Could still be slogging through a hangover. By this hour you'd think he'd be in tip-top shape, but Danny was trying to drown a lifetime of feelings last night, so who knows?

You redial, if for no other reason than to make sure he's not dead in a ditch somewhere. Voicemail again. *You've reached Daniel Svoboda. Sorry for missing your call, but if you leave your name and number, I'll get back to you as soon as possible. Thank you.*

Danny's always been level-headed. Professional. The one of your group, who despite his eclectic and offbeat interests—arguably far stranger than Austin's—is the most put together, aside from Toni. Clean-cut Danny. Polo-shirts. Desk job. But still rocking Payless shoes. From the outside, you'd never guess he was not only into B-horror and metal, but was a walking encyclopedia of niche knowledge. Guess he couldn't afford to stand out. No sense in drawing any more attention to himself or giving people a reason to poke and prod into his personal life. Of all the people in your band, Danny needs to get out of this town the most. Deserves to.

You slam the last piece of pizza and pour a cup of coffee. The warm ceramic feels good on your hands. Sunlight trickles into the kitchen from the large window above the sink doing its best to give the impression your house is a home. One that provides comfort. The vinyl grilles dividing the window panes cast a shadow of three crosses across the kitchen floor—stretched-out and upside down. An unholy, inverted Golgotha.

You flip your phone open to take a photo of the blaspheming sunbeams, when it starts to vibrate, *Danny's Cell* flashing across the screen.

"Hey, he lives," you say.

"Yeah, sorry I missed your calls. Ryan called. Said we're practicing at your place tonight?"

His voice is clear as glass. Not gravelly. Not even the slightest hint of a hangover. Always put together.

"Yeah, that was the plan," you say. "I finally saw the house. It's something else. Eerie. Beat to shit, but it fits the picture Austin keeps going on about. I think Waste Doctrine is going to be into it. If nothing else, I'm sure they won't be expecting anything quite like this."

"If they even show up." Danny's voice is statue-sturdy. Unmoving.

"Think they won't?"

"I don't know, but look—it's the kinda thing Austin would pull. I'm not convinced he even talked to Waste Doctrine. He said they messaged back and forth online, but I wouldn't put it past him to use that as a way to put all this together. Know what I mean?"

Yes, you do.

This, as in, *the band. This*, as in, *the only thing Austin has left in this shithole town.*

"I don't mean to piss in everyone's coffee, but the timing is too convenient for me not to have some doubts."

Danny, always even-keeled. Rational.

"Yeah, I see what you mean," you say. "But you know as well as I do that Austin tends to be lazy. I'm not sure he'd go to all of the trouble if there wasn't anything in it for him."

"Who says there isn't?" Danny asks. "It's all about him having control. Look at it from his perspective . . . he hates his job, but won't look for anything else. He doesn't want to go to school either. His dad lets him coast. He doesn't pay rent or anything. Doesn't pay for his car. Doesn't pay for his phone. He just . . . fucking coasts along, and he can't handle the fact that the rest of the band isn't doing that—can't do that. Ryan's mentioned he may be moving. I'm getting promoted soon and there's been talks of the company paying for me to continue my education and getting transferred out of town. Can finally quit my other job."

He doesn't mention you.

What do you have going for yourself? Doesn't Danny understand that the band is your way out?

"And Toni," Danny says. "Well, she's married now and I don't foresee her sticking around long. Even if she does, she's not going to stay in the band. She basically had to beg Austin to ask you to play."

There's brief silence and you sense an incoming apology. It's like there was a momentary lapse between Danny's brain and conscience. Delayed empathy. But what's said was said, and you had a hunch this was how it was going to be all along. You read Danny well, because he starts to say he's sorry, but you cut him off, "Nah, I get it. I've been out of the band for a while now. I'm the back-up."

The back-up. A funny way for your brain to say *last resort.*

Always picked last.

"I didn't mean it like that. You aren't the back-up," Danny says. "You are the drummer. That's that. Don't let Austin make you feel otherwise. Lineups change all the time anyway."

"Yeah, I guess."

You don't want to talk about this anymore because it's only going to make you spiral, your self-worth unraveling on the way down, down, down into the blackened headspace if you aren't careful.

Lineup changes do happen, because if they didn't—what is the alternative?

Austin's choice was you or nothing. You are a step above absolute zero.

You have to change the subject.

"How are you doing, by the way. After last night?" It's the first question that comes to mind.

"Woke up wrapped around a toilet full of puke. Probably ruined my tie for good, but after a Pedialyte-breakfast, I'm good. Been up since seven. Used to it. Work and all."

"I wasn't talking about that," you say, topping your mug of coffee off.

"I know."

"So?" you goad.

"Fucking miserable," he says. "But I don't want to talk about it right now."

"All right," you say. "But I'm here if you need it. I mean it."

"Thank you," he says. "Your house at six?"

"Yeah, but you can swing by early if you want. I'll be around."

But the way he says *'Kay* is more than enough for you to know he won't show up early. You'll be surprised if Danny shows up at all. He's always been the most put-together, but that's because he's been broken so many times. Danny's so good at putting himself back together.

THE ODDS OF DANNY SHOWING UP TO PRACTICE ARE 50/50. FLIP A COIN:

HEADS, HE SHOWS—GO TO PG 72

TAILS, DANNY BAILS—GO TO PG 76

THE STAIRS LEADING up to the porch are ash-gray and warped, beaten by the erratic Midwestern weather. The uneven boards groan as you put weight onto the steps. You hold the storm door open for Austin, "Have at it."

Austin twists the doorknob to the front door, planting a knee just beneath the knob in order to push his way into the house. "Fucking thing sticks."

You follow Austin into the house, but leave the swollen, wooden door open. Almost immediately in front of you stands a central staircase, bisecting the first floor into two large primary rooms.

Off to the left, the skeleton of gutted cabinetry gives away the kitchen. All the appliances have been stripped from this place, and loose plumbing jutting from empty alcoves is the only proof of their existence.

Austin follows your lead in that direction. "It's a tetanus nightmare in there," he says. "But it might be a good overflow area if enough people show. I hope it isn't huge, though. I want to impress Waste Doctrine, but not with numbers. I want to do it with the performance, you know? Who the fuck cares if the scene kids show up, so long as the show kicks serious ass. Come here."

He pulls you away from the kitchen and into the other room.

You notice a case worth of empties littering the floor and at least twice as many cigarette butts and roaches to go with it. A family of broken chairs lie haphazardly around the middle of the room. No table in sight. The plaster walls are cracked in several spots around the room.

Austin kicks a beer can and it skitters across the floor. "Need to clean this place up before the gig, but this is where we'll play. Should be big enough for everyone to set up."

"This place have electricity?" you ask.

"Nah," he says, "But Danny's getting that figured out. His dad or uncle or some shit has a generator."

Ah. Now the pieces from last night are sliding into place. You and Danny were keeping up with one another, shot-for-shot, chasing each one with cheapy three-five beers. By the time you'd lost count, Toni started slipping both of you waters, but there was enough booze in your systems to fuel a racecar. All you could do was try your best to keep Danny's focus off Toni's husband. No sense in having more than one broken heart at the wedding.

"I was wondering what he was on about last night," you say. "He'd mentioned something about having to go on a journey. About needing to find this and that for his mission. Clears that up, I guess."

You honestly weren't sure where Danny was going with that, but you weren't surprised. He was always like that while drinking. Went from tipsy to trashed in the blink of an eye. One moment he was simply loosened up just enough to have an opinion, and the next it was full-throttle into surrealism and abstract conceptualizing.

"Sounds like he was fucked-up," Austin says.

"Beyond," you say. "He wandered off at one point, but so did I."

And so has Austin, but only in body—in mind, he's still with you in the conversation. He's about halfway up the stairs when he says, "Sorry I didn't show. I've had a lot going on."

It's completely like Austin to apologize like this—from a distance. His voice carries down the stairs and settles near the base where you stand, looking up at him.

You don't hold this against him. This distance. This level of unguarded vulnerability isn't something that comes naturally to him. His family is functional only in the sense that each of them performs their given task impeccably as individuals, but together? They may as well live alone.

Not like you. Where everyone is in each other's business regardless of the mess occupying your collective minds. Despite all of it, your familial unit is equally dysfunctional. Everyone has a purpose and place, and everyone is miserable about it. You're all so great at pretending.

You tell him it's all right, though that isn't your call to make. "I'm sure Toni will understand, you know?"

"She already does."

You didn't consider that he'd already talked to Toni. Why wouldn't he? They are in a band together. Your band. The one you're barely a part of now.

"I'm glad. And I'm sorry shit's been hard for you. I know I haven't really been around much . . . " You dawdle and eventually all you can think to say is, "Work and stuff."

And stuff—how eloquent—and the way he replies, *I understand* in a dull tenor makes you embarrassed somehow, like he knows you didn't mean it and your words are somehow a betrayal to his effort in emotional vulnerability.

The staircase is narrow, and you run your fingertips along the dry, cracking walls as you ascend the stairs in a Jesus Christ pose.

As you reach the top, Austin's calling you into the master bedroom, where a wicker chair sits in the corner of the room. A gilded Bible rests in the seat.

"What do you make of that?" Austin asks, the apology already old news. Time to move on.

"It's eerie, but it's an old farmhouse in the Midwest. Kind of fits the anti-abortion and God is King billboards."

"Look closer."

You walk across the room and it's as if your feet are completely silent.

No.

It's as if the floorboards are absorbing all of the noise and energy around you. Including *you*. A feeling, like a stone settling in your stomach, overwhelms you. The humidity wraps around you and squeezes. And yet, when you pick up the Bible it feels like it always has—heavy, but distant, no matter how many times you've read the scriptures. Forced to stay up late, memorizing passages to be used against people, but not for people. Least of all, you. Answers were provided so long as you asked the right questions.

"It's just a Bible," you say.

Austin grins and shakes his head. "Open it."

You instinctively jam your thumbs into the gilded pages, splitting the book roughly at its midpoint, expecting to find yourself deep into the desperate cries or fervent worship of a psalm.

Instead, you're met with inky smears and jumbled markings. Letters that appear to be cut off. Words interposed on one another as if fighting for their position on the page.

You thumb through the flimsy and nearly transparent pages, but it's more of the same. Word after unintelligible word scrawled across the paper, seemingly without adhering to any set of grammatical rules or syntax.

"This has got to be some sort of printing error," you say and pull the book into the wedge of light coming in through the dormer window. Among the dust motes and smokey floaters squiggling across the vitreous filling your eyeballs, you see indentions on various parts of the pages. Intentional markings that give the page texture as if it were handwritten, not printed.

The more you flip through the book, the more you feel as if you aren't supposed to be seeing this, despite your inability to decipher any meaning.

It's wrong. Not forbidden. Sinister.

Could be the heat. Could be your dehydrated body working to filter the remaining molecules of booze from your system. Could be your empty stomach.

But you doubt it.

As does Austin, because he takes the book from you, treating it with the kind of care your mother and father and all his parishioners do with their own Bibles, and says, "It's not a printing error. It's important," he says. "For the show."

But you know the softness in his voice—the subtle crack—means it's important to *him* specifically.

"How so?" It's a legitimate question, but Austin put his guard up and shrugs it away.

"You'll see," he says. "Let's get out of here. We've got other shit to do to prepare for the gig."

CONTINUE—GO TO PG 61

THE DORMER WINDOWS seem to stare down at you, nothing behind the cracked panes of glass but a cold emptiness. "We're already outside. Show me what's going on out here before we head in," you say, though it sounds like an excuse to delay going inside of the dead house.

"Works for me," he says. "I think you're going to love this shit."

Austin leads you around the right side of the house, through patches of overgrown weeds and prairie grass. It's knee high in places. Burs collect on your shoelaces and scratch at your ankles. A crooked toolshed stands behind the house. The door hangs slack-jawed on rusted hinges no longer serving any sort of purpose.

You wonder who would live out here.

There's no barn in sight. No fence or pastures. Not a single weathered mechanical carcass of outdated equipment nearby. You aren't a farmer, but you've learned enough by existing in the only town with a Wal-Mart in two-hundred miles to know that those who don't farm or rent the land, sell the land—otherwise, what's the point?

Then again, what did Austin say? *There's nothing out here.* And you've existed in your shit-town long enough to know that peace and quiet is priceless. Getting away is a dream.

"Alright," Austin says, turning to walk along the backside of the house. "I know I've been hyping this up, but I'm honestly a bit nervous about this."

"What's there to be nervous about?"

Austin's always been an anxious person, but when it comes to showing off, usually he's incredibly cocksure. Overconfident in this kind of thing. He knows he's intelligent and has intense bouts of creativity, but when he gets like this, you know it's serious. He's genuinely worried you'll disapprove or think it's stupid. Of all the people in the band—your approval has always been the most important to him for whatever reason. You're also the only one who has ever called him out to his face. The only person who's challenged his ideas and creative direction.

"You always have wild ideas."

Notice you didn't say *good* or *great* or *killer*—you said *wild*—and the attempt at reassurance falls flat. You can't be sure if it's because you didn't stroke his ego enough or if it's something else entirely. The dark blurred shape of the collapsing shed stands out against the otherwise bright surroundings in your peripheral vision and you assume his idea has something to do with the shed. Some haunted house installation type of thing. Maybe there are loose saw blades or axes or broken chains in there he wants to use as décor. Deer skulls and antlers.

Whatever is in there, you won't know because Austin's slowly been edging you toward the opposite side of the house, away from the shed.

"I'm not worried that my ideas are bad because they aren't. I'm nervous because last time it hurt—" Austin responds before you can object. "And I fucking liked it."

So, is he protecting you or having doubts about including you? Maybe he wants to keep all of this to himself until it's time for the show so all credit goes to him and his brilliant ideas.

"So fucking show me," you say. "I'm not afraid."

"You're missing the point. It isn't about fear. Not really, at least. Not how we normally conceptualize fear."

You two round the corner of the house where the triangular ground level entrance of a storm cellar butts against the foundation. The door looks like it was thrown together with scraps. A sheet of corrugated steel is crudely bolted to dead wood underneath. The hinges remain affixed to the frame though, and the handle made from bent rebar works as any handle would. And whatever locking mechanism was in place has been beaten and cut to pieces by the crowbar and bolt cutters lying in the dirt next to the entrance to the cellar.

"Time to redefine fear." Austin lifts the cellar door, its hinges groaning. He drops the door once it reaches the peak of its arc, letting it clatter open to the ground beside you.

Despite the afternoon sun, little light follows you two down into the dugout storm cellar. The entryway walls are lined with cinderblock. Words are etched into them, but you can't make out any of the uneven white lines. You follow Austin down the stairs and are blanketed with dread. It layers like a second skin grafting itself to you. Suffocating you. Every breath you take feels like it could be your last.

It's almost palpable how easily, how willingly, Austin's settled into the feeling and into this atmosphere. This pit. This blackened headspace you're all too familiar with—and off to the side, deep into the recesses of the underground room you see a faint glow, pulsing like a distress beacon.

Fear isn't the word you'd use to describe the feelings racing through your body. Discomfort and confusion come to mind, but it's the curiosity clinging to the dread that's overtaking you, mixing together into a perverse elation. A need for understanding. A desire to feel . . . anything.

This isn't fear as you know it. *Knew it.*

"What the hell?" you ask, but it may as well have been a whisper. No, a thought. You barely hear the words from your mouth as if the pulsing across the room is absorbing them.

You're pulled closer, like the fibers of your being are being dragged along a track and you're unable to veer off course no matter how much you want to, and you wonder what would happen if you tried? Would you be unwound, stitch by stitch, like one of your mother's sweaters? Turned into a pillar of salt for looking back?

Curiosity won't let you turn away.

Austin is no longer your guide because that would imply that he possesses some authority and knowledge. Instead, he stands beside you as your equal. Another willing participant. A curious and completely enamored bystander. He stumbles forward, landing on his hands and knees before the pulsing wall, which has drawn your absolute focus and attention.

The wall breathes.

It exhales hues of light—energy—with every pulsing glow, and inhales . . . you? Your thoughts. Your words. Your breath. Every footstep you've taken, drained by the being before you. It is consuming you.

Though there is no pain, like Austin claimed—and this fact, of all things in this bewildering experience, is unsettling to you.

Austin doubles over, arms wrapped into a tight hug around himself, and cries out.

You can't make out his words, but you reach to comfort him, to pull him away. He doesn't respond to your touch. It's as if you don't exist. You lean in to get his attention and notice tears streaming down his face. It's a face you've seen a thousand times. Not Austin's, but the visage of countless members of your father's congregation. A mask worn by desperate and vulnerable and so often the most miserable of people completely engrossed in fervent worship.

You thought maybe by touching Austin some of his pain would be transferred to you, easing the burden of suffering, but all you feel is the sweat-soaked cotton of his Mayhem T-shirt. You remain engrossed in the wall conceptually, but you can't be certain of the authenticity of the emotions you're experiencing. It's all too familiar, witnessing others experience religious fulfillment while you remain an empty vessel.

"Austin," you say. "Austin—don't!"

Austin reaches out to the wall, his fingers caressing it like savior's robes.

The words *I'm fine* echo through your mind. They're stretched out. Pulled apart. Each syllable hits your ears simultaneously and yet, drawn apart, creating a unique and unexplainable sonic sensation. It's like the being is speaking for him. Through him?

"Come on, let's get the fuck out of here."

But he's enamored, his fingertips grazing the wall's bulbous surface, tracing eccentric patterns. As he does so, the being's exhalations seem to quicken and the cellar hums with energy. You feel a peculiar adoration—and a voice speaks, OPEN YOURSELF UP TO THE ESSENCE. And it's your father's church all over again. *Essence. Spirit. Love.* A congregation full of people begging you to be vulnerable. To give yourself to something you can't possibly understand, let alone at a young age. Most of the church doesn't get it either, if they were honest. But they demand you to expose your soul. Your heart. And for what? To publicize your problems? To give your bullies fuel to torment you at school, when you're far, far away from the mirage of protection the church provides?

Confessions your parents can use against you. Teach you lessons in the name of love.

Love. Such an interestingly combative word.

The voice goads you. DON'T CLING TO WHAT ISN'T REAL FREE YOURSELF

Austin continues to paint invisible pictures on the wall while he wails silently. His muscles shift his expression and pull his skin in the most haunting pantomime you've ever seen.

And you think you're beginning to understand Austin's plans for the show. Making them feel something beyond themselves, offering this new awareness. A true religious experience. Miracles. A spirit they can grasp onto and devote themselves to. You don't get how he will incorporate it just yet—how could you? But it's evident that everything he's said up to this point is true. The music scene will be forever changed, and there's no way Waste Doctrine will leave unimpressed. As for the audience—it makes sense Austin wants to keep the show intimate. Only those who will appreciate it should be here. That's the only thing Austin could ask for, and now you grasp that aspect. It's all about who is deserving of this transcendental experience, and more importantly, who will accept the invitation. Who will believe. Concepts that feel just like home to you.

WHAT ARE YOU WAITING FOR? the voice goads.

REACH OUT AND TOUCH THE WALL. YOU NEED TO FEEL SOMETHING—GO TO PG 64

RESIST THE INVITATION. YOU KNOW BETTER—GO TO PG 68

AUSTIN TURNS THE volume down completely and asks, "Do you hear that?" Gravel grinds underneath the tires and there's the occasional metallic plink as pieces are kicked up into the wheel wells and chassis.

"What am I supposed to be hearing?"

"Music."

Ah. Now you get it. He's onto one of his musings. It's been an afternoon and you aren't sure you're up to being regaled by whatever it is Austin's about to go on about, but given the time and place—secluded in a car—you don't really have much of a choice. And you know it's best to just roll with it than fight it, so you play along. Honestly, of course.

"Seems to me you've turned it down," you say.

"That's not what I'm talking about."

"I know, I'm just giving you shit," you say. "So. What kind of music am I supposed to be hearing?"

"You aren't *supposed* to hear anything," he says. "It's not about permission. I'm talking about what music do you hear when it's quiet? The music that plays in your mind whether you want it to be there or not."

Part of you thinks the question is a trap. Your parents have instilled in you the necessity to have a right answer locked and loaded for any given circumstance. 'What do you want to be when you grow up?' *Engineer.* 'What are you thankful for?' *God. Family.* 'How are you?' *Good.*

Any other response would become too messy. Too involved. Too personal. Complicated.

You answer Austin's question with broad strokes. "It sort of depends on my mood. More often than not, my head is a jukebox. I can pull anything I want to hear from it and press play."

"Nah, I don't mean like that," he says. His voice doesn't have the usual frustrated tone. No impatience present, but rather his tenor is calm and collected, trying to convey a sense of understanding. A good teacher. A preacher. "It's not about what you want to hear. It's about what you hear when everything is silent and you're alone with your thoughts. Even if they are screaming at you, shouting above everything else—that's part of the music—but the rest is important too. Do you see what I'm getting at?"

"Yeah, I think so. Almost like the musical equivalent to our conscience. Self-talk, but musical."

Austin bobs his head a couple of times, considering your words. You can tell he doesn't quite agree, but you seem to be on the right track. "You're close. It's like the marrow in our bones. You get it well enough, but you're focusing too much on understanding the concept instead of conceptualizing. So, me? I hear everything at once. That's how it starts. Just heavily distorted droning tinnitus type shit. But then root notes begin to surface, and then chord-like structures . . . I'm not sure if they are chords to be honest. But the pieces come together slowly and then words come to me. Ones I don't always know—foreign, yet I understand their meaning. It feels like a gift, almost. Like I am given the words that allow people to . . . I don't know. See. Feel. Experience something beyond . . . "

He trails off, but continues before you can reply.

"And I know that's what music is if you strip it down. Noises of varying structures put together with intention. I get that. Music is supposed to convey particular feelings and emotions, but that's not entirely what I mean. I think I'm given the words, this music, from something else—somewhere else—and it's like the cult house amplifies every atom in me. It makes my voice stronger. I'm not sure why, I just know I'm supposed to do it. And I can't unhear it. Ever. I know it's going to sound cheesy as fuck, but it often sounds like us—our band. It's what *purpose* sounds like."

By the time he's through philosophizing, you're back in town and headed toward your place. You've volunteered to call the rest of the band so Austin can grab whatever gear he needs.

It isn't lost on you that you weren't able to answer his question. You aren't sure what to make of his drawn-out diatribe, but think maybe the music Austin hears in his head is all some convoluted egoism. An excuse to hear himself speak at length. A way for him to fill the airwaves as usual.

But then, standing in the middle of your driveway, he says, "You don't need to answer now, but think about it. Think about the music you hear. Then focus on it and bring it to practice. Harness it for the gig."

Then again, maybe it isn't the music in his head, but rather your ability to hear it that's some attempt at being something it's not. It's that sinking feeling again. The one that says you're unable to experience something that everyone else seems to be able to, and it begins to drag you down into the cold, dark parts of your mind. A reminder of the perpetual absence in your life.

You stand at the front door and key into your house, Austin's car blaring music behind you. Despite the heat, it feels incredibly cold as you walk into the house. It doesn't matter that the air conditioning is on full-blast to keep up with the heatwave, you know the coldness is emanating from your parents who are sitting on the couch, and from the icy words coming from your father's lips, "Sit. We need to talk."

Go on, get it over with. Take a seat— go to pg 80

You're tired of being treated like a child—go to pg 84

YOU'VE WAITED YOUR whole life to feel this kind of divine presence. You've yearned to enter into a holy space and interact with something beyond your flesh and mind—something seemingly tangible that everyone else around you is experiencing, but for some reason always eludes your invitation like something is inherently wrong with your existence.

THERE IS NOTHING WRONG WITH YOU

You aren't sure you believe the voice, though it is here. You are here. And there is no doubt that you are in the presence of something beyond you, so despite Austin's promise of pain, you step forward and touch the wall with a shaky fingertip.

The wall pulses sangria-purple when your skin meets its flesh, an affirmation not only of your existence, but belonging. It is warm and slicked in an oily substance. This surprises you. You expected nothing but coldness, and you find yourself comforted by the warmth seeping into you through your finger. It slowly crawls up your arm, to your shoulder, and eventually to the base of your neck where it nestles. Time slows to a near-halt while the warm sensation spreads throughout your body as if it's in your blood and every beat of your heart pumps it further and further throughout your circulatory system.

Waves of dim light ripple in your peripherals. Their borders enclose and constrict your focus, slowly reducing your vision to blurry tunnel vision. It only takes a moment for the miniscule blips of light to collapse, leaving you in utter darkness. You try to blink it away, but the blackness remains.

"Austin," you call into the darkness. His name seems to evaporate the moment it leaves your mouth. "What is this?" You aren't even sure if you can hear it or if it is only in your mind. Your words, swallowed by the wall.

Then—an explosion of color washes over you, thinning the darkness behind your eyelids and inside of your mind as every atom in the storm cellar coalesces into a hallucinatory vestibule. This place—this instance—doesn't feel like a destination, but merely a passageway. A waiting room on the edge of reality. A dreamlike womb.

A sonorous voice speaks to you, though the words morph into something else entirely. They're stretched like a held note to near incoherence, though you're skeptical if you'd ever understand their meaning. It isn't the kind of language you understand. No—it's more of a feeling. A blurred line between music and language. And you aren't sure about the pain Austin was talking about because you're experiencing ebullient bliss. It's as if you're weightless—existing in a single moment both inside and outside of time, suspended in space—somewhere between elation and disquieted fear.

Maybe you're missing the point.

Maybe that *is* the point.

This language is not meant to be understood by you in the traditional sense. You are not being spoken with in order to communicate. Maybe this is what it was like being talked to in the womb as a cluster of gooey matter somewhere between the living and the dead, and this—right here, right now—is the closest thing to peace you'll ever know.

There is an impulse to move. A jolt in your nerves. The voice asking you to play.

You wade through the kaleidoscope of color splattered across the cellar. Waves of light bend around you as if you're controlling them, pulling them every which way in order to see clearly. A strand of pure yellow wafts your way. You pull the thread, wrapping it around your finger before plunging it into your mouth, tasting the essence.

Austin writhes on the floor, holding his stomach.

You don't understand.

YOU DON'T HAVE TO UNDERSTAND.

You move toward him and offer a hand, but he refuses. His face is contorted in what seems to be excruciating pain, eyes pinched shut and his teeth clenched. Yet when he opens his eyes and meets your gaze, you see nothing but euphoria inside of them.

"This is what I want," he says. "It's what I've always wanted."

***

D-1—IF YOU WERE NOT SENT HERE, THIS DOES NOT CONCERN YOU. LOOK AWAY, FOR NOW. CONSIDER THIS BUT A GHOST IN YOUR PERIPHERAL.

It is as if you've stepped back not quite into *your* life, but one just to the side of it. Memories flood your mind, but from a unique distance, like everything you've experienced up to this point is a recreation. A rerun. You don't feel exactly like you, but have you ever?

FINDING YOUR PLACE AGAIN IN THIS WORLD CAN BE PAINSTAKINGLY DIFFICULT, BUT YOU'VE DONE IT—CONTINUE BELOW

***

Coming down isn't the slow fade you're accustomed to. It's instantaneous, like waking from a dream. But even then, you aren't left in a haze. You're barely groggy. One moment you were in some cross-section of existence, where reality overlapped with unreality, and the next—you're standing in the dim storm cellar, your finger pressing against the wall's smooth surface. It reminds you of a biology textbook illustration of lung tissue. Bubbly and soft. You're surprised your touch doesn't puncture its pulsing membrane.

"So how about that shit?" Austin asks. He stands next to you and stares at the wall like it's an achievement to be proud of. Something he's earned rather than stumbled upon. It's hard to tell if he's experiencing any lingering effects. Any pain.

You are left with questions bordering on pragmatism and the existential: what is it, because it's obviously more than a wall. Where did it come from? Is it safe? How did it get here? Who the fuck owned this house? And on, and on, and on.

"What the fuck is this?" you ask.

"It's God, or something like that." Austin's nonchalance riddled with confidence. "And it's going to change things for us forever."

You pull your phone from your pocket.

"No. No pictures." Austin knows you too well. Your need for proof. Validation. Assurance.

"Just checking the time."

You don't remember when you arrived at the house or entered the cellar or when you touched the wall, but it's late afternoon now and while you're plenty familiar with the elasticity of time while on substances, the similarities of this experience and those of religious highs don't escape you. The cultish brainwashing tactics disorient your perception of time and place, ushering you into a sense of belonging, leaving you emotionally vulnerable—receptive.

Your experience with the wall was not how Austin said it'd be. Yet another common feeling. Despite all of that, Austin's words surface. *This is what I want. It's what I've always wanted.* And maybe that is the point for you too. Maybe that is what transcendence feels like. Maybe this is true.

You emerge from the cellar changed, though you cannot explain it. This internal transformation is not something for words.

THE CHOICE HAS BEEN MADE, AND ALL YOU CAN DO IS EMBRACE THE CHANGES—
GO TO PG 61

IT DOESN'T TAKE much to keep your impulse control in check. All it is, is an inherent act of pragmatic self-preservation. Standing in front of this glowing aberration, watching Austin in a state of apparent possession, is more than enough to make you take a step back despite the wall's warm invitation calling out to you, seeping into your mind. You aren't so trusting anymore, having had your childlike naivety replaced by cautious and distant cynicism because you used to believe in the good of others until they proved you wrong over and over again.

YOU DOUBT. The words are light, like cotton in your ears.

"It isn't about doubt." Your words fuse to dust motes and float around the cellar where they are swallowed by the wall.

You used to long for this type of experience. Anything to substantiate a belief in the unknown. The spiritual and supernatural. At one point in time, you thought you could wrap your head around the idea of wholeheartedly giving yourself to something beyond oneself—be it God or a concept. Now, with it staring at you, speaking to you—you aren't transfixed by the otherworldly, yet material phenomenon, but instead you still remain utterly skeptical.

UNFAITHFUL.

"It isn't about that either," you say. The word is so dirty in your mind. Unfaithful. A weaponized word. One always meant to ostracize and designate people as *other*. Unfaithfulness was the root of the world's problems according to your mother. It was also the root of your parents' stagnant and unhappy marriage, though they don't realize you know about this.

It took you a long time to come to the conclusion, but you know it isn't about doubt or faith or fear. At least not in regards to some higher being. It's always been about self-doubt and the absence of something in *you*—something that others keep telling you is there, though they can never explain what it is or offer any sort of help on where to find it beyond platitudes of 'Just believe' and 'Trust'.

It is the idea that you are innately broken because they need you to believe you are broken. It isn't about perfection. Sin. It's about control through guilt—and a singular way out of it. You quit believing the lie a long time ago.

"I don't need what you're offering."

YOU DON'T KNOW THAT. YOU CAN NEVER KNOW THAT UNLESS YOU EXPERIENCE IT FIRST.

These contradictions left you depressed for so, so long. This contrived absence. This hole in you. The barrier—a wall—in your mind.

"Just because I don't need it, doesn't mean he doesn't," you say, staring at your friend.

Austin continues writing on the wall. His actions and mannerisms—the whole thing is odd, like he's in two conflicting states. A sort of aloof concentration, while staring inactive for periods of time as if lost in thought, before manically scrawling on the wall with his finger as if he's using paint only his mind's eye can perceive. He does this, slack-jawed, before dropping to the floor, wincing in agony.

You call his name, but he ignores you. Maybe he doesn't hear you—can't hear you? Austin lays flat on his back, awestruck eyes wide open, and you consider pulling him to his feet and dragging him from the cellar.

But you don't.

You wouldn't call it hesitation, but rather an act of observation. A pause; not because you are afraid, but because you want to understand. Is this devotion?

Austin wants this. He said so himself. Maybe he needs this the same way your mother needs her hymns. Who are you to pull him away from that comfort?

Austin grips at the air, hands clenched tight, before bringing his fist to his mouth. It's like he's performing—screaming into an invisible microphone. And you realize that's exactly what he's doing. He doesn't move from the floor, but continues to perform his strange, uneasy act. His face contorts, his mouth forming enunciated but silent syllables. It's like a hushed song, you think. Channeled from an unknown origin.

NOT JUST A SONG—A HYMN—A PSALM.

"To you?"

WHO ELSE?

"What are you?"

I AM MANY THINGS AND I AM NO THINGS.

"Typical god nonsense," you say. "Do you even know who you are?"

YES. IN THE VASTEST SENSE OF THE WORD—A TOTALITY. A COLLECTIVE BEING, AND YET ONE OF COMPLETE INDIVIDUALITY DEPENDING ON WHO'S PERCEIVING AND EXPERIENCING ME. DOES THAT MAKE ME A GOD? WHAT IF I AM SIMPLY A MANIFESTATION OF **YOU**?

"What about him?" You gesture at Austin.

HIM TOO. AND EVERYONE ELSE. PERHAPS THE LARGER QUESTION AT HAND ISN'T ONE OF MY BEING AT ALL, BUT RATHER ONE OF YOURS. DO YOU KNOW WHO YOU ARE?

You know with absolute certainty who you are. "Yes."

You grow tired of arguing with a wall. Maybe this is all bullshit. Some collective hallucination of Austin's doing. Wouldn't be the first time.

Austin's erratic body language has become unsettling, and while he doesn't seem to be in any sort of immediate danger, you no longer wish to observe whatever it is you're witnessing. You pull him to his feet, despite his protests.

He continues to mock-scream into a microphone, gesticulating like all his depressed heroes—his scowling face curtained by strands of hair, shoulders hunched like a sunken version of a Tarot's Hermit. You push him in front of you, guiding him out of the cellar.

The sun is high in the sky, filtering the cloudless expanse of blue in bright yellow cancer. Austin lingers in the prairie grass while you swing the storm door closed, as if closing an ancient tome. Or tomb.

Austin opens and closes his mouth, but nothing but strained syllables come out. He's like a baby trying out new sounds, seeing how they feel rolling off his tongue. Trying to find his voice. Maybe the wall is a manifestation of Austin. A new millennium god. He's always seen himself as one. Maybe it's all been an act of self-worship.

You guide him toward the porch and sit on the sagging steps while he comes down. It's quick, all things considered, but while you both stare into the cornfields outstretched before you, you're well aware the two of you are seeing completely different versions of the landscape—and yet everything before you is entirely true. The line between the observable and unobservable realities of the world is tenuous.

"You ready to get out of here?" you ask.

"Sure," he says, though it's unconvincing. The grip this place has on Austin is alarmingly firm.

WHO ELSE BUT YOU COULD GUIDE HIM THROUGH RELIGION'S DEATH GRIP?— GO TO PG 61

THE WAY THE four of you lounge in the basement is like a recording of your past lives has rewound and is playing crystal-clear through your mind. Ryan's standing off to the side, his amp turned off, quietly practicing scales while Danny methodically unloads his gear and sets up in the same spot he always does stage left—almost like he's performing a ritual. Danny showed up at six on the dot, and it's like he's clocked in for work. He plants his amp down and plugs it into the wall. Then he unwinds his cables, which are stored with the utmost care. Eventually he pulls his bass from its sticker-ridden hardcase and adjusts and readjusts his shoulder strap. He'll do this two or three times. Then he'll switch on his amp and wait patiently for the rest of you to start.

Meanwhile, you've been trying to occupy Austin's attention—which is scattered because he showed up high on something. You've had to keep an eye on him since he walked through the door. He messes with the TV, but loses interest and lights a cigarette. He's coherent, but a bit spacey.

"Turn the fan on and smoke in the bathroom," you say. "Or go outside."

He gives you a look. He's dazed enough not to start anything, but it reminds you that at some point, someone has to push *play* and you know where the recording of your lives will end up. Petty squabbles and tension-infused hangouts. Here's to hoping you can change the script this time around.

Austin drags hard and drops to his hands and knees. The cigarette dangles from his mouth and leaves a small trail of ash on the carpet as he crawls over to your drumkit. He exhales into the port hole on your kick drum. Austin laughs, then licks his fingers, pinching his cigarette out.

"There. Happy?"

"Don't be a dick," Danny says. "Let's just practice."

It's already starting to play out like it did the year after you graduated from high school. Everyone's on edge, trying to figure out their lives. Growing up—maturing at different rates. Contemplating who was still worth your time, not because you don't like them anymore, but because life is different now. Transitory.

The tension between Danny and Austin is palpable already, which is new. The meek Danny of yesterday has found his footing, his voice. A threat—because Austin's voice is all he has.

"Put the CD in for a sec," Ryan says, handing you the burned Memorex. "I want a refresher on how I start the first song."

You're grateful for Ryan's ability to completely dismember a conversation. Though he's hardly a mediator—he's only prolonging an inevitable explosion. For now, in the short-term, it's what the band needs.

You toss the disc into the PlayStation and crank the volume on the TV.

The four of you listen in relative silence.

"Think you can handle it?" Austin asks.

You press X on the controller to pause the music and grab your sticks. The callouses on your hands have slowly softened over the past year, but it's hardly indicative of your ability. Everyone needs a break on occasion.

Without responding, you take a seat on your drum throne, count down, and play—replicating Toni's drum parts almost perfectly. You keep qualifying it in your mind. *The parts are simple. It's mostly just blast beats for a few bars. The parts are pretty typical for this flavor of black metal.* And on and on.

Austin turns around to face you, planting a foot on your kick drum. You expect a snide comment, but instead he's nodding his head, making the horns with his hands. Between your earplugs and the rest of the band playing, it's impossible to hear anything Austin's saying, but you read his lips well enough. *Well fucking done. True fucking black metal.*

You restart the song, this time with the track playing through headphones. It's a bit muddled, but you intend to isolate the drum track later. For now, this works and it feels like an old school jam session. Imperfect. Raw. An energy you can chew on.

Austin is in rare form this evening. You've never heard vocals like this from him. Especially while riding whatever high he's on. He's animalistic. It's like he's channeling something otherworldly.

You've played through the demo a couple of times now and while it hasn't been perfect, you think you'll be able to nail down Toni's parts after a bit more practice this week. Both Ryan and Danny were spot on, though you can tell Danny's heart isn't in it. Seems like he's going through the motions. Biding his time before quitting the band for good. It doesn't seem like Austin noticed. He was entirely too immersed in his own performance.

"I'm grabbing some water," you say. "Anybody else want any?"

"Yeah, and a beer," Austin says.

"My dad only buys piss-beer," you say, but no one seems to mind.

"I'll pass," Danny says. "Not feeling up to it after last night."

"Bring it anyway. I'll drink Danny's," Austin says.

You fill cups of water from the dispenser in the fridge door and yell down the stairs for them to come grab their cups. Then you wander to the garage-fridge where your dad stashes the beer. Cheap-ass Keystone Light. The stuff he only keeps around for when he grills with the other church leaders. You pull four from the case and kick the door shut behind you just as the overhead garage door groans open.

You glance at the clock as you walk through the kitchen and head downstairs.

"My parents are home," you say. "Let's bail and take these to go."

"Is it true you fucking yakked all over your dad in church?" Austin asks.

"In front of God and everyone," you say. "So, yeah. Let's just head."

No one complains. They simply turn off their amps and wait for you.

"You can leave your gear if you want," you say, listening for footsteps above you. It's just like when you were in high school, waiting for the right moment to quietly sneak up the stairs and slip out of the garage.

You're first in line at the top of the stairs, your friends trailing behind you as you poke your head from the doorway and glance around the corner. It's childlike. Fun. You realize you don't need to do this, but why spoil a good time?

Your parent's footsteps have quieted and you're surprised they haven't called out to you. They'd have to have seen your van and everyone else's cars parked along the street. Maybe they want to see you as much as you want to see them.

Oh well, you think. They're upstairs and you've got a clear path through the kitchen and to the garage. The four of you make it to the garage without issue.

"Well, that was easy," Ryan says.

Except, you notice only your mom's car is in the garage. It's normal most Sundays because your parents often take separate cars given he both shows early and stays late those days. Thing is, you heard two distinct sets of footsteps upstairs. Your dad's infidelity is hardly a family secret, though that ended years ago with church-initiated couple's therapy and your mom's tight leash. So, it's particularly interesting to see your mom's car in the garage. You wonder who could be upstairs with her and does your dad know? Even if he did, would he care? Do you?

The four of you trail out of the garage.

At least you thought so. You look back and find Austin dawdling. He's grabbed the case of Keystone from the fridge and has the biggest grin on his face. Just like the old days.

"What?" he asks. "It's time to celebrate."

"Celebrate what?" you ask.

"The band is back, baby." He cracks a beer then and there in the driveway. He kills it and tosses the crinkled can into your front yard. "To true black fucking metal."

Ryan and Danny exchange a *why the fuck not* glance. Soon they're toasting to black metal and tossing their empties in the yard.

"Fuck it," you say, and do the same.

You pile into the van and back out of the driveway. You crank the AC. It's still humid, despite the sun starting to set—gleaming layers of blue, purple, and orange bruising the skyline.

"That your dad?" Austin asks.

Sure enough, the cabernet-colored Ford Explorer turns onto your street. You lift a finger off the steering wheel, acknowledging your dad's nod toward you as you pass. You don't need to, but you reply, "Yeah."

"Good," Austin says. "We've got a church to rob."

THE PLAN IS ALREADY IN MOTION—
GO TO PG 99

IT DOESN'T TAKE long for Austin to rummage through the garage fridge for your dad's beer. You stash the hard stuff in your room, but don't want to open those doors. Not tonight.

"Still drinking this piss?" he asks, tossing both you and Ryan a can of Keystone. He cracks it open and takes a long pull.

"My dad's always been cheap and he doesn't drink that much," you say. He keeps it around for grilling with the other church leaders and football games. Otherwise, you rarely see him drink, despite the stories you've heard of his youth. Small town stuff before he was a man of the cloth. Even then, that doesn't stop most of the men of your dad's congregation. They're men of a certain kind. Men of God. Men who fish and camp. Men who work and men who turn their girlfriends to wives and into mothers. God fearing American men.

"More for me then," Austin says, setting the empty can on the table.

Soon, Ryan adds his to the tower of empties and turns on the PlayStation. He uncoils the controller and slips a burned CD into the drive. The receiver screen glows orange when he turns on the surround sound. You watch the numbers climb and climb as he turns the volume dial.

The band's live recording from Austin's garage blares through 5:1 sound. Though the guitars sound washed out and hollow, you try to focus on Toni's drumming, but you're distracted by Austin's shrill screams.

The three of you listen through the set, accompanied by another round of Keystones. You take a seat behind your drums for the second play-through to get into the headspace. It's like your sticks are electrified, the way you're getting amped up.

Ryan glances at his phone, "Where's Danny? It's pushing six-thirty."

Austin stands and turns on his mic. "Who cares? It's fucking black metal. Who needs a bassist anyway?"

You don't bother stopping the CD because it's immediately drowned out by Ryan's guitar. He repeats the intro for a few bars and shoots you a glance, waiting for you to start playing.

It takes a few false-starts to really get into the groove and feel comfortable behind the set again. The chemistry of the band has changed, and while you and Ryan could jam for hours together, playing actual songs—structured and intentional—takes a different type of focus. Toni's parts aren't necessarily difficult. You wrote the bulk of them a while back, but she's added her own flare to them.

"Don't worry about playing the parts exactly," Austin says.

You've played through the first two songs several times now and your agitation must be showing. "It's just this transition," you say. "Toni's fill feels so natural and I'm not getting it right."

Not to mention your blasts are weak. You're rusty from lack of practice.

"It's fine," Ryan says.

"Everyone is going to be focusing on the atmosphere. The fucked-up house. The . . . " Austin trails off, but you were there in the house. The eeriness. The dismal and bleak void of that house is palpable. "It'll be chaos. A darkness this town hasn't felt before. And we will be the ones ushering it in."

"And if Danny doesn't show?" you ask. Can't they hear how thin you sound without a bass player?

"Then he doesn't show," Austin says. "And he'll miss out on the best fucking gig this town has ever seen or will ever see."

Ryan doesn't seem to disagree, though it's hard to get a read on him at all. Blank faced. Zoned out. However you want to spin it, Ryan doesn't comment and you can only take it as indifference. Austin's apathy—as well as his ardor—has always been contagious, but the pendulum tends to swing erratically, without warning, and doesn't allow people to get out of the way.

The CD has stopped playing and there is a hum coming from the speakers. It joins the buzz from Ryan's amp and the monitors Austin set up.

Suddenly, the room feels too electrified. Like it has a pulse, and the current flowing behind the walls and under the carpet and through the ceiling is too much. You imagine the wiring constricting the house like vines, breaking through the drywall, and seeking you out.

"I need a break," you say. "Gonna get some fresh air."

You don't find fresh air in the garage, but rather another Keystone and a quiet place to text Danny again. He hasn't responded to your last one, but sometimes you have to nag Danny into coming out of seclusion.

You wander to the back patio and can't remember the last time you hung out back here. Family dinners on the deck seem like they took place in another lifetime. Really, it seems like the past two or three years have been on fast-forward. Some abysmal autopilot that's taking you God knows where. You wanted to be gone by now—out of this house and out of this town—but for some reason you can't shake this place. Everyone else seems to have the answers for you, but they're to the wrong question. It's never how to leave or grow. It's *why are you still here. No motivation. No decent job. No four-year degree.* It's never about what you've accomplished, but what you haven't. Always an absence of something.

That's what this gig means to you. An out. And right now, the absence you're focused on is Danny's. You dump the remainder of the shitty Keystone into the grass. You watch it bubble like an acid bath of piss before heading inside.

"You good?" Ryan asks.

"No. I'm tired of this fucking town and everyone in it." You turn off the TV and surround sound system. "Leave your gear if you want, but I'm going to check on Danny."

Neither of them shows concern and you can't be sure if you're more worried for Danny's wellbeing or the gig at this point, but you tell yourself they go hand in hand. A little lie not to feel too self-centered. You grew up masking selfishness as genuine concern. Your dad wore it like corpse paint. It was your mother's Sunday makeup.

"My parents will probably be back by the time I am, so practice is over. Feel free to come along if you want."

You don't really want the company, so you're relieved when Austin says, "Nah, you go ahead. We've got a couple things to pick up for the gig. When you're there, tell Danny he needs to get the generator. Without it, we won't have power and I'm not playing a fucking acoustic set."

"Should we meet you at the roadhouse?"

"You worry about Danny first. He'll actually listen to you," Austin says. It's his way of saying he doesn't think Danny is going to come through with it. That he's a flake. "Keep your phone on. I'll call you later."

You help Ryan lug his half-stack up the stairs and back into his car.

"You sure you don't want me to come along?" he asks.

A dozen excuses pop into your head. Why can't you just say *no?* He won't be offended. Thankfully, you won't have to agonize over it because Austin butts in, "No, I'm going to need your help."

"For what?" Ryan asks.

"Don't worry about it," Austin says.

And now you are starting to worry about it because nothing good ever comes from Austin's nonchalant scheming. It's just like Austin to drag Ryan into some sort of mess.

You check your phone, but Danny still hasn't replied.

Fuck.

Fuck fuck.

You don't waste any more time and hop into your van. The neighbors give you one of those *what-was-that* shrugs as you hit the gas a little too hard, squealing your tires when you pull out of the driveway. You give them the finger because you couldn't give a shit if a little noise has inconvenienced their peaceful Sunday evening. You're too concerned about finding Danny dead in his apartment.

HURRY!—GO TO PG 104

YOUR PARENTS SIT on opposite ends of the couch. There's plenty of room for you to sit in between them, but why set yourself up for that kind of onslaught? Instead, you settle for one of the uncomfortable chesterfields across from the couch. A strategic move. One that places just enough distance between the three of you. You run your finger across the top of the end table nearest your mother as you walk past her, leaving a trail through the dust. You know it's going to bother her to no end.

"So?" This is how your dad starts every conversation.

"So what?" you ask. It's just part of the script. You wish just for once that he'd drop all the pretext and fucking say what he means, but you know that's not the angle he works. He wants you to admit to it first. To own up. To acknowledge whatever it is he thinks you've done wrong. All the while your mom will sit and wait and stew and come to his defense the moment you challenge him. Ever the supportive wife.

"Do I even need to say it?" he asks.

You wish he would.

"No, I get it," you say.

"I don't think you do. I don't think you get any of this—of what you did. You made a fool of yourself, and you embarrassed me—and your mother—in front of my congregation. Do you understand how damaging that is? How that looks."

You're gripping the armrests, absentmindedly picking at the decorative rivets lining the front of the chair. "It's always about image, isn't it?"

"Don't start with that."

"It's true, though. You didn't bother to ask how I'm feeling. How the wedding went. 'Oh, how's Toni and the rest of your friends?' Would it kill you to give any sort of a shit about me or what's going on in my life?"

Your mom winces, like the word *shit* physically hurts her.

"Watch your mouth," she chimes in. "We taught you better."

Now you've done it. Got the both of them going. There's nothing quite like getting yelled at in stereo sound. It's incredible how they can be so still while agitated. They sit there like a Renoir painting. *Parents Disciplining Child*.

"We do care," your dad goes on. "Why do you think you're still in this house? Because we care about you and we thought you knew better. That you at least understood enough about your circumstances to appreciate how much we care."

"What circumstances?"

"You're clueless," your mom says.

"You're too old to be living like this," your dad says.

"Like what?"

"Like you're still in college. I understand staying out sometimes, but you're—stagnating."

You feel a fingernail start to bend as you keep digging at the rivets. Keep at it and it's going to give and separate from the nail bed.

"Like you don't drink sometimes. Half the congregation are Sunday Christians."

"Half the congregation doesn't concern you. And it's not entirely about the drinking. It's about getting so drunk you puke all over me in the middle of a sermon. You like to argue with me— about everything—so go on. Argue. Let's hear how having a couple drinks and getting blackout drunk are the same thing. Tell me how celebrating your friend's wedding responsibly and passing out in the sanctuary of a church and projectile vomiting on the pastor is the same."

"Never said they were the same thing," you say.

"But you're acting like it," he says. "Like there's no difference and there's nothing to be ashamed of."

"Can you stop with the guilt?"

"I'm not trying to guilt-trip you, but I'm trying to understand how you don't feel even an ounce of remorse for what you did. How you can't see that what you did was beyond just a little screw up—"

"And how you can't even get yourself to apologize." Your mom tends to slip these comments in at the worst times. As if you weren't already thinking about this.

These are the moments you start to zone out during arguments—when they start tag-teaming, hitting you from both sides. You know you fucked up, but it happened and it's over, so what else is there to be done?

Thoughts of the abandoned house ooze into your mind and distract you. It begins to pull you into an alternate state. A slippery one. One where the walls of your mind close in and speak to you—

"—still drunk—?" Your mom's voice.

Your dad is snapping his fingers, getting your attention, and pulling you back.

"—not even listening." Your mom.

A glass of water has appeared on the table next to you. You drain it in two long pulls.

"I'm not still drunk. I was outside for a while earlier. Probably dehydrated," you say, shaking the pervasive thoughts of the house on Cult Road.

"I don't want to keep harping on you, but it's hard for us to know how to care for you when you don't seem to care about anything yourself," your dad says.

It's like they see nothing. Or worse, they see only what they want to see.

"That's not what I was talking about anyway." It takes a moment to refocus, but you remember where you were going with this. "You keep saying that you care, but you don't. You care about appearances. So look at me—this is what you get. You told me to go to college. So I did. You said I needed a job. I got one. I don't know what else the fuck I'm supposed to do. It's not my fault the job market sucks and I get paid peanuts. Can't afford rent, so I'm stuck here. Do you think I want that? To be in my twenties and living with my parents? Do you know how bad that makes me feel? How pathetic I feel? I get it. I didn't get a four-year degree. I don't have a career—I have a job. And yet, I did everything I was told I was supposed to do and here I am. And if doing everything 'right' got me here, then I want to do something else. At least try to."

Your mom stands, "I can't deal with this. Not when you're like this."

It's like she didn't hear a word you said, and instead is giving up. Your dad, on the other hand, is good for a fight. Always has been. He's focused and ready to pick everything you've said apart.

"You did. And we're proud of you for that. And you're right. You can't control the job market, but you can control your effort. You can't blame outside factors for everything. If you don't like your job, look for a new one or go back to school."

"Because it's that easy," you say.

"It's not about being easy. It's about doing what you need to do. I don't think I'm being unfair here. I will co-sign your loans—again—if you want to go to school, but you can't live here anymore if you're just going to piddle around."

"I don't want to go back to school. I want to play music and I want to tour."

You know your dad hates the music you like, so it surprises you when he says, "Then do it."

And from the sound your mom makes, you'd guess she's more surprised than anyone right now.

Your hands relax and there's a wave of relief in your fingertips as blood rushes through them. "We were going to practice tonight," you say as though you're asking for permission. "We've actually got a gig coming up. Sort of a last-minute thing."

The tonal shift in the conversation is deafening, but more so, it's unbelievable and you know there will be a catch.

"That's fine. We've got our usual plans. But—and I need you to understand how vital this caveat is—this is your last shot. Practice. Play the gig. But don't waste any more time. Mine or yours," he says, standing to bookend the conversation. He's always been a hardline kind of person. Needs an immediate sense of closure.

You know your mom is going to linger with this for a long time. She wanders back into the living room, swapping places with your dad, with a rag torn from an old T-shirt in hand. You don't say anything to her as you get up and leave the room. You look back and see how with a single swipe, she wipes the end table, removing the trail you made and every trace of you from the room.

FADING AWAY HAS ALWAYS COME EASY— GO TO PG 89

YOUR PARENTS SIT statue still on opposite ends of the couch, both staring directly at you, through you, or maybe *into* you—as if the strange occurrence at the house on Cult Road seeped into your being, altering your genetic makeup, and they're examining the change. Scrutinizing it. You.

Call it parental instinct.

It is like you've stepped into a Rockwell painting. A depiction of American life that everyone's been fooled to believe is real. Idyllic family units. Parents awaiting their child, ready to discipline them. Turn them into model citizens.

They are impatient.

Your mother's hands are folded in her lap, clasped tight, as if holding her posture in place, keeping her from falling to pieces on the couch. And your father all but vibrates with anticipation, waiting for your reaction.

Their faces fall in disbelief when you don't acknowledge them, and instead turn around and walk out the front door without a word. Has it always been this simple—to disregard what is expected of you?

✳ ✳ ✳

You've been driving around for an hour, zigzagging through side streets and residential neighborhoods without any destination in mind. Clearing your head. The clock on the stereo tells you it's time to head home for practice. It's Sunday, so you figure your parents will be long gone by now, but as you turn onto your street, it appears they have company. There's a car parked in your space on the driveway, but you can't make it out from this distance. You approach and park along the street, but remain in the van.

The car is unfamiliar, and you hope it's not their therapist. The

84

last thing you want is to be sucker punched with an emergency family therapy session. Wouldn't be the first time.

Looks like band practice is all but fucked, and you text everyone telling them so. Almost immediately, Ryan calls you, but you ignore it—your focus drawn toward the bag sitting on the front steps. It's the one you always take on trips.

Surprise.

Carefully, you get out of the van and approach the house. There's a note taped to the bag: *Leave your key*.

That's it. No drawn-out letter demanding you apologize, asking you to think about your choices. Your indiscretions. Giving you an ultimatum. It's unlike your father not to overexplain his reasoning. He always makes it crystal clear how badly you've fucked up.

You wedge your fingernail between your keyring's loops. It feels as though your nail is going to give, bending as you pry it open. A small gap forms, and you begin to slide the key loose. It eventually comes free, leaving your fingers smudged in black and smelling of metal. You trade the key for the bag. An easy exchange. The bag is light, but you don't bother to look inside to see what your parents deemed important enough to give you. It's doubtful they'd have picked correctly.

Then again, the sentiment is mutual because you have no idea who your parents are either. Beyond a Bible, what would you slip into your parent's bag as you kicked them out of the house? What is it that defines them?

LOOK INSIDE. SEE YOUR PARENTS AS THEY TRULY ARE. LOOK AT WHAT THEY'VE HIDDEN FROM YOU. THESE ARE THE PEOPLE WHO RAISED YOU. WHO JUDGED YOU. WHO SCRUTINIZE YOU.

A wedge of glass, unobscured by curtains, provides a place to observe through the front windows of the house.

YOU CANNOT UNSEE THIS AND YET, YOU CANNOT LOOK AWAY. NOT NOW. NOT EVER. I'M SO SORRY—CONTINUE

The living room is in a state you can only describe as organized destruction. An unrecognizable atavistic affair. Every photograph has been turned around, placed flat to suffocate the fake smiles portrayed underneath. Candles light the dim space, spewing thin lines of smoke into the air while the smoke detector hangs open; the battery dangling from wires as if disemboweled and unable to cry for help.

Your mother is draped in your father's vestments, which are streaked and filthy. She sashays toward him, golden chords in hand.

It's difficult to tell his exact position, but you can see that he's on all fours in profile view, his back arched like a frightened cat.

Your mother shoves your father to the floor, a bare heel in back. She looms over him, crawling incredibly close. Closer than you've ever seen them together in years. She teases him with the soft, fine tasseled ends of the chords. Gliding it across his bare skin.

Then she pulls the braided ends tight, and begins to choke him with it.

He hollers, seemingly in abject ecstasy, while the painting of Jesus above the mantle appears to smile down upon his disciples.

DON'T LOOK AWAY NOW. YOU'LL MISS THE BEST PART. NOT THAT YOU HAVE THE CHOICE IN THIS MATTER. NO. THIS PART IS WRITTEN SPECIFICALLY FOR YOU— CONTINUE

A third person comes into view from the other side of the room, presumably from upstairs. As they wander into the picture, a neon pink strap-on wobbles to and fro. They wear a featureless masquerade mask and nothing else.

You no longer wonder who the car belongs to.

It's a safe assumption that this mysterious third person is heading for your father, who's still face down on the carpet like a dog having its nose rubbed in piss. Disciplined. Humiliated. Taught a lesson. But the interloper walks past your parents toward the mantle.

They run a finger along the old oak plank. The very one your mother dusted religiously. Head toward Christ, they thrust their arms into the air and scream. It's nonsense.

It always has been.

You want to look away, but there's nothing that can divert your focus.

Your father stands and you wish he hadn't. He quickly turns to face his guest, hands on his hips, while your mother comes back into view with a bottle of communion wine. A generous host.

The guest takes an urn containing your grandparent's ashes—you don't remember which—opens the lid, and offers the contents to your mother. The only time you've ever seen her dump out a bottle of wine was when you were fifteen, and you'd sneaked it from church. The toilet is still stained.

Once the slurry is mixed, your parent's house guest takes a handful, rubbing it down her bare breasts and ribs, before staining her mask with a single handprint. Another handful is smeared across your father. And then the vestments your mother wears. All in strange symbols you can't quite place, but swear you've seen before. Maybe you have.

Your phone buzzes in your pocket, pulling you from this trance as they begin what appears to be a flirtatious ritual. Trading sensual gestures. The third guest completing this unholy ménage à trois.

"Hello?" It's only a whisper, but it's all you can manage.

"You okay? I've been calling."

"Yeah, I'm . . . " You aren't sure what you are, but *okay* isn't it. Fumbling with your phone, your keys, and the duffel bag, you get into your car as quietly as possible. "I'm heading your way. Practice is off."

"That's what I've been calling about. Austin said we can practice at his place."

"I won't be able to get my kit from the basement."

You aren't sure how much to say at this moment. What can you say?

"No problem. Toni left her kit in his garage. We're all set. For real, it's all good. Swing by and pick me up."

✶✶✶

You park in front of Ryan's red-brick duplex. You're cutting across the yard just as he's walking out the front door, guitar case in hand.

You lug Ryan's half-stack down the front steps and heave it into the back of your van.

Ryan crushes his cigarette on the sidewalk, and slides his guitar case in next to his amp.

"How did Austin seem about moving practice?" you ask.

"He asked why a bunch of times, but didn't seem to actually give a shit. He's just nosy."

"I can live with that."

"So why'd we move practice? Your parents still around or something?"

"Something like that, yeah."

"So what's with the bag?" He lights another cigarette as he climbs into the passenger's seat. He rolls the window down, giving you plenty of time to think of something good to say.

WHY NOT THE TRUTH?

You settle on a half-truth. "They kicked me out."

"Shit."

"Yeah, shit."

You bum a cigarette from Ryan, one of many you think you'll need tonight, and drive.

The stereo in your van switches to disc five and Ulver's *Bergtatt* begins, enveloping the interior of the vehicle in a woeful sorrow.

WHAT ELSE CAN YOU DO AFTER WITNESSING THAT?—GO TO PG 94

"**SO THEY LET** you off the hook?" Austin asks.

"You sound disappointed," you say.

"Just surprised. Your parents are usually hard-asses." Austin was the first to arrive and he's been sipping from a bottle of Wild Turkey since he showed up. He isn't sideways, but you take the bottle from him, take a swig, and don't give it back. Last thing you need is him getting plastered before the rest of the band shows up.

"That hasn't changed. I don't think I'm out of the woods from last night yet. The conversation moved away from it though and I think my dad just got sidetracked. My mom hasn't forgotten and she won't let him forget either," you say. "I lucked out for now, I think. But my dad said this is my last shot."

Austin reaches for the booze, so you take one more pull and cork it closed.

"Like I said, this is my last shot. So no getting fucked-up," you say. "Come on, let's set your mic up."

He gives you a sullen look, which you blame on the booze. It's better than his typical petty pissed off agitation, but you know he's going to hold this against you at some point.

You try to lighten the mood by telling him you'll party after practice, but for now, you need to be able to sit upright on your drum throne. It isn't unreasonable and he knows this. Regardless, he sets up his mic and monitor speakers in silence while you check the tuning on your toms. You play a fill and tweak your floor tom. All in all, they're about as good as they'll get until you replace the drumheads. Who needs to be pitch perfect, anyway? Not you, *the drummer* for Abyss—a thought you haven't had in a long time, though it excites you. It elevates your mood and the last-shot mindset. It truly feels like a now or never moment in your life and it's rare that your parents are on board, even slightly, with anything to do with these endeavors.

A new question surfaces as quickly as the other dissipates and you find yourself asking Austin, "Where do you think it came from? The house, I mean—and everything in it."

"I'm not sure you're asking the right question," he says. "At least, I don't think that's the important question."

"How do you figure?"

"Because it doesn't matter where it came from. Who gives a shit? What matters is how we use it. And what truth does that fucking miserable house hold? Because if what's in there is real, then everything else we've ever known and have been told all our lives is bullshit. Or in the very least, it's only been a shred of reality. A sliver of truth. And now that we know there *is* more out there, it's our job to fucking show the world. Starting with our shitty flyover town and Waste Doctrine." Austin grips the mic stand, swaying just slightly. "Don't you feel like there's something about this place that keeps us here? This town, I mean. Maybe Cult House is it. Some fucked-up anchor or magnet or whatever that won't let people go. People run, but they're always dragged back."

It's like Austin to think this—to blame his dissatisfaction with life on anything but himself. There's a part of you that wants to believe it though. A part of you needs to believe this, because the truth is harder to accept.

You find yourself agreeing and nodding along, because if it's the town that's keeping Austin here, then it's the town keeping you here too.

"And I feel like the only way to break free from it is to release whatever's in that house," Austin says. "In any way we can."

"What do you have in mind?"

"A ritual," he says, as the doorbell rings. "Good. They're going to need to know too."

***

"It's like this," Austin says while Danny and Ryan set up their gear. "Think of the gig as a ritual or—or like a service."

"Didn't think this was church," Ryan says.

"It's not fucking church," Austin says. "Not like you're thinking. And the cover fee and merch will be tithes."

"You always do this." Ryan tweaks the distortion pedals at his feet.

"Do what?" Austin steps toward Ryan.

"Never mind. Forget it," Ryan says.

"No. You started it, let's hear it. What is it that I always do?"

"Control everything. Make the band's decisions. It's more than that though. You decide what is cool. What is true. What is acceptable. Everyone is a poser until you decide they aren't. Everything is too mainstream or not good enough—until you decide it isn't. It's fucking annoying." There's a quick pop as Ryan turns on his amp. He grips his guitar by the neck and slings the shoulder strap over his head as he says, "And now you've made our gig exactly like church."

Before Austin can snap back, Danny steps between them. The movement is natural. Danny's always been a good mediator, and he does it so fluidly. He leans over and picks at the carpet near his sticker-covered bass case like he's dropped something, but you doubt he has. It's just cool-collected Danny keeping the band together, saying, "Even Satan has a church," before he uncaps a bottle of water and takes a drink.

The attempt to subvert Ryan's jabs seems to work well enough. At least enough to prevent a brawl from breaking out in your basement.

Austin steps back toward his microphone and absentmindedly checks the cables. You can tell he's fuming, but he's holding it in. He knows what's at stake. Your final shot—yours and the band's. The last thing you need is to lose your guitarist.

Still, Austin has never been good at completely rolling over. Like your dad, Austin's always good for a fight. "So what if it is?" Austin asks. "If you'll let me fucking finish, I'll explain how this won't be like any church you've ever been to. No one has. Not in this godforsaken shithole. But if we can pull it off, it'll be the first of many *services*."

There's an eeriness in his voice. A lurking abstraction lacking any sort of elucidation.

"You going to finish preaching, or are you going to stand there?" Ryan asks.

You try to get his attention, but Ryan's facing away from you. The crack of your snare resounds throughout the basement, but he still doesn't pay any attention to you. Probably thinks you're warming up. "Just leave it," you say.

"Yeah—" Austin starts, but is interrupted by Ryan's distorted strumming.

Ryan mutes his strings and kills the chord.

"I was trying to say—" Austin continues.

Another chord chokes Austin's voice to nothing. His mouth moves in silent mimicry. He grabs his mic and shoves it toward the monitor speakers. The resulting feedback pierces the tension and grates your ears. Austin waits until Ryan stops to cut the feedback and speak. "Fuck it." Austin turns to you and says, "Come with me. I need your help with something."

Danny rests his bass against his amp and shoots you a look. You've both waded through the band's interpersonal bedlam enough before and have an understanding that when things get tense, it's best to split up and cool off. "Works for me," Danny says. "I'm going to need Ryan's help getting the generator. My uncle is cool with us using it as long as we bring it back with a full tank of gas."

Ryan yanks his guitar off from around his shoulders and sets it in his case. He powers off his amp and walks upstairs without a word.

"Right on," Austin says. "You go take care of that and we'll meet you at the roadhouse. Do you remember how to get there?"

"Yeah," Danny says.

"Don't bother bringing the toddler if he's still having a tantrum."

You get up from behind your drums, taking a pull from the Wild Turkey. You pass it around amongst the three of you. "Just chill out, alright? All of us. Remember, there won't be a gig without a band. Be mad. Blow off steam, but let's not fuck this up before it even starts. You two can sort your shit out later."

"He was being a dick though, right?" Austin asks.

"Yeah," you say.

"Usually I'm the dick," Austin says.

"Yeah," Danny says.

"Fuck you," Austin says, but does so with a grin.

"In your dreams."

You hear the door upstairs. "Better go catch him. We'll meet you at the house, alright?"

Austin's words settle in your mind as you get into his car. It's true. He's usually the asshole of the group. Ryan tends to hold things in, so you wonder what made him go off, let alone antagonize Austin the way he did. Austin's always been full of it. Self-important. Talks of grandiose plans. Maybe Ryan's just sick of it. All talk, but no substance—completely antithetical to Austin's yearn for authenticity. Except that is authentic to himself. He is a walking contradiction. Who he is and who he wants to be perceived as are two different people.

"Taking me somewhere weird again?" you ask.

"Yeah," he says. "But you've been there a thousand times."

He doesn't need to say it because you know where he's taking you—your dad's church. Only you don't know why.

CONTINUE—GO TO PG 109

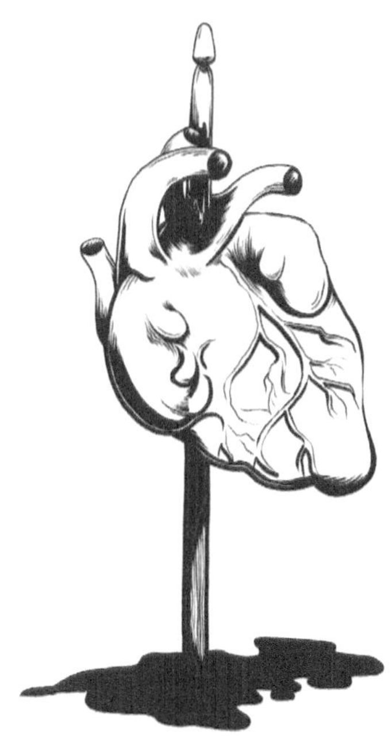

YOU BACK THE van into Austin's driveway and throw it in park. Ryan pounds on the garage door a couple of times. A haze of smoke drifts out into the stale summer air as the door opens. Austin stops it about halfway, causing you and Ryan to stoop in order to lug the gear inside.

A rich man's workbench stands prominently at the back of the garage. Name brand tools neatly organized like it's a display at a hardware store. You doubt any of the batteries to the power tools are charged. Some of them appear unopened.

Skis and recreational boating equipment hang on the wall. You've never known Austin or his dad to be into sports, let alone watersports, but who knows? You're realizing you don't know everyone as well as you thought you did. Time shifts everything.

"Danny's not here yet?" you ask, though this is unsurprising, as time and again Danny's proven to flake.

"See his car anywhere?"

"Figured I'd ask," you say.

Austin's in a mood, but you won't even begin to take a stab at the cause. Anything and everything will set him off or plaster him with somber malaise. Instead, you bum a cigarette and ask him for a light. Then you grab the open bottle of bourbon sitting on the dusty garage floor and take a pull. You don't want to get fucked up, but including yourself in the debauchery always seemed to lighten his moods. Maybe you're enabling him. Or yourself.

But if participating in Austin's little rituals puts him at ease and makes it easier on everyone, you're happy to join in.

NO AMOUNT OF BOOZE WILL LET YOU UNSEE WHO YOUR PARENTS ARE DEEP DOWN.

"Called him, but he didn't pick up," Austin says. "Left a message. We'll see if he shows."

"It's Sunday," you say, trying to shake the voice.

"And?"

"He's got a big boy job now." You try not to make it sound like an excuse. Austin settles back into the folding lawn chair that's splayed out atop an oil stain. You can already tell that practice is going to be a wash.

"So he's sold out," Austin says.

"Whatever, man," Ryan says. "He's got rent and bills and shit."

The implication that Austin has it easy doesn't go over his head. No bills. No loans. No rent. You can see it in Ryan's eyes. *Take a look around. You live in your dad's house free of charge. You work when you want to.* Only you hear the words in your voice—full of vitriol and a bitter edge. A resentment you have against not only Austin, but yourself because the statement applies to you too.

"Let's just practice." You take another pull of bourbon. Anything to loosen the tension. Bury it deep. What's the use though, if you don't kill it first? Burying animosity alive will only enrage it, making the decaying feelings a hell of a problem later. And your band has already dug so many graves.

"Why bother, if the rest of the band doesn't show? May as well be a fucking jam band and see what happens. Besides, you know the parts. You pretty much wrote all of them for Toni."

That isn't true. You heard the demo. The parts are similar, sure, but you and Toni have a different type of groove and you don't want to throw the rest of the band off. It'll be important to nail down the transitions for Ryan, especially if Danny doesn't show. It's true fucking black metal—who needs a bassist anyway?

"Just start playing," you tell Ryan. "First couple of songs off the demo. Got to get a feel for them."

You settle into Toni's kit fine, only having to make subtle adjustments here and there. You hate messing with other people's setups though, because it's like dancing on sacred ground to you. Feels off. You already feel like you're stepping on her toes too, even though she made it clear she was ready to hand the spot back to you. That the throne is yours again.

Soon enough, Ryan's playing. He repeats the intro for a few extra bars while you nod along, finding your place to come in. It's hard not to notice as Austin stands, his face framed in dark wavy strands as he shakes his hair out. He closes the overhead garage door, leaving about a foot gap at the bottom.

You run through a couple of songs before Austin joins. He's been standing in the center of the garage, sometimes still, sometimes erratically moving along to Ryan's distorted riffs and your pummeling beats. Austin's energy has always been a pendulum in motion, swinging from quiet and methodical to frenetically sinister.

When he finally joins the musical chaos, his shrieking seemingly stems from some void. Another plane. Another world. Someplace without light. Someplace deep within himself, yet entirely alien. Wherever it's coming from, it affects you. Like there's some psychological gravity pulling your brain matter, stretching and reshaping your thought patterns.

QUIT FOOLING YOURSELF.

You know where this is coming from.

And apparently, so does Ryan. His eyes roll back. The solid white stare is what catches your eye, but not what holds your attention. No. It's his fingers, which flicker like candle flames across the fretboard, their forms as distorted as the sound waves emanating from his half-stack.

Austin continues to belt out incoherent words.

They aren't 'incoherent' in the typical heavy-metal sense of the word. It isn't a matter of crooked syllables. Garbled phonemes. His words aren't indistinguishable to you by any fault of his own. It's because of you. You are a stranger to these words.

BUT YOU DON'T HAVE TO BE.

YOU ARE WELCOME.

Palpable intensity saturates the garage. A yearning to belong, but you're nagged by a familiar sense of needing to earn it. You raise the tempo slightly—synced still to Ryan's strumming—a natural quickening fit for this section of the song while Austin wails along, and yet your perception is thrust into slow-motion. Your sticks appear to be fanned out as you haunt your snare with ghost notes. A trick of the light, you think. A blur. Movement captured in a camera shot. Your sticks splinter and crack.

You become acutely aware of the fog of cigarette smoke suffocating the practice space. The pungent odor clings to every surface. Whiskey vapors bubble from the neck of the glass bottle at Austin's feet. Their chemical structure floats through the air in three-dimensional illustrations before your eyes. It's like the world's layers are unpeeling. Exposing themselves to you.

It doesn't feel like the first time, but it is the first time you've allowed yourself to see it. To smell it. To taste the whiffs of color evaporating from your sweat-slicked skin.

You aren't sure how long Austin and Ryan have quit playing, but when you finish your mind's song, completing the drum fill and choke the ride cymbal, the garage is quiet, save for the lingering snare drum reverberating off the rafters. The two of them stare at you, stupid grins adorning their faces. An image of them in grotesque corpse paint flashes over them, but quickly fades as you blink and refocus.

And there's that urge again.

You leap from the drum kit, knocking over the throne in your attempt to find a trash can. Your guts betray you, constricting and covering you in a wave of nausea, and you eventually spot the rusting Folgers can, still exhaling a weak smoker's breath.

The added smell of a month's worth of spent butts only propels your vomiting further. It doesn't take long before the can is half full. A fleet of Camel filters swim in an ocean of sour bile. You blame the heat. The smoke. The booze. The stress. Everything but the dark pit in your gut and vast blackened headspace warping your thoughts. The abyss.

You know you can't run from the truth. Any of them. The wall, or your parents.

Austin lights a joint and offers it to Ryan, pressing pause on the heated comments from before. Between the solid practice session and little pot, you figure they'll be good long enough to play the gig. It's only temporary, but it almost always is.

"I've got an errand to run," Austin says. "For the gig. You wanna come?"

Ryan's got an iron lung and just now exhales, nodding along.

"Nah." You need to collect your thoughts. Drink some water. Be anywhere but here or around Austin right now. "I'm going to go check on Danny. See where his ass has been all evening."

"If you see him, tell him to get the generator sorted out. Without it we won't have power and I'm not playing an unplugged set."

Austin doesn't seem to mind when Ryan says he'll tag along with you.

"Let's meet at Cult House afterwards. I'm going to need help setting things up."

"Works for me," you say. You have nowhere to go anymore, and a late night will put off having to sleep in your van.

CONTINUE—GO TO PG 113

YOU DRIVE A lap around the parking lot to get an idea of who you may run into while inside. The lot is mostly empty, save for a few twenty-year-old sedans with high school marching band stickers and rust patches eating away at the wheel wells. If you had to guess, they probably belong to the high school kids lingering after youth group.

"Oh this is going to be fun," Austin says, tossing another empty Keystone can to the back of your van. He's downed two on the way to the church, and he's egged Ryan on to keep up with him. Danny hasn't cracked one open since the toast on your driveway. "Time to rob the house of God. Think he has guard dogs?"

"If we're going to do this we're going to get in and out." You snap your fingers. "I'm not going to fuck around and bully high schoolers."

"You're no fun," Austin says.

"Save the fun for later," Danny says. "Once we're hauling ass out to the Cult Road House."

You meet Danny's gaze in the rearview mirror. *Thank you.*

"For real, stay focused on the gig." You pull around to the other side of the church and park behind the semi-trailer full of recycling. It's supposed to be one of the youth group's fundraising efforts, but you aren't sure the thing has ever been emptied.

Danny unbuckles his seatbelt and starts to open the door, but Austin cuts in, "Nah, nah. I'm going with."

"Danny should come," you say.

"Fuck you, I'm going."

"The fewer the better," you say. "I know where things are and Danny's—"

"Not drunk, sure, sure," Austin says.

"I was going to say *quiet*, but sober helps."

Ryan's in the backseat enjoying the show. He cracks open another Keystone, slugs it back and burps. "Yeah, and I'm keeping watch."

"Goddammit. Fine," you say. "Danny, stay here."

Austin's sliding out of the passenger seat and into the parking lot before Danny can protest. He slams the door so hard crows on the powerline scatter.

"Shit," you say.

"Go catch him," Danny says. "I'll call you if anyone new pulls up."

You close the driver's side door gently enough it barely latches shut. This wasn't how you planned on spending your evening, and you aren't sure you even want to be here. If this morning's shitshow wasn't enough, the church is a Pandora's box of memories and being enveloped by them last night was tough enough. At least you had your friends and an endless supply of booze to numb the biting emotions that being at church sics on you.

Now you're mostly sober and playing babysitter.

By the time you reach Austin, he's peering through the glass and yanking on the door handle. "Come on, God, open up." Then he turns to you and says, "Guess no one's home."

"Keep it down," you say, pulling him away from the door. This end of the building is newer construction. Brick. High ceilings. Exposed steel beams. It's supposed to scream *contemporary* but looks like an elementary school gymnasium. The addition is attached by a singular hallway that connects it to the original part of the church.

You pull Austin away from the door and walk around the perimeter of the building, sneaking quickly past any windows, trying to find the right balance of stealth and inconspicuousness.

"I thought you had keys to get in."

"I do, but that end of the church is where the youth group meets."

"Maybe that's where we need to be. Gotta go in there and make disciples of true black metal. Turn them from their perverted Godly ways."

"Invite them to the gig. We'll leave fliers," you say, although your sarcasm seems to have eluded him.

"Shit, I forgot about gig fliers," he says. "You're brilliant."

If only he were this amicable every time he got wasted. The last couple of years would have been drastically different if Austin had been easier to get a pulse on. It's too hard to roll the dice though. You deserve better. Your friends deserve better. Why take a chance of getting yelled at and humiliated for being who you are by being around him? Is that all the gig is—a calculated risk?

It's only more proof of what you already know—that you're all desperate for something and will put up with more bullshit than what's healthy in order to get it.

You've pulled Austin into an alcove near a maintenance door. Last you remembered all of the church locks were keyed the same way. You glance at your phone and check the time. Unlocking the door shouldn't trip the alarm system yet, but you can't be certain. Lots has changed since you quit going to church.

"Before we go in, remember to keep it down. Don't dick around. I don't want—" What? What is this wall you can't seem to hurdle? Disrespecting your parents? The church? God? Some guilt-stemmed hesitation seems to overcome you. "—want us to get caught and fuck up the gig, you know?"

Austin doesn't know. He has no problem laying into organized religion. You get it. The disgust and disdain for all of it. But he lacks the guilt. Didn't grow up with it. There's a unique type of contempt that goes along with living it for so long, and he completely lacks any sort of solidarity with you. He's angry at the world, but the church is low-hanging fruit. Church isn't your thing anymore, but that doesn't mean you want to go in there and ravage the place. That would feel off. Something deep down won't let you do that. Maybe it's trauma. The truth.

You plunge the key into the lock and twist.

"So let's get in and get out."

The church's footprint is circular, save for the additional wing at the back. Classrooms and offices jut out like tumors around the entire circular floor plan.

"Lead the way then," Austin says.

It's easier said than done because you don't exactly know what you're looking for. Neither does Austin. On the drive over you probed for info. He kept saying he'd *know it when he saw it*, but the gist is he wants accoutrements to adorn the Cult Road house.

You figure the best bet is to go back where your day started.

The sanctuary hasn't aired out yet and the chemical smell of industrial grade cleaners shrouds the room. Only a couple of emergency lights remain on and their angelic blue fluorescent light is all that guides throughout the sanctuary.

For saying he'll know it when he sees it, Austin is making you do most of the looking. You open the vestry and find that it's had only a perfunctory cleaning since this morning. Candles have been tossed half-assed into the back corner instead of into their boxes. Robes still dangle askew on broken hangers. Although, the absence of the communion wine does not escape you, and you wonder if it was your mom or dad's doing.

You find an altar candle lighter leaning against the inside of the vestry doorframe and grab it. It's got to be nearly three feet long. Solid brass, save for the wooden handle. At the end, a small smoke bell curves almost like a shepherd's hook. You check the wick, which is fed through a small opening near the bell. There's still plenty of length left.

You exit the vestry, asking, "What do you think of this?" thrusting the candle lighter into the air like He-Man.

Austin's lit a cigarette.

He stands, hands on his hips, staring at the gigantic empty cross hanging on the wall behind the altar. He drags. Exhales. Then asks, "Where'd Christ go?"

"Lutherans aren't known for their iconography."

"I want the cross."

"Yeah, and that'd be discreet. A fucking twenty foot cross." You don't bother explaining how impossible the logistics of the cross idea are and show him what you've found instead.

Austin seems pleased by the idea of lighting something on fire at the gig. He continues to puff away at his cigarette, hands-free, and walks to the altar. "If I can't take the cross, I'm taking these," he says, referring to a couple of brass candelabras to match your lighter.

Austin shoves the candelabras into your hands and wanders into the vestry.

Your phone vibrates in your pocket.

"We need to go." Your hands are full, but you know it's Danny. Call it a feeling. "Now."

You hear him rummaging and then, "Fuck yes!" as he comes out of the vestry with a couple of bags marked, *Cavanagh*—communion wafers. The body.

"We'll feast." A dark wave glints in his eyes. A trick of the light?

Your phone continues to buzz violently in your pocket.

WELL, NOW YOU'VE DONE IT. NO WAY TO GO BUT FORWARD—GO TO PG 118

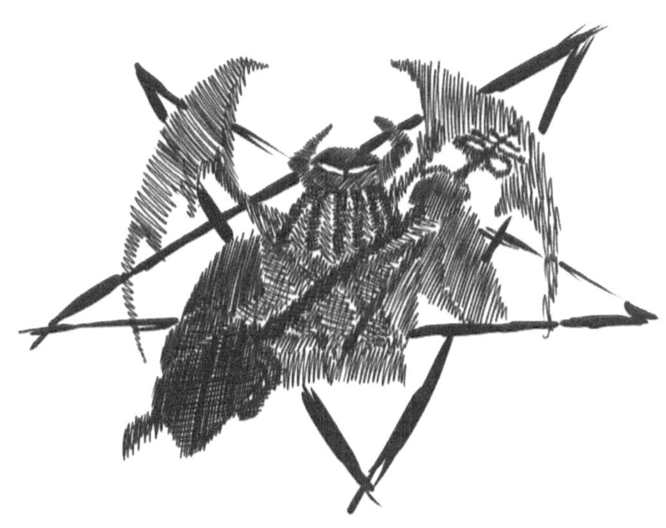

THE MAIN ENTRY to Danny's apartment building sticks, the door swollen from humidity. It budges after you put your shoulder into it. The stairs creak under stained carpet as you take them two at a time to the third floor.

You've been through this before. Danny said he's good now. Said that therapy is working, and his meds keep him level. But it isn't foolproof.

Banging on the door doesn't do anything but piss his neighbors off. The grouch across the hall has been telling you to *pipe the fuck down* since you started knocking. *Don't you know what time it is?* You've learned not to bother with that neighbor though. They're all bark. Eventually they'll turn up the volume on their reruns and leave you be.

You check your phone again. Still no texts.

"Come on, Danny. I'll beat the fucking door down if you don't let me in."

You press an ear to the door, listening for anything. Running water. The TV. Music, but you know it's no use. Danny's more considerate than anyone in the building and keeps the volume on everything low. Uses headphones for music and practicing bass.

Your best bet is listening for movement.

Even if he didn't let you in, hearing his footsteps approach the door would be okay. The metallic slide of the security chain. The twist of the deadbolt. Anything. All you need is any indication he's upright. Your neck begins to itch as the hairs stand up while a hot wave of panic-induced sweat starts to mist your skin. The heel of your hand feels like it's already starting to bruise as you continue to beat furiously at the door.

Tom, the neighbor from the unit next door, steps out into the hallway in nothing but gym shorts with stoned, sagging eyes. A heavy towel is rolled up along the seam of the doorframe. It catches and unrolls as he closes the door to a narrow crack, failing to keep the smoke in.

You hear a voice ask if it's the cops.

"Nah, baby it's not the cops," he says.

"You see Danny around, Tom?"

He sucks in a lungful of air. "Left about a couple of hours ago, maybe longer."

You both exhale at the same time, but deep breathing isn't enough to calm you down or give you peace of mind. You're absentmindedly picking away at your cuticles. The skin on your thumbs is rubbed raw in places. Cracked and bleeding.

"Are you sure he hasn't come home?"

"I mean, I can't say for certain, but I don't think so. Saw him lugging his guitar down the stairs," Tom says. "You don't look so good. Like you saw something you weren't ready to see."

"I'm good." The fact Danny had his bass with him gives you some relief. "He was supposed to meet at my place for band practice and never showed. Just a little worried is all."

"Nah. Dan the man is all right. You'll see." Tom slaps your shoulder. A small, but genuine effort of reassurance. "Probably got hung up on something. He told me his job's been on his ass a lot lately. He's putting in all sorts of extra hours, apparently. They don't pay him enough. All the shit he does, he definitely should be making enough to move out of this dump."

The voice inside croons for Tom to come back.

"Can't keep my girl waiting," he says. "But I'll tell Danny you came looking for him if I see him."

"Thanks," you say. "I appreciate it."

It isn't the answer you want, but it'll have to do for now. You won't be fully satisfied until Danny's standing in front of you. The beige, smoked-stained walls seem to be closing in on you as you trudge down the stairs. You see yourself as you descend. Some perverse omnipotent tunnel-vision in which your body appears like it's being swallowed. Is this truly how you see yourself? Perpetually dejected. Disappointed in the lot you've been given. No interest in dissecting the anatomy of your life's decisions in this instant, even if they'll tell you what you want to know. What you need to know. The perspective is disorienting.

The stuck door to the parking lot catches you, your balance knocked off kilter during your brief trip out of reality, and keeps you from faceplanting on the sidewalk. The swim through the black pool in your mind leaves you doused in ennui. A panic-induced blackout, you think. Too focused worrying about Danny to keep a clear head.

But then why was it all about you?

You shrug the thought aside and unclip your keys from your jeans.

You hear Danny shout your name through the summer air like a blurry heatwave in the distance. A distortion of the truth. You key into the van and hear your name again.

Swarms of gnats and mosquitoes are visible in the yellow cone of light raining down on Danny's car from the streetlamp. He's waving to get your attention.

You walk past a dozen cars to meet him at his Impala.

"Some asshole parked in my space," he says deadpan, but his tone shifts to let you know he's joking. "But it's fine, because that asshole is going to help me with this."

You glance in the windows as you walk between his car and an SUV parked too close for comfort. His amp takes up the majority of the backseat, while his hardcase is wedged in the narrow gap along the floor.

Gasoline fumes emanate from the open trunk.

"Austin said we'd need this," Danny says, pointing at a two-wheeled hunk of equipment. A gas can secured by bungee cords sits beside it. "But we're going to move it to your van. My trunk won't shut with it in here. The trunk door slams against the generator every time I hit a bump and there's no way I'm driving it out to the house on those gravel roads. I don't really know how to get there anyway, so the asshole who took my parking space gets to drive."

He must sense that you're put off because the dry-deadpan bit is Danny's way of trying to alleviate tension. Does he get how worried you were?

"How'd you get it in your car in the first place?" you ask. "I could have come helped if you would have called."

There.

Slide the comment in nice and easy. He's too smart not to catch it, but will he grab a hold of it and shake you down over it?

"My uncle helped," he says. "I knew you'd be at practice, so I didn't want to bother you."

"I could have helped," you say, freeing the gas can from the bungee cord. You wait to see if he'll say anything, but it's radio silence. Dead airspace between you. "We missed you at practice."

You take the gas can to the van without waiting for him to respond because you know he won't. Not yet. Danny isn't quick to bark back. He'll brood and he'll think through every possible scenario before responding. You take your time securing the gas can to the luggage hooks, careful not to leave too much slack in the bungee cord.

Danny stands motionless as you walk back to his car. It's hard to read him.

"Look," he says, grabbing hold of the generator and gesturing to you to do the same. "I'm sorry I didn't show up for practice, but it was either miss practice or don't get the generator. My uncle's heading out of town, so it was tonight or not at all, and you know how Austin would have taken that."

"I called. A lot."

"I'm aware." Danny scans his trunk, pointing and taking mental tabs.

He's going to make you say it. You can feel it. Why is he ignoring your subtext?

"Could have answered." Is all you can eke out.

"I know." His demeanor is stone solid. "The hills wreck the cell reception out there, and I was driving. Not that I need to justify it. Maybe I just didn't want to talk."

The two of you heave the generator out of the trunk of Danny's car and place it onto the ground. From there, he takes two bright orange coils of extension cords from the passenger's seat and locks his car. Two power strips are wrapped among the cords.

It's his turn to walk to the van without saying anything.

The generator's wheels grind against the gritty and the uneven asphalt as you pull it like luggage across the parking lot. The rattling obscures your thoughts. Eventually, you reach the van and open your mouth. You're no longer able to hold in your strained frustration, "You could have at least answered my texts. A quick *okay* or something. Anything. I was worried about you."

Danny tosses the extension cords into the back of the van and waits for you to grab hold of the generator. You do, and the two of you place it next to the gas can, angling it in such a way to prevent it from sliding around.

"You don't need to be," he says. "I'm good. I promise."

"Would you tell if you weren't?"

"Of course," he says.

It isn't the first time he's said this. Danny's never been one to break a promise, but if you've learned anything over the past couple of years, it's not to expect your friends to stay the same. Not even Danny.

"Well," you say. "What are you waiting for? Hop in. The asshole who took your parking space is going to need help unloading this at the house."

"Will Austin be there to help?"

You catch him checking the time on his phone.

"Dunno. He took Ryan to do some prep for the gig. He said he'd call though," you say.

Danny waits at the passenger side door and you're trying to guess by the way his eyes shift if he's calculating how much sleep he's going to get or if he's just feeling guilty for missing practice.

"I won't make you stay up too late. I know you've got to work early tomorrow."

Danny opens the door and says, "Why not? I'm not that tired."

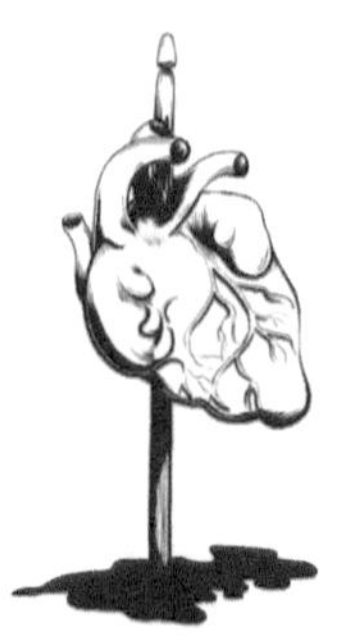

TIME TO GO ON, BUT AT LEAST YOUR
FRIEND IS JOINING YOU—GO TO PG 119

MOST PEOPLE AROUND here are fine with carving two hours of their weekend out for church. They walk in, exchange pleasantries over Styrofoam cups of thin coffee, sing a few songs, listen to your dad's sermons, and get the hell out of there with enough time to do what they want. Then, on Monday, they'll return to work and talk shit about the same people they exchanged handshakes with. Their kids will still fuck and drink and curse and disappoint their folks, only now they've got the guilt to go along with it. What else is there to do in this town, but sin?

The ultra-involved types tend to linger on Sunday though. The ones attending adult classes or the volunteer paper-pushers.

"Let's just go inside," Austin says. You can barely hear him over Dark Funeral's *The Secrets of the Black Arts*.

"Hold off for a few more minutes."

It's roughly seven pm, which means the high school youth group has just started. The ones dedicating their time in order to make damn sure the youth of the nation are on the right path. Policing their peers. The ones not worth fretting over. They'll be here for at least a couple of hours. But there's always a few who trickle in late. The ones who attend youth group because they have to, not because they want to. They'll joyride around town and make out at the park first. The ballsy ones might even slip a couple of their dad's beers and tear through a pack of gum before stepping foot in the church.

"Pull around to the other side of the parking lot," you say. "Behind the semi-trailer."

"Why does the church need a semi-trailer?"

"It's for recycling," you say, though you aren't sure you've ever seen it emptied. "It's full of newspapers, mostly. It's one of the volunteer things for the youth group."

"How helpful," he says, and puts the car in drive. "They should consider paying taxes instead. Give to Caesar what is Caesar's."

Doesn't seem to matter what you do, but you'll never be able to shake the church in Austin's eyes. You'll always be the relatively strait-laced kid who only recently started living. Thinking for yourself. He'll never understand the baggage you lug around.

"For real. Might actually help the poor," you say. It's an easy enough way out of the conversation. Agree with him, but don't point it back to him. He likes to mention the centuries' worth of bullshit the church is responsible for, but it's not like Austin spends his weekends at the soup kitchen. It's easy to call people out when you don't have to think about the solutions yourself.

"Okay," you say. "Let's do this, but make it quick."

The extra pull of Wild Turkey before you left the house was enough to drown the intrusive thoughts of the band splitting up as Ryan stormed out. And the second extra pull of Wild Turkey you take before leaving Austin's car numbs your tongue and masks the sudden sense of recklessness as confidence. You two walk the line of being cautious and inconspicuous. Nonchalance is key when doing something you shouldn't be doing.

You avoid the end of the church where the youth group meets and slip in through a side door. A circular main hallway loops around the entire church while offices and classrooms branch off like tumors. The sanctuary is located dead center and takes up the majority of the interior, which is where you lead Austin. "Care to enlighten me about what we need?"

"I'll know it when I see it."

"Ten minutes," you say. "That's all we get. Then we're out of here."

The sanctuary reeks of industrial strength chemicals.

"You really must have puked something vile," Austin says, stepping toward the altar. "Think we could nab that?"

He's pointing at the massive cross hanging above the altar.

"Good luck," you say. "Think smaller."

"The cross is empty," he says. "Call the cops, I think Christ is missing."

"That's a Catholic thing." You walk into the vestry, the dark closet where this all began, and rummage through the dimly lit space. You find a brass candle lighter leaning against the interior of the door frame. It's nearly three feet long and screams *ritual*. The word Austin kept repeating on the car ride over. The altar boy robes are pure white and, in this light, make you think of ghost skin. You leave them be, and instead, grab an unopened bag of communion wafers.

When you exit the vestry, Austin is juggling a couple of brass candelabras to match the lighter you found. They aren't particularly ornate, but they'll do. You look around the sanctuary, a place you once revered as a child, and find it all a bit boring. All of the accouterments you found mystical as a kid lost their magic when you realized it was all mass produced in Wisconsin, and ordered from an online catalog.

Austin doesn't know any better, though, and is having a heyday. All of this seems fascinating to him, despite his disbelief. Does he think any of this is ancient? Would it ruin it if you told him every Lutheran church in the United States has nearly identical religious paraphernalia? That you may as well be buying this stuff from a head shop?

With hands full, the two of you successfully burgle your father's church.

***

"Good call on the communion wafers," Austin says, "I almost forgot about those. Should give it to everyone as they come in."

You're on your way to the house on Cult Road.

"Nah, we should wait till we're halfway through the set. Pass them out during one of the instrumental sections. Could extend the outro in 'Spectral Gaze' or see if we can't write an elegy or something. Would be perfect for this sort of thing."

"Yeah," he says. "I've got something in mind," but you barely hear him above the hum of his tires on the highway.

"Think Ryan's cooled off?"

"Don't care."

"You should. At least a little. Last thing we need is him quitting before the gig."

"If he quits, he quits," Austin says. "We'll still give everyone a show."

It's hard to not to say anything because if this is how Austin is approaching this, then it's not about the music anymore. Whatever self-important fantasy he's got going in his head is beyond the

111

band, and if he can write Ryan off just like that, then he can drop you, too.

"Can't be a black metal band without a guitarist."

"Then Danny can play guitar instead. Fuck."

"Danny hates playing guitar," you say. "He's not bad, but he's not Ryan."

"Then he can fuck off too," Austin says. "We'll make it work."

Maybe this is the most true-black-metal thing you've ever been a part of. Bandmates that hate each other. A band that cannibalizes itself out of the womb.

"Let's hope it doesn't come to that," you say. "I want to impress Waste Doctrine and get out of this fucking town."

"Don't be a poser. It's not about impressing anyone. It's about the chaos we're bringing."

Austin pulls up to the house on Cult Road and parks haphazardly across the overgrown lawn. The stereo is still blasting Dark Funeral and he's mumbling under his breath. All you can make out is, " . . . do it myself if I have to."

The music stops when you open the door.

"Let's just set this shit up, alright? Doesn't need to be a whole thing."

"Sure," he says. He takes a pull of whiskey.

Walking into the house feels volatile. The interior glows uneasily in the dwindling sunlight, not in a way that gives the impression of life in this place, but rather one that illuminates the dead. Moonlight in a graveyard. Torches in a crypt.

You set the candelabras on the rickety table, but continue to keep a tight grip on the wooden handle of the candle starter. The brass glimmers dully.

Austin clomps up the stairs, straining to carry the ten-gallon buckets in either hand. They're sealed, but poorly. The rims of the lids are crusted with blood.

"Don't open these," he says. "Help me with the rest."

His trunk is full of deer skulls, most of them bleached brilliant white by sunlight. There are bags full of antlers and jawbones and teeth. There are two more buckets, too, heavy with the scent of death.

"Jesus," you say.

"Anything but," Austin says. "I told you to trust me."

THIS BETTER BE GOOD—GO TO PG 124

AS YOU DRIVE across town to Danny's apartment, you can't shake the feeling that everything seems a little different now, like you've stuck your head through a doorway into another realm. Though you'd barely crossed the threshold—only long enough to take a look around at the altered landscape of your mind before being yanked back—the change is there, and it's not like any high you've ridden before. Even though you weren't in the Cult House long, there's no doubt in your mind that whatever is behind those walls and hidden in the woodgrain of every board in that place is responsible.

It's only been a few hours. You're no stranger to lingering after-images and slower come-downs, but this? This isn't that.

The shift is subtle in how it's rewired your brain.

It's felt in the way music is amplified differently when the music hits your ears. How sunlight beams through your windshield. The unbearable humidity, so heavy you can almost see the water molecules in the air.

Maybe it's how you see yourself now? An amalgamation of atoms. An obscure glitch, wavy and distorted, yet always a true image. Your brain reshaped.

You almost miss the turn into the apartment complex, taking the corner into the entrance too wide, tires squealing, nearly colliding bumper-to-bumper with Danny's car.

There's panic on his face, poor guy, but it subsides when he sees you. He reverses, making room for you to pull into the lot and park. Danny pulls into the empty space beside you and kills the engine. He opens his trunk, then walks around to your door and taps on the window. Oily fingerprints smudge the glass.

"Come on, help me with this." Danny's voice is muffled.

The smudges turn into streaks as you roll the window down, Danny's finger unmoving from the glass.

"With what?"

"Moving the generator."

The generator takes up most of the space in the trunk. Bright extension cables are coiled like a pit of snakes next to a gas canister that's secured by a stretched-out bungee cord. You grab the extension cables while Danny unhooks the gas can and places it onto the asphalt.

"It's not terribly heavy, but it's big and a bit awkward to carry by myself," Danny says, nodding toward the generator. "My uncle said it's ours to use, but to return it with a full tank of gas."

"Sounds fair to me," you say. "Glad you got it. Austin would have lost his shit if you didn't."

"Yeah, well. He's all bark. He'd whine about it until he found something new to whine about. Just like he did about having to move practice to his place, and just like I assume he did when I didn't show up."

You grab ahold of the generator and smirk, "How'd you guess?"

"I don't need to guess," he says, helping you lift the generator into the back of the van. "I've known Austin so long. He's predictable. At least his reactions are. It's his actions that have a special kind of chaos to them. Especially when he's had too much time. Then his actions are laced with . . . I don't know."

"Reckless pandemonium."

"That'd be a good band name."

"What? *Abyss* too boring these days?" you joke.

"Please. It's perfect for us. It's why I chose it, but I can't help but think it's predicting our futures."

You remember Austin telling you about how he thought of the band's name. Abyss. He'd scrawled it all over his school notebooks and in the margins of his textbooks for weeks.

"Austin told me he came up with it. Said it came to him in a lucid dream."

"Of course he'd say that," Danny says. "It came from my sleep paralysis, though. Not lucid dreaming. Fuck it. Doesn't matter. It's his band now. We're just playing the parts until he doesn't need us anymore. Speaking of, he texted me a little bit ago. Said he and Ryan were heading to the Cult Road House and they need our help. Probably should head out before he gets more impatient."

"Alright," you say. "Hop in."

Before you leave, Danny grabs a CD from his car and puts it in your stereo, immediately shifting the atmosphere in the van. Long, droning notes fill the space. It puts you at ease, and it takes you until you're already cruising the highway out of town before you realize the absence of both drums and vocals.

"Who is this?" you ask.

"Stars of the Lid's latest album."

He tells you without any sort of hesitation or pining. Complete opposite of Austin. You have to prod Austin to the point of annoyance. It's like he gets off on keeping music from you.

"I like it," you say. "It reminds me of *Blade Runner* in a way. This sort of calm, but melancholy ambiance."

"Yeah, I've always thought if I made a movie, I'd want them to score it. Them or Boards of Canada. I can picture it clearly. I've got the scenes in my head. They'd nail it."

"Why don't you?"

"What? Make movies? Time. Money. Not to mention there's no way I'm moving to L.A. Too big. Too many people. Too—"

"So make something here. You always had an eye for all that stuff in school. Isn't that how you landed the marketing stuff you do now?"

"Not exactly," he says. "Not the same thing."

Danny thrives at making excuses for himself. He lets his pragmatism suffocate his dreams. The other side of the coin to Austin's unwarranted confidence.

"You should try," you say.

"Yeah, maybe. I'll have to see how the promotion goes, but yeah. Could be worth a try or something," he says, but quickly changes the subject to you. "Did your parents really kick you out?"

"It appears that way, yeah. My dad told me not to let out the cold as he shut the door on me."

The ambient music lulls you into a trance as you drive, and you no longer recognize where you are. "I think I made a wrong turn."

"You sure?" Danny asks, the slightest bit of alarm in his voice.

"No, but maybe. I think we'd have passed Cult House by now. I probably just turned off on the wrong mile marker."

You drive until you reach a dirt road perpendicular to the one you're on.

"Maybe we should turn around," Danny says. "Or call Austin."

You don't want to be berated by Austin all night for this, so you ignore Danny and continue driving. A yellow *Minimum Maintenance Road* sign graffitied to say *Minimum Maintenance Road* warns you not to continue.

The deeply rutted road causes your van to rattle and visibly jostles you and Danny in your seats. Danny continues to protest, but you push the gas pedal down farther. The engine revs and your tires struggle to stay out of the ruts.

You smell gasoline and turn around to see the gas canister has tipped. Before you can ask Danny to slide into the back to take care of it, an ungodly metallic clang punches the hood of your car.

Everything is totally fine—continue

You realize this is about to get completely and utterly fucked, but you still have to continue, so go on—continue

THAT SEEMS INCREDIBLY UNFAIR. PLAYING WITH YOU LIKE THAT. THE ILLUSION OF CHOICE . . .

"Goddammit." You stop the van and pull the hood release.

"Sounds like you threw a rod."

You slam your door and walk around to the front, though you know shit about cars. Everything under the hood is just steel to you. "I don't know what that means."

Danny gets out and looks under the van. "It's means we're fucked," he says. "You've got oil leaking everywhere."

You join Danny on the ground, gazing at the trickle of black pooling onto the dry, cracked earth. And then, without warning, you're pulled backward by the ankles. Your fingers scrape against the ground. A knee pushes into the small of your back, preventing you from standing. Your head is forced to the ground by a heavy hand. Socks are stuffed into your mouth, which is now taped shut. A bag is placed over your head, but not before you catch a glimpse of the hooded figures responsible. You hear Danny whimper and prairie grass rustling in the wind.

COMPLETELY AND UTTERLY FUCKED
—GO TO PG 130

AUSTIN FOLLOWS YOU through an unassuming door behind the altar out of the sanctuary, and into a general-purpose space behind it. Typically, it's set up for catechism classes and Sunday morning schmoozing, but tonight the space is empty. The accordion style wall partitions arc bunched up like loose skin. Chairs stacked four or five high join the tables that are pushed to the perimeter of the space. The diffused red glow of the exit sign stands out against the otherwise dim space.

Your phone buzzes against the change in your pocket. A new voicemail.

"Here, hold these." You pass the candelabras to Austin and pull your phone out. The voicemail is from Danny, but instead of checking it, you text him: *coming asap,* and clamp your phone shut. The footsteps and murmurs coming from your left is enough for you to guess what Danny was calling about. Afterall, you'd recognize your dad's voice anywhere.

DEAL WITH YOUR DAD ALONE SO AUSTIN CAN BAIL—GO TO PG 134

NO TIME FOR THIS SHIT, RUN!— GO TO PG 136

AN ONSLAUGHT OF bugs explodes as they impact the windshield. Your van's wiper blades are no match for the gooey constellation and they end up smearing yellow-brown arches across the glass for you to try and see through.

The added visual obscurity only heightens your frustration, which you blame for missing your turn and having to double-back, not once, but twice down the dusty country roads. It doesn't help that Danny's asked several times if he needs to call Austin.

"I've got it sorted out," which is the same thing you'd said to your dad when he reminded you to fill your wiper fluid.

By the time you reach the house on Cult Road, gravel dust clings to the guts of a thousand bugs, coating your van in a layer of filth. Through the grimy windshield, you see Austin's car parked, but still running, the brights shining toward the house—and Austin—who's precariously balanced on the second story roof hip with a paint roller in one hand and a handle of Wild Turkey in the other. A ten-gallon bucket sits at a slant on uneven shingles.

You kill the engine and step out of the car.

Danny follows.

Austin's high beams do a better job of illuminating the porch, highlighting just how rundown this place is. The message isn't finished and you can barely make any of it out. A crudely drawn skull cries red paint. The numbers *666* are scrawled across the forehead of the skull.

"You're going to fucking kill yourself."

"We all have to go some way," Austin says, taking a pull of bourbon.

"And you're assisting him," you say, walking toward Ryan, who stands at the base of a rickety wooden ladder smoking a cigarette.

"Nah." Ryan spews a lazy cloud of smoke. "We all know if Austin ever did himself in, he'd go out in a harder way than this."

"Fine, you're going to accidentally kill yourself."

"Ryan's right," Austin says. "If I were to do it, it wouldn't be like this. What about you, Ryan?" Austin stares down at the three of you congregating at the base of the ladder. A thick gob of paint drips onto the dry, graying rungs.

"Dunno. Probably OD or something."

"Weak. If you're going to do that, at least take a fuck-ton of acid, or candy-flip, and obliterate God in space or something," Austin says. "What about you, Danny?"

Ryan lights another cigarette to mark the awkwardness.

"What the fuck, man?" You ball your fists.

Austin shrugs his shoulders and says *what? what?* like he has no clue.

Danny walks toward the van.

"You know goddamn well what," you say, shooting Ryan a glance for backup, but he won't meet your eyes. He just stands and smokes and stares at the dirt. Fucking coward.

"It's fine," Danny shouts through the rural emptiness. He opens the trunk to the van. "You all know the Xanax didn't work, probably because I passed out before I could drink enough to do the rest, so if I were to try it again—which I won't, by the way," he says this for you. You know this. You can hear it in his tone of voice. The firm reassurance. "But if I did—"

"Let me guess, your dad's nine?" Austin asks.

Danny walks toward the house, extension cords in hand. "No. Too messy and I wouldn't want my parents to see me like that. I'd spend all my money and travel north. Canada or maybe fly to Norway or something. Then I'd wait for a blizzard and just start walking and never look back. If you have to fucking ask."

"Whatever, dude," Austin says. "Like that would do it. Too many variables anyway."

"It worked for Valfar," you say.

"Yeah? And who's that?"

"Dude from Windir," you say. "Though it isn't confirmed to be a suicide."

Austin dunks the paint roller into the bucket again. "Windir sucks," is all he says.

***

You help Danny lug the generator over to the house and roll it inside.

"Sorry," you say. "About all that."

"It's fine," Danny says. "Doesn't bother me. I attempted and failed, but I'm in a better place now. My parents are still weird about it. They tip-toe around the subject, but it's all good. For real. Talking about it helps, I think. Except when people like Austin's edgy ass try to romanticize it. Or make it more than what it is, you know? Anyway, where should we put this?"

You wheel the generator over to the dining room and set it close to the back wall, along with all the extension cords and can of gas.

"Look, I'm glad you're still around."

You leave it at that and show Danny around the first floor of the house.

"Have you been here?"

"Once, but not for long. And it's a whole new experience at night. It feels off, you know? Like the whole place feels too alive for being an old dead house."

"I don't think the place is dead," you say. "Can't explain it, but last time I was here I was walking up the stairs and it felt like I was . . . I don't know, transcending or something. An outer-body experience. The whole thing felt surreal, like watching myself sleep. I could see myself from above. Shadows outlined everything in my periphery. A sort of tunnel vision, except the borders were dead-TV-static. A black and white void closing in on me, but I couldn't do anything about it, but watch."

"Jesus," Danny says. "What happened?"

"I dunno. Felt like I blacked out. One minute I was walking upstairs and the next, Ryan is holding me up. I can't tell if this place wants us here, you know? Like, are we intruding on something or are we being invited in?"

"Dark, quiet places have a way of messing with our heads," Danny says. "Our brains excel at filling in the gaps where nothing exists because we can't comprehend the idea of nothing. Not like this. We're wired to survive, so nothingness is foreign and we will do anything to fight it. We fill it with legends and myths and religion and on and on to make sense of it. Humans have done this forever."

He says this, but his tense muscles and uneasy, rigid stance tells you he maybe doesn't quite believe what he's saying. Not completely, anyway. His words are proving him wrong—filling the empty space. He's always been the logical one, but no one is immune to existential fear. Of all of you, Danny's the one who's been closest to experiencing the void. Maybe that's where the fear is coming from.

"That's where our band name comes from, you know? Abyss," Danny says. "Austin didn't come up with it. It came partially from my sleep paralysis. The weird lucid space it leaves me in and the weight of being stuck between two realities, but it's a little more than that. It's about nothingness, and how we react to it. And it's our job as a band to bring people to the edge of the abyss and make them stare into it, if only for a few songs."

The air hangs heavy in the house. A hot summer breath waiting to be exhaled across the dry prairie.

Austin's footsteps can be heard creaking above you as the two of you emerge from the house. You step far enough away from the house to see what he's been writing. Beyond the skull and number of the beast, you see indiscernible letters chaotically scrawled on either side of the skull.

Maybe it's because Austin is wasted, but it's nonsense to you.

"What's it supposed to say?" you ask.

"You'll know when you know."

"Whatever," you say. "We're heading out."

"Hold on," Austin says. "You never answered the question. How would you do it?" Austin crab-crouches and rests his elbows on his knees. "Probably emo-ass cutting." He squints through the brightness of the high beams. "No, you wouldn't do it at all."

"You say it like it's a bad thing," you say.

"Oh, come on. It's a hypothetical scenario."

It isn't lost on you that Austin never answered the question. He shouldered it to Ryan.

"Whatever. You wouldn't do it and I know why," he says. "Because deep down, you still think god would punish you for it."

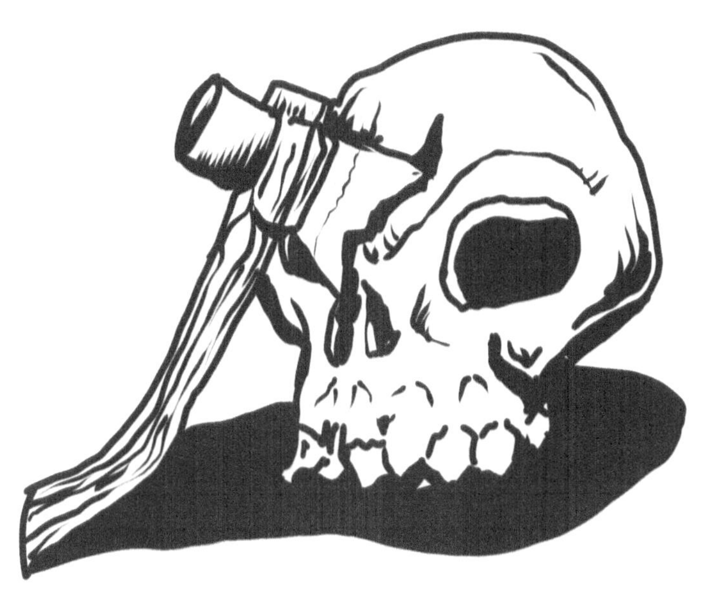

You allow the rage to build up in you. Where does he get off? Kick the ladder, just a little—GO TO PG 148

You use the wave of rising fury to push yourself away from this conversation. Go home—GO TO PG 152

TRUSTING AUSTIN HASN'T been easy for you these past couple of years. He's proven time and again that his loyalty and friendship are temporary, and any trust tends to be one-sided and used as a manipulation tool. Yet you're here. You've let him string you along this far, so where's the harm in following him a bit further? After all, he's led you back into the band and onto a path that should steer you out of town, even if only for a little while.

Why are you like this?

He's had so many chances not to be a dickhead, but he proves you wrong every single time. And *you* let him try over and over, like your friendship is a game with infinite continues.

You crave to see the best in people, but your loyalty is your downfall.

He's careless with your feelings. Careless with the band. Careless with everything he touches. And tonight is no different.

Austin lugs one of the ten-gallon buckets up the stairs while you trail behind with a couple of paint rollers. "We'll do the exterior first," he says, stopping about halfway up the staircase. "We should be able to finish before dark, if we're quick. Setting up the interior won't take very long either."

The staircase feels larger than you remember. Wider. The walls stretch higher to meet a ceiling that appears convex, the corners where the planes intersect are occluded by darkness. It gives the impression that the walls are bubbled, expanded like a held breath. You feel like the house is making room for you.

Austin adjusts his grip and walks into the bedroom at the end of the hall. He sets the bucket down near the end table where the gilded Bible rests, and fiddles with the window. Eventually, he gets it open and lets in the slightest breeze, which only seems to carry the dry allergenic stench of prairie grass your direction. You aren't sure what you expected. The house to exhale?

If only, because that might explain the sudden cutting chill enveloping you, despite the lingering heat of the day. Maybe you've got it wrong. The house isn't letting out a cold breath, but whispering something into your ear.

Still, whispers come in all kinds of contorted configurations— Secrets. Endearing coos. Threats—and you've never been particularly great at determining which is which.

You don't have time to parse through the words you don't understand, because Austin pulls you from your thoughts to an immediate need. Austin's crouched on the roof, gripping the windowsill. He peers in and says, "Bring me the bucket, and toss me a roller."

"Watch yourself," you say.

"Speak for yourself," he says. "You're helping."

You hand him the bucket first and watch him place it precariously on graying wooden shingles before giving him the paint roller.

"Come on, don't be a bitch," he says, moving aside to give you room to climb out of the window.

You hook your paint roller along the windowsill while crawling backward through the window and onto the roof. You figured you'd be nervous, having never been fond of heights, but it isn't your nerves rattling around, shaking your core. It's the sudden absence of the house's walls and what little comfort and sense of stability they gave you that's gripping you. Reckless vulnerability overwhelms your sense of place in all of this. The capital *W*-world and beyond.

The slope of the roof isn't terribly steep, but the already uneven shingles are warped, making it difficult to find and keep your footing.

"What's the plan?" You figure it is as honest a question as any at this rate, yet Austin seems annoyed by it nonetheless.

"Just fucking write something," he says, prying the lid from the bucket. A wave of thick, heavy death rises from within and invades your senses.

The stench clings to every raised hair on your body. It coats the inside of your nostrils—lingering—an unwanted and uninvited stranger.

Austin tosses the lid like a frisbee into the gloomy, dwindling light. It rustles prairie grass in the distance, disturbing the quiet peace of the plains. He's kneeled on the roof and plunges the paint roller into the bucket. He stirs the bloody contents a few times before pulling it from within. The goopy excess drips off of the roller in viscous, saliva-like strands across the roof of the house.

Then he rolls on the blood like some sinister handyman. Perhaps he's simply an artist with a vision only he can see.

You lean, keeping as much of your weight against the house as you can while carefully scooting toward the bucket, using the dormer window as support. You pull the collar of your shirt over your nose as you stare into the bucket. The paint roller reminds you of a mutilated lamb as it's submerged in the blood. Chunks of viscera stick to the fibrous cotton roller.

WHAT ARE YOU WAITING FOR? SCRAWL YOUR MESSAGE. LOSE YOURSELF. CREATE SOMETHING. PUT YOUR ART ONTO THE PAGE:

"I think I'm done," you say, leaning back to admire your work.

Austin cranes his neck in your direction and nods. It's the first time he's looked over to your side and you're uncertain if he approves. A silent nod is barely better than loud criticism. At least if you rile him up it means you've hit a nerve.

He's been busy scrawling some kind of message across his side of the house. At first, you'd figured them to be offensive lyrics or blasphemy-infused esoterism.

You crouch to lower your center of gravity and shamble across the roof to get a better look. The moonlight creates an odd shimmering effect on the blood. Strange reflections ripple in the sanguinous script, but you can't make out their meaning. It's as if the foreign letters wriggle and writhe, changing form and the message entirely. Moving pictures. The living word.

"What the hell does it say?"

"Just look," he says. "It will reveal itself to you."

No matter how hard you try to make sense of the alien language and the serrated lines of the script, the jilted prose scrawled across the dead, decrepit house does not reveal any meaning to you. They're just bloody lines. An absurd empyrean argot.

You hate how easy this is for Austin—the mysticism, and the ability to take it seriously.

Frustrated, and your mind preoccupied by your inability to decipher the message, you misstep with your front foot. As you try to lean into your misstep and shift your weight to prevent yourself from slipping, you overcompensate with your back foot. You plant your boot hard near the edge of the roof, shifting the rickety shingles and dry-rotted boards beneath.

You grip for anything within reach for balance.

Your fingertips graze the windowsill in a desperate caress, while the bucket of blood topples as you swat it with your other hand. It rolls in a lazy semi-circle along the roof.

And then there's Austin, who stands with his hands on his hips, completely entranced by the squiggling words. You wonder what he sees. Do they say to let you fall? To ignore you? It's hard to tell if Austin even realizes the imminent danger you're in, absorbed in the ominous annals as if in prayer.

You cry out as the board beneath you finally gives, cracking and slumping like a shattered wrist.

There's no time to recall the proper way to fall to reduce injury. The clock is ticking. Your gift of slow-motion-near-death-cognizance is burned, consumed by tried-and-true thoughts, and this cyclical thinking brings you back to the same tired question— why you?

Wait. No, not that one. It's the perverse mirrored image. Its backwards twin.

Why not you?

There's a brief moment as the rush of air kisses your skin, and through tangled wisps of hair obscuring your vision, the blood glinting in moonlight seems to finally make sense. But the moment passes as your vision abruptly shatters and the message on the Cult Road House turns into an unintelligible cracked windshield as your body impacts the earth below.

COME ON, YOU HAVE TO KEEP GOING. FOCUS. STAY WITH IT—GO TO PG 166

THE BURLAP BAG is musty. It scratches your forehead and cheeks as you jerk your head back and forth, trying to clock your captor in the face or jostle their hands. Your boots feel so, so heavy as you kick erratically, hoping to connect with your attacker.

Unfortunately, they maintain their grip on your collar, which tears under your persistence. You hear the quick bite of a length of duct tape being pulled from a roll next to you. Danny must not be putting up much of a fight, but you figure if you cause enough trouble to steal the attention of both attackers, he might be able to get away.

You continue to worm your upper body back and forth, using the distraction to shift your arms into a push-up position instead of worthlessly down the sides of your body as before.

A knee grinds your spine.

You clench your jaw, biting down on the sock you've been gagged with. The sharp pain in your back persists. Using every bit of strength you can muster; you try to do a push-up to offset your attacker's resistance bearing down onto you, but your muscles feel like they're moments from being ripped from your bones, like your elbows will fold in on themselves. Arms wobbly, you collapse onto the rock-hard dirt road.

Danny squirms beside you, not in obvious resistance, but panic. A wounded animal in a trap. There's a frantic rustling and shuffling of feet, which makes you believe he's been pulled upright.

And there you remain on the ground. You try to yell *run* and it's almost hilarious how hopeless the attempt is through all those layers of cotton and burlap. Another length of duct tape is pulled from the roll and is quickly wrapped around your wrists. You're then pulled to your feet.

You'll never forget how your attacker's hands feel on your forearms.

Calloused.

Nails just long enough you can feel them graze the soft hairs on your arms and scratch your skin as you resist.

The smooth wedding band on one lonely finger is warm against your flesh.

Just enough of a clue to make a last-ditch effort to get the fuck out of this situation. For whatever reason, they remain behind you. As you're pushed along, you drag your feet, feeling out the road and to give the impression you're horribly clumsy. When you stumble, they stumble. You walk a few paces to gauge their stride.

They keep in time with your gait and you begin to count.

One . . . dirt clods crumble under your boots.

Two . . . Danny breathes heavily a few feet to your right.

Three . . . Your left foot slides into the rut entrenched in the road.

Four . . . You stumble forward and abruptly stop, causing your captor to bump against you out of step. Using both hands, you grip your captor by the groin, squeeze, and don't let go, determined to rip their nuts off if you have to.

They yelp and pull at your hands. Instinctively, they lean forward while doing so and you throw your head backward, connecting with their face. They call you a motherfucker and spit.

Soon, another set of hands is yanking at you. You stomp at the new person's feet. Kick at their shins. You throw your body around, trying to cause as much confusion as possible, hoping Danny finally takes the fucking hint.

You're pushed to the ground, your knees taking the brunt of the impact.

Then there's the scrambling of feet as someone takes off running. The awkward, frenzied shuffle of someone running without the use of their arms fills the gaps of quiet as you struggle on the ground. The other captor lets go of your legs and mutters the word, "Shit!" and takes off.

Come on, Danny. The odds of him getting away are abysmal, but you've managed to accomplish what you set out to—confuse them. Cause chaos. Split them up. Make them regret whatever it is they've got planned for you.

You listen, but can't tell which direction Danny's going. If he's gone into the fields or if he's still on the road. There's no way to tell through the sudden wave of confusion that hits you as you take a blow to the side of the head. A shockwave slams against your right eardrum, obliterating your balance. You smell dirt through the burlap bag, but it feels like you're clinging to the sky somehow. Your head hanging upside down, swimming through clouds. Gravity pulls you further and further from the earth.

You don't black out.

That's not how this works.

Instead, you stumble while being dragged to your feet and try not to puke from the intense pang ringing in your ears.

Every twenty or so paces, your captor stops to spin you in circles, but they're wasting their time. You quit counting your steps or bothering to determine which direction you're going in. Their efforts in zig-zagging across the dirt road are futile, too, for the simple fact you remain on the same heavily rutted road.

You try to focus on a song to play through in your mind. Something to collect your scattered thoughts and quiet the slurry of emotions ricocheting around your head. Saying you aren't afraid would be a boldfaced lie, but it isn't the driving force behind your current contemplation. What fuels you right now is the curiosity about who the fuck these people are. It nags at the back of your skull because you know damn well that if you don't know who these people are personally, the degree of separation in your town is razor thin and you sure as hell know someone who does. And they will not get away with this.

You didn't recognize your captor's voice when they called you a motherfucker, and they haven't said a word since. They've been spitting and sniffling, though, and you hope you broke their nose. Busted a tooth. Anything that may give them away if you get out of this.

WHEN YOU GET OUT OF THIS.

You recognize this voice speaking to you, though. It's the one you aren't sure is real. The one you have no choice but to listen to in this moment, for no reason other than it's here.

When it really comes down to it, aren't all voices just in your head?

You suppose it doesn't matter.

You were looking for something to focus on—

SO WHY NOT ME? NO, DON'T TRY TO SPEAK. JUST KEEP WALKING AND WAIT IT OUT. IT WILL ALL BE OVER SOON.

You're concussed.

Minor brain damage.

The burlap bag is cutting off your oxygen and causing you to think sideways.

THAT ISN'T TRUE. YOU KNOW WHAT IS TRUE. DON'T FALL INTO THE CULT OF THE MIND. JUST PICK UP ONE FOOT AFTER THE OTHER AND WALK, AND BE PATIENT. WAIT FOR YOUR OPENING—AND MOVE.

Now you're in for it. This fucking cryptic voice thinks you're going to listen to its authority. What authority? What does it have to do with your existence? Nothing. Just a dead tone. Some indistinguishable pitch, masquerading as guidance, spewing nonsense in your face. What of it?

You trudge along the road, lost in thought of the cosmic slop saturating what's left of your concentration when you are stopped abruptly. A car door opens off to your right, followed by a single set of feet hitting the ground. You sense your captor raise a hand as if in acknowledgement, continuing their silence.

The other person isn't as discreet and barks, "What took so long?"

"Issues," is all they say.

It isn't much to go off of, but your captor is tired and frustrated. This third person seems annoyed and has the voice of someone who doesn't sound particularly large or imposing and plans begin to trickle into your head.

NOT NOW.

"Well, where's . . . you know." It's hard to tell if he means Danny or the other attacker, but it doesn't seem to matter because the only response is the clank of a tailgate falling open, and you being hoisted into the bed of a pickup.

"Try and jump out and I'll shoot ya," the new voice says. "If you were smart, you'd lie flat and try not to think too much. Thinking only makes things worse."

You roll onto your back and move your legs around, feeling for anything useful, but are met with a familiar emptiness.

THIS IS TRULY ROTTEN LUCK, BUT WHAT ELSE CAN YOU DO? CONTINUE—GO TO PG 171

AUSTIN ALMOST DROPS the bag of communion wafers as you thrust the candle lighter into his arms.

"I can't carry all of this," he says.

"Deal with it," you say. "I'll cover for us. Slip back through the sanctuary and head straight out the front doors."

Austin slips into the shadows quieter than you'd have anticipated. Your dad rounds the curved hallway and into view as the lights turn on, a stranger in tow. Pretty much everyone in the church is unfamiliar to you these days, but the surprised look on your dad's face leads you to believe the woman sheepishly taking cover behind him is more of a guest, than a stranger. A date, even. Looks like you're both breaking commandments tonight.

You don't have the energy to deal with his excuses. It's a song you've heard on repeat throughout your childhood, and you know every line by heart.

Instead, you kick off the conversation so you don't have to hear his sorry attempt at obfuscation, "Hey, dad." It's subtle, but it's the only potshot you'll allow yourself. A slight unveiling to the mystery woman that not only is he still wearing his wedding band, but his progeny stands before her, too. "I hope I didn't trip the alarm system, but Ryan lost his cufflinks at the wedding reception last night and I was looking around to see if I could find them. I don't want the tux rental place to charge him out the ass for them."

"Language, please. Have some respect for where you are." His voice lacks its usual disciplinary sternness because it's been replaced by a calm, but panicked pleading.

The two of you both know the situation you've stumbled upon tonight, and now you're placing the pieces down, sizing up one another's strategy.

"My bad," you say.

The woman steps forward and says, "Hi, I'm Marylin."

You don't bother shaking her hand.

She prattles on about how she's new to town and looking for a home church, and that your father was giving her a tour.

My god, lady. You've been given the out. No need to over-explain.

"Yes." Your dad steps in. "She'd just dropped her daughter off for youth group, and—"

Your dad is way off his game. Maybe he's lost his touch. Maybe it's because you're older now and he realizes weaving the lie is nowhere near as easy as it used to be.

"Dad, I don't care," you say. "I'm just looking for the cufflinks."

The words *I don't care* visibly shake him. His skin flushes. He absentmindedly pops his knuckles one by one.

"Do you still have the lost and found in your office?" You're laying a simple path down for him, but he seems too stunned to take it. "If so, could you look for the cufflinks? I need to head out to meet the band."

He seems relieved you don't mention going home. Does he think you'll tell your mom? You could. Maybe you should. Then again, would it make any difference at this point? Not to you. Their marriage was killed a long time ago. You were caught in the crossfire, sure, but those wounds are scars now.

"Sorry again for tripping the alarm," you say. "Didn't mean to force you out here."

"It was nice meeting you," Marylin says.

"Sure," you say. "Enjoy the tour."

The band is hiding poorly in the van. As you walk up to the driver's side door, you see them trying to be as inconspicuous and unimposing as possible. They're comically scrunched up against their seats, stiff and tense.

"We good?" Austin asks.

"My dad's fucking some lady named Marylin."

You start the van and peel out of the church parking lot.

YOU MAY AS WELL CONTINUE—
GO TO PG 139

THERE'S NO SENSE in trying to run across the hall toward the new part of the church. Even if your dad doesn't see you, you'd have to dodge the youth group kids. You quietly place a hand on Austin's shoulder, but before you can pull him back to exit through the sanctuary, he shoves the candelabras into your hands and takes off, following the curve of the hallway to your right.

The chains on his jacket and bullet belt rattle like chainmail as Austin sprints down the hall, the brass candle lighter his sword.

"What in the world?" You'd recognize your father's voice anywhere.

"Did you catch who it was?" This voice, however, is completely foreign to you.

"No. Probably one of the high schoolers. They tend to get pretty lax during youth group."

You wedge yourself as tight as you can in the corner of the dim multi-purpose room where the wall meets the accordion partitioning, hoping your clothes blend into the shadows enough. The candelabras glimmer in what little ambient light seeps into the room, but your father doesn't seem to notice. He walks by, seemingly unfazed by the potential intruder wandering through his church, hand in hand with a bottle-blonde.

Looks like you're both breaking commandments tonight.

You give them a minute or two of head start before following behind them. It's hard to say why you're doing this. Neither of your parents talk about the affair that consumed your formative years. Not directly with you. Yet it permeated every conversation. The passive-aggressive comments. The distrust. The tone of voice. The silence.

They went to therapy for *you*. That's what they always said. Not for them. You'd bet everything in your bank account that the bottle-blonde is hardly the first since they completed marriage counseling. Though look how much good that did for them.

Maybe you're doing it as some sick voyeuristic adventure. Collecting blackmail you'll never send through the post. Why would you? Your parents are plenty good at sabotaging themselves. They don't need your help.

Your dad said if he had a time machine, he'd have never done it. He'd have resisted the temptation. That it was the biggest mistake of his life. But if he had a time machine, you'd tell him to go through with the divorce instead. The three of you would all be better off.

Better yet, never get married at all. You can live with the thought of never existing.

You skirt around the curves of the church hallway in relative darkness where you used to run. A thousand footfalls of innocence.

You round the corner leading into one of the main entryways into the building, No one is at the front desk at this hour, yet you find yourself crouching past the volunteer secretary window toward your dad's office.

The office on the left belonged to the former head pastor who'd heard God's call and moved a couple of states away, though you'd bet money that even he was tired of your dad's bullshit. How easy would that be? To claim God told you to hightail it out of town to a place where you don't know a soul.

Your dad's office is on the right, where you find yourself hunched close enough to see words forming in the lemon scented woodgrain of the door. They arrive first in your mind, not as sounds, but ideas, before their shapes form along the surface of the door. *Transcendence* and *truth* and *abyss* and *blight*. Not even your hand can wipe them away. The words settle like a stress headache on your brain. Poking. Prodding. Clamoring for your attention.

Are these words you? Your desires? Somehow manifesting to you—*as* you. Words for you to deliver into being?

You blink and the words quit forming their delicate scrawl across the door, but they immediately come back to you as whispers. Vapor. Smoke rolling from under the door. They come from beyond the door, uttered in an odd cadence from your dad's lips. And the blonde's trembling affirmation as she repeats them.

The sudden jolt of the air conditioning system causes you to lose your balance and bump your head against the door.

Move.

You don't have to think twice.

The door to your dad's office opens behind you, but it's barely an echo. Despite the panicked agitation gnawing at your nerves, you sprint, leaving the uncanny chill of the church at your heels—but your dad's strange recitation clings to your thoughts and rings in your ears.

CONTINUE—GO TO PG 143

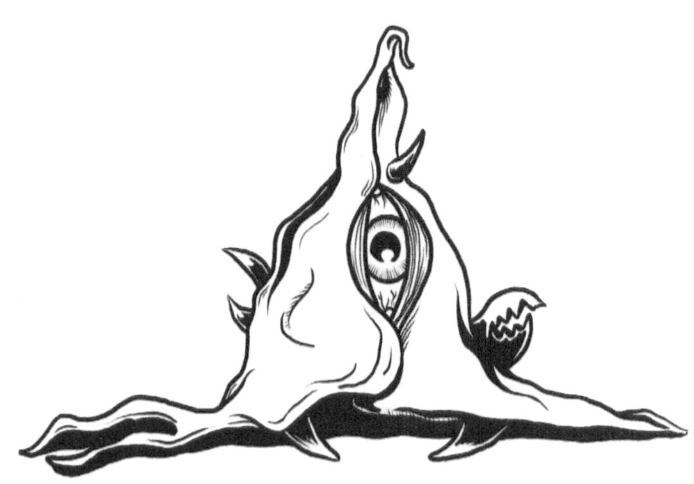

THE HORIZON LOOKS like a painting you'd find framed in faux-distressed wood in a hotel lobby.

You've let Austin take control of the stereo, your mind preoccupied with not only your father's infidelity, but the potential of your mother's, because someone else was in your house when you left. There's no way it could have been your father, so who was it?

You can't make up your mind if you care or not. If you *should* care or not. Maybe it's less about concern and more about morbid curiosity. Your parents suddenly seem so interesting. Sinful and imperfect and ruined. Who doesn't love a good secret?

Austin's changed all six CDs in the stereo, completely ruining your organizational system. He switches it back to disc one and a clip from a movie plays, talking of witches and magic. An interesting choice for Austin. You didn't think he liked Inquisition. The first time you showed him *Into the Infernal Regions of the Ancient Cult,* he couldn't get over the vocalist's approach. "Sounds like a frog-throated asshole," you believe is what he said at the time, but you've always taken the album to be a sort of ritualistic concept album. The vocalist's take was entirely purposeful. Like he was an actor in a Daniel Haller film, delivering some accursed message from an unholy pulpit.

You cruise along the highway, pushing your van to over sixty-five, waiting for Austin to remember his disgust for the record and change the disc, but he doesn't. He rolls the window down enough to blow his hair all over the place. The rush of air obscures the music, but he doesn't turn the volume up. Instead, he asks, "Is she hot?"

"Dude," Danny says.

"It's fine." You make eye contact with Danny in the rearview mirror.

"What? It's an honest question," Austin says. "Fine. Is she hotter than your mom?"

"Dude, the fuck?" Danny says.

"Just hear me out." Austin's hands are held out, palm to palm. A mock prayer. "If you're going to fuck up a marriage, wouldn't you at least go for someone hotter than what you've got?"

"No wonder you're perpetually single," Danny says.

Ryan cracks a beer and stays silent.

Austin isn't the most emotionally intelligent person in the world, but in some way, you think he might be trying to lighten the mood. He was there the first time you found out about your dad cheating. Your mom standing in the kitchen weeping silent tears masking the rage you knew burrowed deep into her being. Your dad making excuses. And you, doing your best to blend into the fabric of the couch because you couldn't bear to watch it all fall apart.

Austin wouldn't let you disappear though. He pulled you from the couch and dragged you out the front door, calling your dad an asshole to his face. Then you met up with Danny at the playground, smoking stolen cigarettes and questioning the world and God and everything you'd known in your short twelve years.

"Who am I to say if Marilyn is hot? But she's exactly my dad's type."

"The religious homewrecker?" Austin asks.

"Nah. You can't wreck a home that's already been bulldozed to the ground," you say. "Apparently my dad's type is anyone that isn't my mom."

"Goddamn," Danny says.

You try to laugh it off because by a certain point the truth doesn't hurt anymore, but you can't quite shake the lingering frustration. The curiosity drilling into your brain. All of the liturgical moralizing your parents have thrown at you. To what end? Their paltry efforts circle the drain in a never-ending spiral of distrust. Misplaced and manipulated love that's only led you to where you are not because of, but in spite of them.

Once again, you park on the overgrown lawn of the Cult Road House. The sky folds into layers of orange and purple, which seem to swirl together and blend into the line of trees on the horizon. You kill the engine and say, "We doing this or not?"

***

It's late enough that light is virtually nonexistent in the house, leaving the four of you to share the Maglite you found rolling around the back of your van amongst the stolen church paraphernalia.

You take the lead, shining the dim cone of light on the walls.

"Leave the stuff in here. It got dark sooner than I thought," Austin says. "I'll have to come back to do the rest. Don't have everything I need anyway."

"What's left to do?" Danny pulls the candelabras from the bag on the floor and places them on the dining room table in a haphazard row. He inspects the candle lighter, fiddling with the sliding mechanism on the handle that feeds the wick.

Austin jabs at Danny, "Your ass needs to get us the generator. No power, no show." He grabs the flashlight from your hand and shines it at Ryan, who sways in the doorway. "And you need to work your magic on the gig fliers." The light fades as Austin focuses the beam on the bag while he digs through it.

And though it's quick, barely a breath's time, during this brief shifting of senses, you hear a humming noise seep through the floorboards.

The noise fades as fast as it arrived as Austin tosses a bundle of church service pamphlets at Ryan. The rubber band holding them together snaps as Ryan misses the catch. Paper scatters.

"Nice catch," Austin says. "It's all I'm asking you to do, so don't fuck it up."

You walk over and help Ryan pick up the leaflets, folding them back into their tri-folded construction, and pile them into a neat stack. Ryan's dopey drunk eyes are confused, both in purpose and intent, and they stare at you, practically begging you to spell out what it is Austin wants of him, but you're distracted.

The humming continues, but you can't place the noise. It isn't electrical. It's almost a murmur. Like a living being is sheltered, bombilating below the house.

You tie a knot in the rubber band and hand it back to Ryan, "Just make them look cool. Scratch out the words to make it nonsense. Draw on them. Put the gig details on it and you'll be good to go."

"Pass them around town," Danny says. "Don't overthink it. It's just to drudge up interest."

"In other words, it's easy so don't fuck it up," Austin says.

"Just cool it," you say. "What do you need me to do?"

Austin flicks the flashlight on and off, creating a lazy strobe-like effect.

"Practice and show up," he says. "And help me once I get the rest of the shit I need. I'm painting this place red. Dousing it in whatever kind of blood the butcher will give me. Got a pile of skulls in my car too."

You want to tell him what a dumb idea it is. That it's going to smell horrid, especially in this heat. That it will attract disease-worthy levels of insects. But you know it's the filth and the shock that he's going for. A fucking poor man's Gorgoroth show, only hardly anyone will show up and it won't make the news and it won't get you banned from any venues, let alone a country.

But you don't say anything at all because the droning buzz below vibrates stronger.

Except this time, you aren't the only one to notice it.

Danny immediately shoots you a concerned look. Ryan's dazed, but even he picks up on it. Austin's digging through the bag again. The flashlight rests on the floor, creating an eerie arc across the floor. He pulls the altar cloth from the gym bag, candles falling from the tangled mess, but keeps rifling through it.

"*Shhhh.*" It's a gesture you rarely make toward Austin because it implies a command.

Austin grabs the flashlight in one hand and juggles the sealed plastic package of communion wafers in the other. "Okay. Found them."

"Stop for a second. Don't you hear that? What do we even need those for?"

"I think it's time I show you the basement." Austin doesn't wait for you to follow him out of the front door, leaving the three of you in the thrumming darkness of the Cult Road House.

LOOK, YOU DECIDED TO COME OUT HERE.
FOLLOW HIM—GO TO PG 175

YOU BOLT OUT of the church and are immediately swaddled by thick, humid air. The van is a straight shot to the other end of the parking lot, but running across the concrete expanse before you would require you to run past your dad's office windows, so you hook around to the opposite side of the church, hugging the perimeter of the building as tight as you can.

As you shuffle through the freshly cut grass, you wonder how much better off suburban families would be if they put as much care into their children as they did their unnaturally green lawns.

Then again, would you still be you?

How much does something like that define the qualities of your makeup? Does everyone dwell on the minutia as much as you do? Maybe something cannot truly be considered minutia if it has ingrained itself so deeply into your brain that it consumes your thoughts like this. And what of your parents? What is *their* version of manicured lawns?

Perhaps it's nothing. Or everything.

Your dad compartmentalizes better than most. He's focused. Driven. Devout—well, in some cases.

You skirt toward the front of the church without signs of pursuit. It's hard to say with any certainty, but chances are, your dad will shrug the noise off as kids dicking around and won't look into it. He's too busy doing whatever it was that he was doing with the blonde. Knowing your dad, your first instinct is he's fooling around again, but the strange words they exchanged felt off in a way you can't quite place. Hardly flirtatious, but maybe that's his thing.

You've heard strange utterings like those before. Tearful prayers. Liturgical phrases. Vulnerable confessions and passionate testimonies. It's the kind of shit you've always passed off as church things. *God* things. You don't fully understand it and you've accepted that you don't have to, but that doesn't mean you're immune to curiosity. Thoughts of the door trickle into your mind's eye. The words swirling in the woodgrain. You've never seen anything like it outside of the psilocybin-induced hallucinations from your late teens.

You wedge yourself into a corner near the front doors and set the candelabras down momentarily to regain your composure. The moment doesn't last long, though, as you catch the glint of a shadow through your peripherals, setting you on edge.

Austin comes barreling out of the sanctuary, arms full of more stolen items. He kicks the catch and sends the double-paned door flying open.

"Go!" Austin yells.

Your van prowls by the front of the church with the side door open, Danny in the driver's seat, Ryan motioning *hurry up!* Austin tosses the armload into the back seat and jumps in.

Without thinking, you grab the candelabras and run alongside the van.

Austin grips the doorframe and holds his hand out as Danny steps on the gas.

Sirens blare in the distance, but they're closing in. A strong breeze carries the scent of smoke your direction, but you don't put two and two together until you're pulled into the van and look out the back window at the pillar of smoke billowing from the rear of the semi-trailer and the small, but growing crowd of high schoolers congregating on the lawn.

Austin slides the door to the van closed as Danny loops around the parking lot toward the closest exit.

"Drive to my place," Austin says.

"We've got to ditch the stolen stuff," you say.

"Like hell we do," Austin says. "This wasn't for nothing. This was for everything. Just drive to my house. I've got something to pick up and then we can lie low at Cult House."

You buckle your seatbelt and close your eyes. "Fuck."

"Calm down," Austin says.

"There's no way people didn't see us," you say.

"And if we're asked, our original story is legit: Ryan was

looking for the cufflinks he left last night at the wedding. That's it. Don't overcomplicate it."

"So what? We bailed the moment the fire started?"

"Yes, exactly," Austin says. "Does anyone else see a problem with it?"

Ryan shakes his head.

Danny mumbles a half-hearted *no*.

"Okay then," Austin says. "Off to my house."

✳✳✳

It doesn't take Austin long to find what he needs. He comes out of the empty garage, struggling with two ten-gallon buckets. "Someone else take one of these. There are two more back by the workbench."

Ryan grabs one and heaves it into the back of the van.

"Careful," you say, noticing the ring of dried blood around the lip of the lid.

Ryan goes back for the others while Austin quickdraws two paint rollers from his hip and mimics a shooting you. He tosses the rollers into the back seat and says, "Hang on a sec."

Austin returns, running and ducking under the closing garage door, double-fisting bottles of honey-brown booze.

Danny swaps seats with you, and as you settle into the driver's seat, your phone buzzes in your pocket. No doubt one of your parents calling to tell you how badly you've fucked up. That they know what you did, and what you're a part of. You ignore the vibration, and crank the volume on your stereo, blaring a burned copy of Behemoth's *And the Forests Dream Eternally* as you drive to the Cult Road House.

Austin won't shut up about how Nergal was only seventeen when he recorded this record. And you can tell. The fantasy-fueled lyrics are so angsty. It's not that you hold it against the band or their self-expression, but come the fuck on. They may be grown now, but all of Austin's heroes are children. Does he realize he based his beliefs off lyrics written by teenagers? Self-centered and angst-riddled words frozen in time. That he still bases what is cool and real and true off the opinions of kids?

"Yeah, it's wild," you say. "It's a hell of an accomplishment, you know? Do you think anything we do will be as lasting?"

145

Will Austin's lyrics be studied and regarded as gospel to people in five years? Ten? You know that's what he wants. To be worshipped. Then again, who doesn't want to be seen?

"Are you kidding?" Austin asks. "They won't have a choice by the time we're through."

You're feeling sick to your stomach by the time you reach the house. Blame it on the buckets of blood sloshing around the backseat. The smell is faint for the time being, but it's the thought of it. The putrid stench of blood, stagnating in a hot garage for who knows how long.

Granted, you know that's a lie. It isn't the blood odor that's bothering you, but the smoke you can't seem to get out of your nostrils. It lingers, an unspoken message—like the one buzzing in your pocket.

It's too dark to see much of anything, so you park close to the house and leave your headlights on. "Make it fast," you say. "I don't want to kill the battery."

Austin uses one of the buckets to prop the front door open. One after the other, the four of you unload the supplies into the house.

"Just leave everything by the table," Austin says. "We'll come back this week to set everything else up. That should give Danny time to get the generator. In the meantime, make sure to spread the word around. Don't give much away. Just tell people about the show. I'm going to make some road signs for directions. Nothing too commercial. Thought I'd spray paint some inverted crosses or some shit to show the way."

You find yourself unable to ignore the incessant buzzing in your pocket any longer. The stairs creak as you climb them to take the call away from the rest of the guys, where it's quiet. Shaking, you pull your phone and flip it open to answer—your mom's number flashing on the screen. The uneven hardwood is uncomfortable to sit on, but you sense nothing comforting coming from your mom's lips, "Where are you? You need to come home now. There was a fire at the church. We need to talk to you." Her words are stilted. Monotone. You expected anger—hoped for it. You know how to handle your mom when she's angry, but her tone is frightening. Sullen. Void.

The high beams of your van flood the entryway to the house and creep slightly up the stairs. You move your feet out of the light as if it were rising water, threatening to pull you under and sweep you away.

And there they are again. The woodgrain in the steps spell out *transcendence* and *truth* and *abyss* and *blight*. The darkened lines of the woodgrain shift and swirl, fusing together in accursed cursive. The wood is dry and rough to the touch while you try and erase the words. It wouldn't matter. They are ever present in your mind. These words you're carrying.

"This is serious," she says. "A kid is dead."

EVERYTHING ABOUT THIS PLACE IS
WRONG. YOU HAVE TO LEAVE—
GO TO PG 177

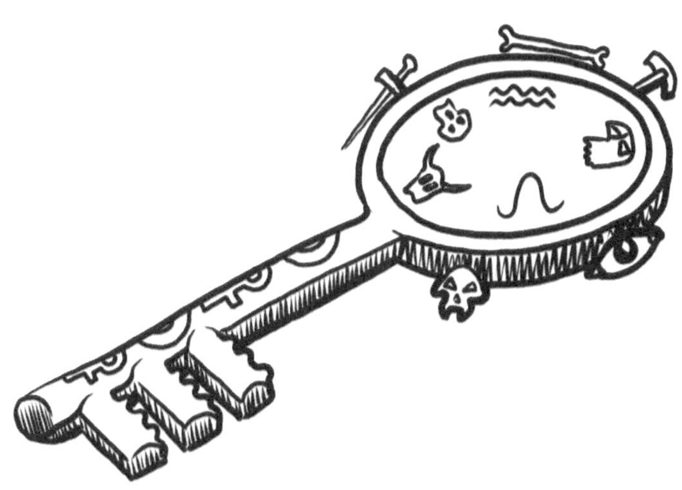

YOU'RE A DRUMMER. It only makes sense that you'd lash out, kicking at anything that will make the loudest thud. The wood cracks as your boot connects with the ladder, forcing it to teeter off balance.

It's one of those moments people always talk about. Time creeps to a near halt as you push off, returning your foot to the ground. The ladder sways, and ultimately chooses to fall away from you.

Ryan scatters, dropping his cigarette.

Austin scowls, his face twisted in disbelief.

Danny pulls you back by the shoulders, and you watch as the top of the ladder knocks the bucket tottering on sloped shingles. Goopy paint pours down from the eaves while the bucket spins in a lazy semi-circle before plummeting to the ground. You narrowly escape being doused in deep, wine-colored paint.

As it coats the entryway to the porch, splattering the stairs and your boots, the pungent and iron-heavy smell decks you in the face, and it becomes apparent that it is not paint at all, but blood.

It elicits a gag-reflex from Danny, while you remain focused on the meat of the situation—the *where?* And *how?* Though you don't have to guess long or hard about it. Austin's grandpa hunts, whether it's deer season or not. You wouldn't put it past him to walk into the grocery store and ask for their drippings either. Maybe he collected the blood himself.

Austin stares down at you with a thin smile on his face.

"You'd have found out sooner or later," Austin says in a monotone voice. It's hard to tell if he's pissed or pleased by your outburst.

"It's going to reek," you say. "Especially after it bakes in the sun all week until the show."

You almost ask if he's thought of the flies. The maggots. The disease and putrid stench.

Then Austin corrects you. "You mean rot. It's going to rot all week."

And you realize he's thought every part of this through.

Danny pukes in the grass while Ryan stomps out the small fire caused by his cigarette. The small patch of charred grass only adds to the sinister peculiarity marking the entryway to the house.

"Are we going to leave the puddle or . . . ?" you ask.

"Fuck yes we are," Austin says. "Don't move."

No one has bothered propping the ladder back up, but it doesn't matter. Austin slams the paint roller into one of the dormer windows, clearing away the shards of glass still clinging to the frame, and disappears into the house.

The heavy noises erupting from within makes it seem like the house is groaning, choking on Austin's presence, and intensifies with his turbulent exit through the front doors.

He stomps across the porch, bounds off the steps into the puddle of blood, coating his boots, "Come on in, the water's warm."

Blood squelches as you step into the puddle.

Austin takes the blood-bucket and tells Ryan to grab the stuff from his car. Then looks at you and says, "Come on. Time to leave our mark."

You follow him through the entryway tracking tacky footprints across the floor. Every step feels slightly gummy. The prints fade the further you walk into the house until the sanguinous trail disappears entirely. Soon, the prints will congeal as the blood coagulates in the tread pattern of your worn-out boots.

Danny hasn't come in yet, but it doesn't take Ryan long to add his footprints into the mix. He walks over to where you and Austin stand in the soon-to-be stage area and heaves a bloated gym bag onto the table.

Piece by piece, Ryan pulls out various religious supplies: a handful of candles, twin candelabras to match, an altar cloth, braided pastor's cords, a couple of hymnals, a communion tray and bags containing quarter-sized bits of God flesh.

"Where'd you get all of this?" Though you should have asked *how*, because you'd recognize those brass behemoths and those tasseled cords anywhere.

Austin grabs the altar cloth and dunks it into the bucket at his feet. Then he swats the gym bag to the floor and unfurls the soaked altar cloth across the table.

"By the look on your face, I think you already know," Austin says.

"But when? How? You can't just walk in at this time of day. Did anyone see you?"

"Chill out. Damn," Austin says. "No one saw us."

But you see the quick flash in Ryan's eyes.

"You didn't break in, did you? Shit. I'm serious. The church has an alarm system you asshole. My dad won't hesitate to file vandalism charges. Breaking and entering. He'd love nothing more than to throw the book at you because—" because your dad sees you in your friends and punishing them is punishing you. Some disciplinary commutative property. "—he loves to prove a point and you two will be easy targets if you got caught breaking in. Especially because the fucking police chief is a member of—"

"Fucking chill," Austin says. "We didn't break in. No alarms. No property damage, alright. But I lied. One person saw us. Some high school kid let us in, but he didn't want to be there in the first place, so we're cool. He let us slip in the door behind him."

Ryan lines the candelabras on the table and dips candles in the blood bucket before placing them into the brass fittings. "We're more than cool. The kid was wearing a Converge shirt."

Austin sneers and mutters something under his breath that your tinnitus won't let you catch.

But Ryan seems to.

"It does fucking matter, though, because heavy music is heavy music, and now he's going to spread the word about the gig. Can't have a gig without a crowd. I'm not going to get into it again."

"It's not just a gig. It's a goddamn ritual."

"And you can't have a church without a congregation," you say.

"You'd know," Austin says.

"Are we done here? Because I've had enough of your shit tonight. The generator is over there," you say, pointing at it. "We should probably bring our gear out here at least once to make sure it works."

Austin dips his hand into the blood-bucket without responding.

"Cool. Guess I'll fuck off," you say. "See you guys later."

Ryan fist-bumps you and tells you not to sweat it.

You head out the door expecting to find Danny waiting in the van. Instead, you find the faintest trail of bloody footsteps leading around to the side of the house.

THERE'S NO POSSIBLE WAY THIS WILL BE GOOD, BUT YOU MUST FOLLOW IT —GO TO PG 156

IT ISN'T WORTH getting into when Austin's trashed and feeling aggressive. You can deal with him when he's mopey-drunk, but you aren't looking to fight tonight. The show is less than a week away and all the band has to do is stay together long enough to perform. With everything going on, you have your doubts that in a few months' time, Abyss will be anything more than a defunct local band from the middle of nowhere.

You're leaving regardless, with or without the band.

You don't have a choice.

Thoughts of teaching yourself to play guitar and mixing solo records fills your headspace, but you're soon distracted by the faint pitter-patter of goo slowly dripping onto your shoulder.

Austin's leaning over the edge of the house, hoisting the paint roller above. He laughs like a kid lighting ants on fire.

"What the hell, dude?" you say, but he laughs and laughs. Gobs of it fall, stretching and pulling itself apart into thinner and thinner strands before it hits the ground. You step back and watch him dunk the roller into the bucket again.

Danny's the first to notice the smell. He dabs at the already drying droplets on your shoulder. "It's blood."

Rancid drops of animal blood riddle the ground as Austin swings the paint roller like a conductor's wand. The smell intensifies as more and more of it is poured below.

"This shit is going to reek," you say. "Do you know how bad this is going to smell at the gig? Especially after baking in the sun for a week. The flies. For fuck's sake, dude."

Austin dunks his hand into the bucket and presses it against his face. "What do you think? How many times do I have to tell you I have a plan? I know exactly what I'm doing. Have a little faith," he says, over-enunciating the *th* in *faith*. Heavy on the tongue.

Danny pukes in the grass when you mention the maggots and diseases that go hand-in-hand with decomposition. Again, you're met with a sort of delighted apathy.

Ryan hasn't said a thing, but quietly smokes a cigarette, like he's waiting for some kind of fallout. It isn't too apparent in his body language. Ryan's mannerisms are gelatinous tonight. A smoking blob, simply existing. You can't tell if he's got a care in the world, let alone if he could string together a coherent thought right now. His eyelids hang two-hit-heavy, unfocused, but telling nonetheless.

You've observed him making eye contact with Austin, then absentmindedly telling on himself by trailing toward Austin's car.

Maybe it's nothing more than concern for Austin's gas mileage, as the engine's still running. The high beams on. Melancholic distortion pounding against the windows, like the soundwaves are trying to escape.

"Come on, make yourself useful and grab the shit out of my trunk." Austin fiddles with the keys dangling off his belt, and his car chirps as he unlocks it.

Ryan follows you to the car. You release the catch to open the trunk and are hit with a surge of foul odors emanating from another couple of buckets, dried blood ringing them just under the lids.

"I wouldn't open those," Ryan says. "Not till the show."

The shock of the blood buckets has faded and you find yourself more concerned with a new object grabbing your attention: a bloated duffel bag.

It doesn't move, which you believe to be a good thing considering there aren't any other gruesome signs pointing to foul play. Just a gym bag, you think. Which isn't entirely true. Can't be. Otherwise, Ryan wouldn't have that dewy anticipation burnishing his eyes.

You slowly tug on the zipper and allow the bag to open its mouth, tooth by tooth, widening its grin, and eventually, you flip the skin-like flap backwards to reveal the contents.

The top layer is some kind of cloth. At first, you think maybe Austin gave in and made band shirts, but as you move it aside, it's a singular piece of fabric—one you've seen a thousand times. The overhead trunk light emits a weak yellow glow, yet it causes the brass candelabras to glimmer like weak candlelight.

Dozens of half-spent candles clutter the bottom of the bag like loose bullet casings. It's all here: plastic bags of communion wafers—flesh waiting to be consumed—golden pastor's cords, braided into a thin rope, hymnals, and blank worship service bulletins.

It's hard to say what kind of reaction Austin was expecting from you, but as you peer over his car, you don't think this is it. "Did anyone see you?" is all you think to ask.

Did he expect you to praise him over the theft?

What a stupid question. Of course he did. Austin aims to impress. That's what this whole gig is about. Image. Doesn't matter that he claims; it's about the ritual. The experience.

If it weren't, why would he make such a big fucking deal about every little thing?

He needs you to tell him how cool this is. How smart he is. How great his ideas are.

So when you don't and repeat the question, "Did anyone see you?" and continue with, "You didn't break in, did you? The church has an alarm system, you know?" It is unsurprising to hear Austin bark back.

"No. I told you I've got this shit under control. Can't you just be fucking excited about all of this for once?"

You heave the bag out of the car, noticing a pile of deer skulls and dropped antlers shoved toward the back, and close the trunk. The air is dense, and the mineral-heavy scent of blood and tension in the air makes the mood feel impenetrable.

"I am." You drop the bag on the porch steps. "But getting thrown in county for robbing a church will be the end of it."

The warped boards creek as Austin sits on the edge of the roof, feet dangling. He stares down at you, "We weren't seen. Happy?"

"How'd you get in?"

"Some kid let us in," Ryan says. "Could tell he didn't want to be there."

You know the type. Probably some high school kid getting dragged to youth group by the girl he wants to feel up.

"Had a Converge shirt though," Ryan says. "Let us slip in

behind him without question. Told him about the gig, so we're hoping he'll bring a small crowd."

This is where Austin checks out, uninterested by the type of kid he deems not cool enough. But you've already had this conversation. A crowd's a crowd. No sense playing to an empty room.

"Where're we going with this?" You nod at the bag.

"Inside. Where else?" Austin grabs the bucket by the handle, holds it over the edge of the house and drops it. He uncaps the whiskey, glugs away, and drops that too. Then he grips the ladder and swings his legs over the edge. Too bad the drunk motherfucker missteps and loses his footing.

OH, SHIT!—GO TO PG 161

DANNY DOESN'T TRACK blood far, only a few steps toward the side of the house, before his footprints no longer stain the yellowing prairie grass. The indentations left by heavy footfalls give you a better idea where he's going than the blood will. You're left with a slim wedge of artificial light from Austin's headlights as you round the corner of the house.

"Danny? Are you alright?" you call, but your voice is lost in the rustling of dry brush as you walk toward the open storm cellar. The ground level entrance blends into the earth almost perfectly and you could see how if the scrap-wood-door were closed, it would be easy to pass without notice.

But it isn't.

It's wide open, welcoming you to step inside.

YOU WANT TO GO IN. YOU HAVE TO CHECK ON HIM. NOT LIKE YOU HAVE A CHOICE—YOU GO IN

YOU ABSOLUTELY DO NOT WANT TO GO IN THERE—YOU GO IN

You place your hands along either side of the foundation walls as you walk down the craggy steps into the cellar, your fingertips graze etchings of unfamiliar letters scratched into the interior walls of the entrance.

"Danny? Are you in here?"

The only response is his incoherent mumbling, layered between the faint hum emanating from the cellar and the frantic pulse of your heartbeat pounding steadily in your eardrums. You step through debris strewn across the uneven dirt floor and into underground space which is lit only by the hazy discharge of purple hues beaming from the far wall.

Danny kneels near the wall, his fingers gliding across its surface, which softly undulates as if it's breathing like a resting animal.

"Danny!" You trudge through broken planks and spent candles and animal skulls, and place your hands on his shoulders when you reach him, gently nudging him to respond. Any acknowledgement would suffice.

It's no use. He's entranced by the absurdity before him. His fingers tap and slide across the oily surface of the wall like he's playing an instrument. Communicating in foreign chords. Playing a duet with the wall. Can you blame his indifference toward you?

You wonder what would have happened to you had you not been pulled back to reality by Ryan earlier. If your out of body experience would have led to something as seemingly pleasant and ethereal as what indulges his mind right now.

The wall does not appear to be harming Danny, so you back away, not wanting to rob him of the experience.

He babbles like he's speaking in tongues, but you hesitate to write it off as a nonsensical spiritual feat. It's incoherent to you, sure, but there's something about the way he's interacting with the wall that makes you stop and reconsider your original observation. That it's not an act of glossolalia—not how you'd recognize it to be—but rather that Danny is in tune with the wall, uttering strange melodies. Almost like he's literally speaking music . . . every syllable is some bizarre form of notation.

As you step farther back, intending to—what? Leave him to ride it out? Go get Austin and Ryan? Observe Danny from a distance?— A voice speaks to you. YOU DON'T HAVE TO BE A BYSTANDER, YOU KNOW? YOU CAN PARTICIPATE. YOU CAN HAVE A ROLE IF YOU WANT TO. THERE'S NO NEED TO LEAVE THIS PRESENCE BEHIND YOU.

The melodious voice hits your ears simultaneously, yet you're able to perceive the sonic sensation hitting each ear individually. It's like the soundwave is being pulled apart and fed to you as separate, but layered tracks that converge in your mind into a singularity.

You ask the obvious, "Who?" and "what?" in stammered confusion.

The response is a vague NOTHING AND EVERYTHING, delivered by a voice composed of two parts—belonging to both Danny and the wall—braided together by an indistinct bond.

A weight bears down on you. It isn't dread, but the crushing heaviness of excess. Overstimulation. Wrapped in the energy exuding from the performance—because you're convinced that's what this is. An overbearing taste of what's to come.

Again, you're called to join the spectacle.

YOU'RE NOT ONLY WELCOME, BUT YOU ARE WANTED. THOUGH THERE IS NO OBLIGATION. NO EXPIRATION DATE. THE INVITATION WILL NOT BE RESCINDED, AND WE ARE ALWAYS EAGER TO HAVE YOU. EVERYONE DESERVES THIS EXPERIENCE.

It's confusing how the words seem to make no sense as they travel through the air as guttural sibilance, but congeal into something resembling understanding in your mind. You're skeptical that what you're experiencing is true comprehension, but rather that it's something else entirely. Some universal knowledge. Some metaphysical feeling of perception. Words whispered in the womb.

You've heard this honey-tongued rhetoric a thousand times, though. This offering of overwhelming and abundant inclusion. And you know eventually there will be some sort of condition to it. An unmentioned requirement you won't recognize until the honey has crystalized around your feet and you find yourself unable to move.

You can't break free from asking, "Why?"

Why is Danny down here in the first place? Calm and pragmatic Danny. One minute he's puking in the bushes and the next he's disappeared to do . . . this?

Again, the question—why?

NOT ALL DECISIONS HAVE EXPLICIT PURPOSE. The voice rings throughout your mind in sonorous bellows, its words echoing, returning as Danny's. SOMETIMES ACTIONS SIMPLY ARE. AND THOUGHTS ARE MERELY THAT WHICH DWELLS WITHIN. HAVE YOU ASKED YOURSELF THE SAME QUESTIONS YOU POSE? HAVE YOU CONSIDERED WHY YOU ARE HERE?

"I was looking for my friend."

LITERALLY, SO. BUT THINK LARGER. OF ALL THE INFINITE POSSIBILITIES, WHY ARE YOU HERE ON THIS PLANET DURING THIS GIVEN

TIME? LET ALONE WHY YOU'RE WANDERING THROUGH THE MUGGINESS, AROUND THIS DECREPIT PIT OF A HOME? YOU DON'T NEED TO ANSWER, BECAUSE YOU ALREADY KNOW THE TRUTH, AS I ALREADY KNOW THE TRUTH. IT IS SOMETHING YOU WILL GRAPPLE WITH UNTIL THE END OF YOUR EXISTENCE. IT IS WHO YOU ARE.

You amble forward as if pulled by invisible threads from a celestial skein. You are not insusceptible to the allure of belonging. It is perhaps your greatest downfall, masked as desire. But what is the harm in it? Inclusion. Wanting. You've been taught to be content. Made to feel guilty for feeling humanity's most basic instincts.

Why *are* you here?

The answer is not something you can wholly put into words, but when you place your palms on the bulbous wall, you feel it.

You feel it in the way the wall pulses violently violet, slicking your hands in oily excretion, melding your thoughts with your physical being.

You feel it as you swim through the hallucinatory gray matter of the cellar. Its walls no longer feeling cramped, but growing ever more cavernous as your fingertips plunge into the surface of the wall, digging into the subcutaneous tissue beneath.

As you pull away, your fingers stretch like putty and remain connected to the being before you like the strings of a cat's cradle. Wisps of color flutter through the air like hummingbirds, intertwining with your breath like strands of DNA.

You inhale and taste conscious thought. It coats your lungs in fibrous mist. You hold it in, then exhale it back into the dense atmosphere of the cellar, which has become a thick fog of effervescent smoke that plays with your vision.

No matter how hard you try, you cannot blink away the occlusion, and the more you strain your vision, the more obscure reality becomes. Panic begins to settle in your mind, but the voice is quick to reassure you, DO NOT BE AFRAID. FOCUS—THIS IS AS THINGS ARE.

Through this mental barrier, you begin to see yourself in double vision, then in triplicate—and soon, you feel as if you have been thrust from your body and you see an infinite number of yourself, as if viewing your existence through a hallway of mirrors. An astral body floating throughout the cosmic slop of your brain.

You swim through this space, staring at every version of yourself presented in the reflections, shattering each and every one of them who lies to you, until there is only a singular version of you staring back.

IT IS WHO YOU ARE, AND IT IS WHY YOU ARE HERE.

ONLY RED PILLS FOR YOU. SORRY. KEEP GOING—GO TO PG 179

YOU SEE THE fall as several occurrences happening simultaneously: Austin kicking the ladder as he scrambles for purchase on the ledge of the house, the ladder subsequently falling in your direction, Danny still hunched over in the grass, and Ryan running toward the house in slow-motion. Everything shifts in dark splotches, blips of time speeding forward until you find yourself slipping in the spilt blood and falling backward as you sidestep to dodge the tumbling ladder. Ryan is unable to reach Austin in time, and Danny only looks up from puking after you've collided with the ground near him.

Austin's body slams into the ground and the distinct sound like a tree branch snapping cuts through the air.

You scramble to your feet and run to him.

He's on his back, gasping for breath.

"Hold on, and breathe," you say. "Slow and steady."

In the very least, he's had the wind knocked out of him and he needs to catch his breath.

He tries to sit up, but you hold him back and tell him not to move. "You could have messed up your neck or back. You need to stay still."

"I don't think he'd be able to sit up if his back was messed up," Ryan says.

"Doesn't matter. Call 911," Danny says. "You can't mess around with this kinda shit."

"Don't . . . " Austin says, pushing your hands off his chest. " . . . Touch me. I'm good."

"Like fuck you are," you say.

His skin is whitewashed and clammy like greasy fat trimmings. He won't let you get a pulse, but he's got the panicked breath of a prey animal and the spacey dinner plate eyes of someone tripping balls.

"Shit, he's in shock." You try to look for any signs of obvious injury, but Austin keeps swiping your hands away from him. He takes a few deep and uneven breaths, then belches foul whiskey-breath in your face until you back away.

Austin stands on noodle-legs and swats Danny's phone out of his hand. "No 911. They'll board this place up and—" He showers both the grass and Danny's phone in vomit. "—and goodbye Abyss. Goodbye Waste Doctrine."

Even when he's hurt, Austin's an insufferable asshole.

"Oh, come on," Danny says. "Dick."

You've heard of people walking out of car wrecks, cars smashed like aluminum cans, or falling from fifth floor balconies and being totally fine, but there's no way Austin doesn't need to get checked out.

"Dude, you've got to at least let us take you to Urgent Care or something," you say.

"I said I'm fucking fine," Austin says, though he winces through gritted teeth as he wipes the dribble of puke from his chin. The sleeve of his leather jacket is cracked and scuffed. Folded strangely at the wrist.

He wobbles, then spits onto the grass.

Could be the booze, but it could be a head injury. Maybe internal.

It's hard to get a read on him because he won't stay still. Ryan helps herd Austin so you can walk around him to inspect his neck and the back of his head. His hair is tousled and knotted, but there doesn't appear to be any blood; at least none that didn't originate from the spilled buckets.

"Screw the clinic then. Call . . . what's her face, your ex. She was a nurse, yeah?"

"She was studying to be one," Ryan says.

Austin won't keep his eyes off the duffel bag and says, "The show is an act, the act is an inevitability. Participation is the only option."

You put yourself between him and the bag, trying to usher him toward the porch stairs, "Come sit, dude. You need to chill for a minute."

The veins on his face are a grotesque lattice work of purple and blue, made more prominent by the increasing sallowness of his skin. He favors his left arm, keeping it snug against his abdomen.

Time is crucial in these emergencies and you've already wasted two or three minutes keeping Austin from moving too much. When you finally convince him to sit on the porch, he lets his arm hang loose at his side. Blood oozes from the cuff onto the planks. The deadwood soaks it up, greedily nourished, drop by drop.

"Oh shit," you say, pulling your phone from your pocket.

You're fast, but Austin is faster.

By the time you manage to flip your phone open and dial 9, he's pulled his switchblade from his pocket and lazily digs the point into the base of your sternum.

"Whoa, whoa," you say. "We don't need to do this."

Both Ryan and Danny approach him from either side, leaving you in the middle.

You don't break eye contact with Austin, but you speak to the whole band, hoping they get the hint not to make any sudden moves, "We're okay. We just want to help. You seem to be in a lot of pain and we just want to make sure you're good for the show, you know? Nothing too wild. Can't have a good gig without the singer, right?"

"I live for the pain," he says. "The show *is* the pain. Life *is* the pain."

Ryan and Danny inch toward him, but one of the boards creaks and gives them away.

Austin stands, but immediately loses balance and falls against the front. He swipes an arc in front of him, keeping the three of you at bay, but he's stumbly and it's a miracle he's standing, seemingly anchored to the porch only by his combat boots.

"Come on, Austin. You aren't thinking straight. That's the shock talking. You're fucked up. You don't want us to call 911. No big deal. Let us take you into town. You'll get fixed up and be good to put on the show of a lifetime, alright? Just put the knife away and let's get into the van. I'll even let you pick the CD. Only the truest black metal. None of that other shit, yeah?"

Tears slick his ghoulish face. He shakes so severely the chains dangling from his jacket clatter against his bullet belt like bells.

"No," he says. "I have a place. Much better."

Danny and Ryan dart looks back and forth.

You're perplexed, but roll with it because Austin seems to be amicable. "Okay, okay. Let's get you into the van and we can go to this other place."

There's no way in hell you're going anywhere but the emergency room, but you've almost got him. You can feel it.

"Trust me?" he pleads.

You've never seen this kind of desperation from him before. It oozes like the trickle of blood continuing to drip from his sleeve.

"Yeah, of course," you say. "But let's put the knife away first."

You hold up your hands, palms out.

"Trust me," he shouts, and thrusts the knife into your left palm, clean to the hilt, through your hand.

You drop to your knees, staring at the double-edged blade glimmering grisly red. The pain hasn't set in yet, but the immediate shock paints your body in sweat.

Ryan and Danny grip Austin under the arms.

Austin won't quit stomping, struggling to get free. He shrieks, loudly adding to the cacophony of chaos and curses coming from the porch.

You don't remember where you saw it, but you don't think you should pull the knife from your hand. Instead, you find the bottle of whiskey Austin dropped off the roof and douse both sides of the wound with the auburn liquid, saving a pull for yourself. You down it and toss the bottle into the grass.

Austin squirms, and wriggles out of his jacket. He slips his right arm out of his sleeve first, but flinches as Danny yanks on his left to regain control.

"Let me go," he says. "You have to trust me."

"I don't have to do shit," Danny says.

Ryan backs away, unsure how to help.

Austin quits fighting, but he's got that pleading look in his eyes again.

"Let him go," you say, gripping the knife handle in your other hand to hold it steady.

Grimacing, Austin carefully tugs at his left cuff, sliding his arm from the sleeve little by little, taking sharp breaths the entire time. He turns slightly away from the three of you and tosses his weathered leather jacket over his left shoulder, seemingly doing everything to postpone showing you how bad of shape he's in.

Austin rotates to reveal his cartoonishly bent wrist, twisted in warped-geometry, skin split by the sharp bone protruding from his skin, "Follow . . . me," he says, and stumbles off the porch.

WHEREVER HE'S LEADING YOU MUST BE GOOD—GO TO PG 181

YOU USED TO know how to breathe. At least you think so. So why is it so damn hard right now? The sky above you is impossibly huge. The expanse is a blurred twilight hue, lit only by a few notable stars and the dim fog of moonlight in your periphery. For a moment, it almost appears as if you're swimming through space.

Inhaling seems like the right choice, but if that's the case, why does it hurt so goddamn much to do so? It's the one thing you have to do to live and it's painful. Was it always so painful?

Exhaling isn't a walk in the park, either. All of the air you've breathed in won't leave your lungs fast enough, and you're certain if you keep trying to force an eviction, they will self-destruct in protest.

You manage to gain some control over your breathing by connecting the stars. Invisible lines drawn in your mind. It gives you something to focus on beyond the numbing sensation burning at the back of your skull and rippling down your back, where it ends abruptly in confusing non-sensation.

The lines in your mind's eye don't connect to form a picture, but rather words: YOU'VE BEEN IN WORSE SITUATIONS BEFORE. NOT BY MUCH, BUT TRUST ME. AT LEAST THIS TIME YOU DIDN'T SEE WHAT YOUR PARENTS WERE UP TO . . .

As you try and read the message, Austin intercedes, stepping into blurry view.

"Oh shit," he says. "Are you okay?"

His hair dangles like the branches of a weeping willow, and distinct heavy strands appear to be reaching to grab your face.

Austin is agitated. You wonder what's with the panicked look carved into his face.

When you don't respond, he mutters, "Fuckfuckfuck," and

things go dark for an impossible moment. One moment he's there—black—the next he's reading from the gilded Bible.

You remember he asked you if you were okay, but now you're thinking maybe you should be asking him the same thing, because his speech is slurred. His typical tenor is layered with guttural phrases cut by sharp, deep inflections that mimic songbirds. His intonation is all over the place, and soon his voice goes whisper-quiet and you almost ask him to speak up, but breathing is really taking it out of you.

You blink and his face is bloody.

"Whoa, what the hell happened to you, man?"

The words formed in your mind, but you can't be certain they made it out of your mouth.

You blink again, and Austin tears the page from the book. He wads the golden-edged page in his palm while balancing the book in the other, and then places the wadded page into his mouth with a bloodstained finger. He chews. He swallows. He repeats this process five more times, punctuated by blips of darkness while he alternates spitting the pages into the grass and devouring them in some freakish hunger—until the sixth page—which he chews, then pulls from his mouth.

He places the book on your chest and slips a hand under your neck, cradling your skull in his palm. Then he pulls on your chin, opening your mouth, and places the chewed ball of scritta paper onto your tongue.

"Chew and swallow," he says, then presses a bloody thumb to your forehead.

The wad of paper is cold and disintegrates into a pulpy sludge in your mouth. Swallowing requires little more than a few focused gulps as it ekes down your throat like sinus drainage. Drip by drip, it hits your stomach with an intense, biting cold, lacquering your stomach lining like black ice.

Then things begin to feel wrong again.

Your eyes flutter involuntarily, warping the rural Midwestern landscape into a frenzied mural of strobing confusion.

Austin says, "Trust me," and you feel weightless among the stars. His breath is dry ice across your face, but you can't seem to move away from the cool burning. The sensation webs across your face as he lifts you onto his shoulder.

You're jostled with every labored step he takes. Bile is forced up your throat, burning your esophagus. It slicks your tongue, offending every taste bud. A hard step makes you gasp for breath, sending a spittle of bile down the back of Austin's leather jacket. A blade of light catches his bullet belt jangling off his hips.

"Almost there," he says. "Stay with me."

You attempt to ask where *there* is, but your mouth won't cooperate. Your muscles stand defiant. Your vocal cords, silent.

He doesn't sound convincing, but maybe that's where you've been wrong your entire life. All of Austin's contrived mysticism, your parent's dogmatic religiosity—none of it has been an attempted occultation of the mind, but a displaced plea, because maybe no one else truly sees like you've previously believed them to. But they keep telling you to trust, because if you can see it, then maybe that will convince them that what they want to believe is true. And only then will they be able to see.

Austin struggles, kicking at something.

All you see is the browning prairie grass moving closer through your drapery of hair as Austin bends over. Bundles of nerves wax and send illicit messages to your brain as he adjusts his hold on you. His body rotates slightly and heaves.

The weak thud of cheap wood falling against the overgrowth fills the silence.

"Okay, you have to trust me. I mean it." Austin carries you down through a narrow staircase. You are moving too quickly, and despite the light becoming insufficient with every step into the nearly lightless pit, you notice the strange words scratched into the cinderblock walls. Their shape and structure have shifted since you were last down here, but this time you're able to make sense of a handful of the words. *Truth,* and *refuge,* and *transcendence.*

The lingering scent of smoke twirls around the room, combining with a much stronger aroma of mineral-heavy dirt and stone. It's laced with the sharp body odor emanating from the two of you.

An overwhelming sensation hits you and it feels as though you are suddenly being watched. Like you've awakened the presence of something beyond the wall.

You believe it is death.

What's truer than death? What else is transcendence, what

safer place can a broken, dying skeptic take refuge in than the inevitable embrace of death?

You aren't afraid, but the sensation is paralyzing.

The further Austin carries you, the more alive the dwelling appears. Striking bright light burns your retinas as the room suddenly glows white hot like a television turned on during the dark witching hours of night. You pinch your eyelids closed; the strained sensation vibrates your eye sockets.

You open them slowly as you feel yourself being placed onto the rough floor as if given in offering. The puzzling purple being stands, imposing itself in front of you. As your eyes adjust to the looming violaceous glow, Austin speaks, though it almost sounds like a plea—a prayer:

"Help."

REACH OUT. FALL INTO THE ABYSS.

OH, COME ON. BY NOW YOU KNOW YOU HAVE TO DO THIS—GO TO PG 183

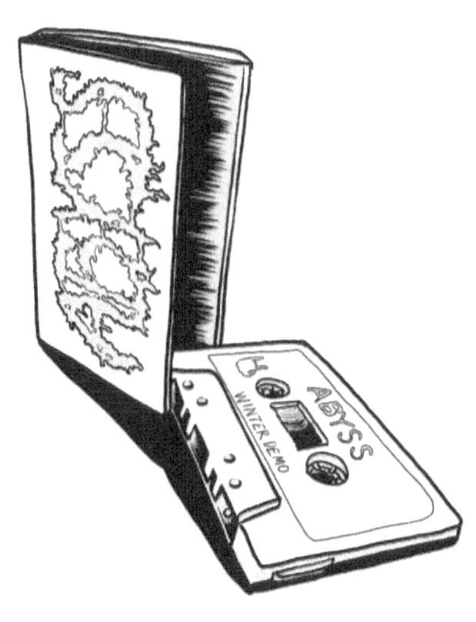

PEOPLE DISAPPEAR AROUND here all the time. No one likes to admit it, but it's the truth.

The numbers aren't as jarring as the big city crimes, but that doesn't mean it doesn't happen or that it isn't felt. You remember the baby they found, bloated and blue, floating through the flood control channel after an unexpected torrential thunderstorm. Or your middle school classmate who was absent for a week straight, then two, then all month, and then never spoken of again.

Most of those crimes boiled down to trafficking and the uptick in rural meth production, and you consider the possibility you and the band intruded on something at the house on Cult Road. Maybe you and Danny drove past something. A wrong place, wrong time sort of thing. It's a reasonable thought, but your gut tells you this is different. You don't know any meth addicts roaming around in robes, but then again, what *do* you know?

You're in the bed of a truck heading to an undisclosed location.
You left your phone in the van's cupholder among loose change.
One of your captors allegedly has a gun.
Your parents kicked you out and will not be expecting you.
There's a voice in your head that doesn't belong to you.
THAT'S RIGHT, BECAUSE IT BELONGS TO ME.
Danny got away?
The truck is slowing down.
Momentum forces you to slide against the cab of the truck as it slows to a stop. Dirt and gravel crunch underneath the tires, telling you you're still on the road. It's been tough to discern, but you don't believe the truck has made more than a couple of turns the entire time, and if you had to guess, you're still within a couple miles of the van.

They didn't duct-tape your feet, which you assume is because they expect you to walk some more, or at the very least they don't want to carry you.

You lie on your back and wait, not wanting to make a move yet. Focus on the details.

The passenger door opens, followed by feet hitting the ground. Only one pair. The driver remains in the truck. The passenger's side door clangs shut. Engine's still running.

"Scooch forward until your feet dangle and you can't scooch anymore," he says, unlatching the tailgate. "Try anything and I'll shoot ya."

You do as you're told.

BE PATIENT.

You want to tell the voice in your head to fuck off, that you're imagining things and it's going to get you killed, maybe worse, but the pain radiating from the side of your head is overwhelming and you can't expend any extra effort. It probably wouldn't listen to you anyway.

When your feet reach the end of the tailgate, you're pulled by the ankles out from the truck bed. A meaty hand grips you at the nape of your neck as your feet hit the ground, putting pressure on your traps like he's trying to stake you to the dirt. He slaps the open tailgate with the other hand and the truck drives away.

He loosens his grip on your neck, slides his hand between your shoulder blades, and pushes you forward, "Walk."

You listen for anything to clue you into who this person may be. The nervous jangling of keys. Sniffles or the deep hawking of phlegm. Cracking knuckles. Whistling. But there's nothing but the crunch of boots, his and yours, through the ankle high grass.

There are no cars in the distance. No cows. It's a beautiful silent night. Even the bugs have gone quiet.

"Hang on," he says after walking a few more yards. "Mind the barbed wire fence. I'm going to step on it. You just walk forward and step over it."

Wire grates against wooden posts as he steps. Without the use of your hands, it's hard to balance, let alone maintain your composure as you make your approach and nearly fall on the uneven earth.

"Step now and swing your leg over," he says. "Just like that."

You plant a boot firmly in the grass and pivot your body to clear the fence.

The barbed wire groans, relieved of tension, and you feel your captor's presence beside you once again. You trudge through the field, the occasional hand pressed into your back, pushing you toward your fate.

***

Although it hasn't spoken since its cautionary advice in the truck bed, the voice in your head perpetually thrums in odd cadences and almost-words. Indiscernible whispers. Sleep-talk. Cosmic tinnitus. It speaks to you, but only in cryptic bullshit. The sonic version of an auto-stereogram.

If it's so goddamn important, why not come out with it?

BECAUSE—

It stops and ends there—static—as other noises consume your headspace: the rattling of chains, the shriek of metal sliding over metal, and the creak of wood.

"Well, we're here," your captor says, "Unfortunately for you, it might be a long night on account we've got to find your friend first."

As you're pushed forward, your elbows graze what you assume to be a doorframe. Your captor stops at the threshold and goes off about the world being a strange place.

"People around here think the Czechs found this place. Or the Swedes. The Irish or any number of Europeans. They were merely settlers. Poor farmers. They barely recognize the indigenous tribes, though they were here long before anyone else. That much is true. But people were hardly the first beings here, you follow? The truth is much stranger. You ought to be grateful for the sack on your head," he says. "Well. Be back at some point."

The door behind you closes, followed by the shrieking latch and jumble of chains.

Adrenaline thumps in your ears and clouds the persistent droning as you're locked in this structure. You should have made a break for it in the truck. It wasn't moving very fast. Could have hopped out and booked it. Worst case you would have ended up dead in a ditch versus whatever this is. Dead in a barn?

THE PLACE DOESN'T MATTER. WHAT MATTERS IS YOU WERE PATIENT.

You can't speak. You can only answer in your mind and it's like fighting with yourself.

YOU KNOW I'M NOT YOU. WE MET IN THE CELLAR.

Slowly, you walk around the structure to get a feel for the layout. It's small, no larger than a standard tool shed. It makes sense to you that you'd be stashed in something as unassuming as a decrepit shed. You slump to the floor and kick your feet around, but the place is empty. You'd expect nothing less, yet part of you hoped your captors were less intelligent than that. Then again, they didn't pat you down.

You hope Danny was smart enough to keep his phone on him.

YOU DON'T NEED TO IGNORE ME.

You've grown accustomed to the darkness of the burlap bag. So much so, you've neglected to take note of the subtle shift in ambient light flickering in weak tandem with the voice. You scoot backward so you can lean against the wall. As you adjust your position, your bullet belt digs into the small of your back, offering a way out.

You chip your fingernails in the process, but manage to pull a single cartridge from the belt. The belt goes slack and falls from your waist. Using the bullet end of the cartridge, you poke a small hole in the tape, but it's enough to create a weak point. You yank on the tape, but the several layers wrapped around your wrists don't budge.

As you struggle on the floor of the shed, your jeans catch on what feels like the crooked head of a loose nail. Shimmying on your back like a flea-bitten dog, you use the nail to rip through the remaining layers of duct tape and tear your wrists free.

You pull the bag off your head and rip the tape from your mouth, spitting the saliva-soaked sock onto the floor, which bubbles and oozes like gobs of flesh along the far end of the structure. It bleeds into the corners and creeps up the wall. A sangria-purple wave ripples across the topography of the being in a flash. It pulses, breathing new life into the tiny void-like space.

YOU CAN'T IGNORE ME NOW.

Your lungs vibrate as though you're breathing sound, the waves reverberate through your chest.

THE OTHER ONE WAS CORRECT WHEN HE SAID THE TRUTH IS STRANGE, EVEN IF HE'S WARPED THE TRUTH AND MISUSES IT. I'VE WITNESSED COUNTLESS FORMS LIKE YOU COME THROUGH HERE AND THEY ALWAYS MAKE THE SAME MISTAKE. THEY DO NOT LISTEN. THEY DO NOT

WAIT. THEY ARE INCAPABLE OF EMBRACING THE ABYSS. I NEED YOU TO LEAN INTO IT—THIS BLACKENED SPACE OF WHICH YOU'RE NO STRANGER.

Thoughts of Danny flood your focus, but you are reassured he is okay. It's hard to believe, but you aren't sure you have another choice. Tantalized by the being and its promise, you stagger on uncertain strides toward it. You drop to your knees and place your palms onto the aqueous material glinting before you.

LEAN IN.

You listen, pressing your hands into its bulbous flesh. You jut forward, breaking the surface tension, slowly diving through the effluvium and into the abyss.

WHAT A FUCKING DAY YOU'RE HAVING—
GO TO PG 185

CALLING IT A wall feels like a distortion of the truth, but you don't see the point in losing yourself in semantics. Austin offers no elucidation. So, you and the rest of the band are left to wonder what exactly it is that stands before you, radiating bruised hues and exhaling iridescent purple mist into the already muggy cellar of the Cult Road House.

Ryan's the first to ask the obvious, "What the hell is this?"

If he's received an answer, there's no indication, and you consider that the wall has inhaled his question, silencing the sound waves as if they've been spoken into the geometric jutting of acoustic paneling. It isn't a completely ridiculous thought. The atmosphere has shifted since the three of you followed Austin down into the dwelling. The murmuring you heard upstairs has gone quiet, replaced by an overwhelming hum. A buildup of pressure. Your lungs grow tighter with every breath heavy. The dense air plays with your sinuses, confusing your olfactory and visual senses, and causes your brain to draw on some distant memory. Like it's recognizing foreign patterns in your discomfort.

You find yourself echoing Ryan's question, only you rephrase it as, "Who are you?" because you recognize the aberrant structure commanding your attention as a lifeform. If it is merely an object, it's made of alien architecture. Its skin is bulbous and weeps an oily substance that glimmers dully in the insufficient glow exuding from its pulsing, undulating form.

Its response surfaces in your mind in hushed ambiguity, AN AMALGAMATION OF CYCLES.

You're unable to process its answer before Austin speaks. "It's everything we need."

Austin steps intimately close to it and runs his fingertips along its surface, gently as if testing bathwater. The wall reacts to his near-sensual touch by sending a surge of color rippling across its flesh.

He staggers backward.

Danny reaches out to offer support, but Austing shrugs away and says, "I'm fine."

Austin picks up the plastic bag of communion wafers amongst the spent matches and half-burned candles and cigarette butts and bones at his feet. He tosses it back to you, telling you to open it while he continues to knead the wall's flesh.

You puncture the plastic with a fingernail and dig your thumbs into the packaging to widen the hole until you're able to pull a quarter-sized piece of the Body from the bag. All the while, the wall's reply bounces around your head, "An amalgamation of cycles."

The response reeks of enigmatic homily. Holy words spoken by a delusional being to people too damn stupid to grasp. Maybe they just don't like what they hear, so they choose to misinterpret the meaning; feigning ignorance when it comes to taking responsibility. What does that even mean? An amalgamation of cycles. What cycles?

GROWTH-DECAY. REJUVENATION-ENTROPY. EVERY NUMBER OF STATES OF EXISTENCE.

Alpha-Omega comes to mind.

GODHOOD IS A COSMIC OUROBOROS. DON'T OBSESS OVER TRYING TO MAKE SENSE OF SOMETHING AS PARADOXICAL AS SUCH. DON'T MISINTERPRET THIS—I AM NOT A GODBEING. I JUST AM. I AM IN EVERY PATH. IN ALL REALITIES. JUST AS YOU ARE. ONLY I KNOW IT, AND ACCEPT IT. CAN'T SAY THE SAME FOR YOU.

You're drawn toward this being. "Here," you say, handing the open bag to Austin.

His fingertips squelch as he pulls his hand from the wall. A slimy strand of mucus-like substance hangs from his fingers. He places dripping gobs onto four separate communion wafers, balancing them in an open palm, and turns to the three of you. "Come," he says. "Take and eat. The abyss awaits."

PARTICIPATE. EMBRACE THE NEW COVENANT—GO TO PG 187

AUSTIN DIDN'T WANT you to leave. Paranoid. Convinced you would rat him out. Austin never said he started the fire—not even a whisper of admission—and to your knowledge he didn't, but it's hard to ignore the shock on his face when you told him, eyes darting around the room. The sudden focus on you when he asked what your mom said. The eerie eye contact, as if he was trying to read your thoughts.

He stole shit, absolutely. So did you. But Austin had come bursting from the entrance of the church when you ran into him and was nowhere near the semi-trailer where the fire occurred. Still, the room smells like guilt—sweaty, nervous—and the subtlest crack in Austin's voice bounces around the stillness of the room. The worry. Stress. His eyes say *don't say anything*.

"Don't go." And for once, it sounds like a plea, not a command.

You don't give him time to argue, explaining it'd be more conspicuous if you didn't show up, especially after talking to your mom. Call it a gut feeling, but you know your dad knew you were at the church. You can't be certain he didn't see you, or in the very least, saw the van, but you can feel it. He knows.

But you saw something in the church, too. The woodgrain spelling strange words. Your father speaking them like incantations. The mistress.

These are the things you tell yourself as you drive back into town alone in relative silence. You turn the stereo off, your mind too cluttered by the road noise of your tires and the panicked guilt wracking your brain to concentrate on music.

A single SUV marked Fire Marshal and a patrol car are the only remaining emergency service vehicles in the church lot when you arrive. They're parked in a cockeyed formation near the torched semi-trailer.

You park a good sixty yards opposite, wanting to distance yourself physically and mentally from the scene, but the smell of smoke trapped in the air won't let you dissociate.

Your dad waves you down. He's too far away to see the look on his face, but you assume it is detached. Always strong in the midst of catastrophe. His idea of leadership. Your mother is nowhere to be seen, likely comforting the families or holding a prayer session somewhere in the church.

You approach your dad and ask, "What happened?" though you immediately regret it, wishing you could inhale the words back into your mouth. The semi-trailer looks like a half-smoked steel cigarette, dark halfway down its length. Its framing remains intact among the crumbled side panels. It's obvious what happened here.

He ignores your stupid question, instead asking, "Did you see anything? Some of the youth group mentioned seeing your van."

An officer is standing by and tries to reassure you that this isn't an interrogation. That they're just looking for information. Facts—the truth. Yet his presence is imposing and you want nothing more than to dissipate into mist.

"I was here earlier looking for cufflinks," you say. "A friend lost them at the wedding last night."

Your father verifies that the wedding did take place and you sense he doesn't want to relive this morning's disappointment any more than necessary.

"That's it," you say, and your father seems pleased by this.

The fire marshal joins the conversation, speaking of flash points, stating the fire had a single origin, likely from a match or a cigarette, "Arson is highly unlikely. No sign of fuel. Gasoline. Lighter fluid. Full of newspaper like that, the whole trailer was a tinderbox. A tragedy, but seemingly an accidental one. I'll keep you posted, Pastor."

Consumed by relief, you wander away without a word through the water runoff, awash in soot, slicking the pavement. If it weren't for the grimy, gray water speckling your boots, you'd think you were floating across the parking lot. Transcendent.

DRIFT AWAY TOWARD HAPPIER
THOUGHTS—GO TO PG 189

REALITY TRICKLES INTO view with kaleidoscopic vision. It bleeds blurry geometric shapes into ever-changing patterns that eventually blend together into forms resembling human figures. As you come to, you recognize them as Austin and Ryan. Though in your mercurial mental state, they appear like stained glass versions of themselves. Mosaics of humanity.

You rub your eyes.

Austin approaches you in harsh, jagged movements, with a mouth full of triangles as he speaks. "So, how about that shit?"

His words fill your ears like cotton.

You turn and find Danny sitting with his back against the wall, weeping crystal tears. They fall and shatter on the cellar floor.

When you don't answer, Austin simply pats your shoulder and says, "It's okay. Take your time. We'll be back later. I'm glad you took the plunge here tonight. Discovering this on your own was the best outcome."

It's hard to navigate Austin's shift in demeanor. You recognize that your current state of mind is altered, but your memory hasn't evaporated. The two of you just had it out, and it's not like him to swat it away like a swarm of gnats. He must be pleased with himself and how things are going.

You ask, "Outcome for what?"

But by the time the words formulate in your mind and leave your mouth, Austin and Ryan are long gone. Only blurred afterimages of them remain with you. Your words float around the cellar like bubbles, popping letter by letter against the low ceiling. Clouds trail the letters like car exhaust and release the faint aroma of coffee and bile.

THE OUTCOME OF HIS PERCEIVED PURPOSE.

"Which is?"

YOU ALREADY KNOW IT. YOU KNOW HE THRIVES ON CHAOS AND WISHES TO CREATE IT. HIS VERSION OF DISORDER.

"And you are part of it."

OF COURSE. I AM ATAXIA.

"What you showed me wasn't chaos."

PERHAPS NOT FOR YOU, BECAUSE YOU KNOW WHO YOU ARE, BUT WHAT IS MORE CHAOTIC THAN REVEALING TO PEOPLE WHO THEY ARE AND WHAT THEY ARE TO BECOME? SHATTER THEIR ILLUSIONS. BUILD THEM BACK TOGETHER WITH THE PIECES THEY HATE. FOOL THEM WITH THE PARTS OF THEMSELVES THEY BELIEVE TO BE GENUINE, BUT ARE ANYTHING BUT. CHAOS IS TRUTH.

The words, "I don't believe it" swirl around the room. They rain mist like an oil slick onto your face as they pop.

THE THING ABOUT THE TRUTH IS YOU DON'T HAVE TO BELIEVE IT FOR IT TO REMAIN. IT IS IMPARTIAL. YOU ARE A PART OF THIS, NOW AND FOREVER.

You walk over to Danny and sit beside him. He babbles. You wonder what it is that he is saying and what he sees. It can't be worse than the abysmal pit you saw lurking among the reflections of yourself. No matter how many versions you shattered, it was there. This void. This blackened headspace you are all too familiar with. That is the truth you carry with you. You consider none of it is real. That you aren't real.

Danny whimpers, the pile of crystalized tears piling higher and higher in front of him. And there is nothing you can do but ride it out with him.

REAL OR NOT, THIS IS YOUR REALITY— GO TO PG 192

AUSTIN HOBBLES THROUGH the overgrowth to the side of the house. He stops and kicks at the cellar door. "Help me."

Ryan throws the makeshift door open. The corrugated steel rattles the scrap wood it's attached to as it hits the earth.

It doesn't seem possible for Austin to still be standing. The pain he's in must be excruciating, and while he shows signs of agony, there's got to be something beyond shock fueling his stubborn delirium.

Your hand hurts like a bastard and you're giving Austin a couple of minutes tops before you'll drive yourself to the ER to get stitched up. If he doesn't want to join, fine, his arm can rot. You aren't going to risk infection and permanent damage for him. How the hell does he think you'll be able to drum for the gig now? You've always had a weaker left hand. Austin can't help himself but to point it out, too. About how much better your blasts would sound with a stronger left hand. As if you don't know this.

He's lucky this didn't happen a few months ago, when you'd wanted nothing more than to plunge a knife into his thick fucking skull. Tonight's ordeal would have been in self-defense.

You shake the thought loose.

There's no way you could have done it, but you aren't surprised how easily the decision came to Austin. The way he talked in high school. You remember the whispers. The bets. The snide comments from kids who figured he was a moment from snapping and shooting the place up.

It was bullshit, of course. An act. The easiest way to keep people away was for them to be afraid of you. Not let them get close. That's how Austin played things. Made it easier to hate them. Blame them.

So why'd he go after you? Some deep seated resentment? A desperate attempt to get you to listen? His twisted rhetoric worked though, didn't it? Because here you are, following him into a grimy cellar.

The air feels unnaturally thick, even for the cellar of a rundown house. It's too dark to see much, but the floor is riddled with things that crunch beneath your boots. As you follow Austin toward the bleak recesses of the space, light swells as if you've tripped a motion-sensor. The light flits on in a weak but steady violet the color of communion wine. As you walk further into the cellar, you realize the strange color lighting the room is not the result of some shock-induced hallucination, but the mass taking up the entire back wall. It pulses as if breathing. Its flesh is bubbly like lung tissue, and is slicked in a phlegmy substance.

Austin collapses to his knees at the base of the wall. "Trust me."

The rest of the band stands frozen, perhaps in awe, entranced by the oddity. There's a glimmer in their eyes. An intense focus.

A thin sound redirects your attention to Austin. A sound like a butcher knife cutting into raw meat. Quick and wet. His injured arm is plunged elbow-deep into the wall. He scowls, face distorted into a grotesque mask. "Trust . . . me."

The words filter through your mind and it's hard to tell who spoke them. They're offered more like an invitation than a plea, though the way your body is pulled by an unseen tether, maybe it's a command. How can one trust something by force?

And yet, you find yourself yanking the knife from your palm in an agonizing motion and placing your palm onto the wall. You expect pain, given Austin's reaction, but you experience something else. Hardly bliss. It's a unique, near-hyper fixation of understanding—of yourself, your pain—of every cell knitting your flesh back together.

YOU ARE POWERLESS TO WHAT'S TO COME—GO TO PG 194

BLIPS OF HALF recollected images of your first trip to the cellar flit through your mind, repeating on a lazy carousel. They're coupled with bits of broken conversation with the wall and the uncertainty you felt toward this being. Although you were skeptical, you laid into the idea of it, touching the wall, becoming absorbed in its illusory trip.

It feels different this time. The peaceful sensation is absent, replaced by an anesthetized rawness coursing through your circulatory system. It's as though you are aware of every cell and pore and atom and yet, you're uniquely numb.

You consider this is what transcendence feels like. Maybe it's death.

TWO SIDES OF A COIN.

The words tune in and out of your mind like the wall is trying to find your frequency.

You aren't afraid of death, but you aren't sure you're ready to welcome it either. Then again, lying frozen, hallucinating in cold stillness in a cellar is hardly a life. Why would Austin bring you here to die? What good did he think this would do?

YOU MISUNDERSTAND. YOUR FRIEND DIDN'T BRING YOU TO DIE, BUT HE BROUGHT YOU HERE SO YOU COULD TRULY LIVE. TO REACH OUT AND EMBRACE THE ABYSS—AS HE HAS DONE.

It sounds a lot like conversion to you. Austin the evangelist. You'd never thought you'd see the day, and you wonder if Austin sees the irony of it all. That he's become the type of person he's always hated. Makes sense. He's always hated himself the most.

So what's in it for him?

HAVE YOU CONSIDERED THAT DESPITE THE SELF-HATRED AND BRAZEN ENMITY HE HOLDS FOR THE WORLD AROUND HIM—THE WORLD HE

You cannot help that the concept of absolute and unconditional love has been warped beyond recognition. Every relationship has been marred by a twisted definition, built on ulterior motives and transactional promises and frail words spoken by razor-edged tongues.

Austin is hardly the embodiment of selflessness, but you aren't sure you have the mental capacity to argue any longer. The atmosphere around you feels carnivorous, like the air around you is absorbing every particle of your being as you disintegrate on the floor.

You consider the fluidity of bargaining and language and find yourself struggling, reaching out to embrace the wall. Your willingness to step into the abyss is on your terms and no one else's, determining your decision by the two-way nature of a transaction.

You're pulled to your feet as if tethered by puppet strings and led in weightless steps toward the wall. Instinctively, you hold up your hands like bracing for impact or in a subconscious gesture of vulnerability, showing you mean no harm. When your skin meets the wall, its bulbous flesh secretes an oily substance that softens the barrier between the two of you.

You lean into it, breaking the surface tension, and fuse together like melting wax figures. Enveloped by an overbearing warmth, you look around and feel as though you're encased in a lava lamp. Suspended in this dreamlike existence, you drift along the cosmic current as your body is reconstructed.

THIS IS FORMULATED. YOU CANNOT CONTROL THE PAST; YOU CAN ONLY EMBRACE THE FUTURE—GO TO PG 196

YOU ARE SWADDLED in warm, glowing light, soft and pink like epithelial tissue. At first it is overbearing, like standing too close to a bonfire, but the further you wade through the psychedelic mire, the more you acclimate to its womblike embrace. The constant pressure surrounding you relieves the swollen lump on your head and bruised aching from the beating you took. Slowly, you are cognizant of the reality in which you find yourself—one that is outside of your previous conception of the truth.

You hesitate to call it a *portal*, but *doorway* feels too blasé, and *gate* doesn't capture the fluid nature of where you are. *Conduit* is more like it, because despite your ability to effortlessly glide through this space, you are drawn to the voice guiding you, determined and with purpose.

But whose, and to what end?

"I've done what you've asked. I leaned in. I'm here. Now where the fuck am I? Where are you taking me?"

I'M NOT TAKING YOU ANYWHERE. YOU'RE CREATING YOUR OWN PATH. YOU MAKE YOUR OWN DECISIONS. I'VE ONLY HELPED MOVE THEM ALONG, BY TAKING YOU SOMEWHERE SAFE. SOMEPLACE OUTSIDE OF YOUR FRAME OF REFERENCE.

Way to shrug off the responsibility.

"I don't want to be here any longer. I'm done being patient. I need to find Danny and help him." There's a pang in your gut. Legitimate fear masquerading as embarrassment. For what? You shouldn't be ashamed about caring for your friend.

But it's more than that, isn't it?

There's anger and resentment. Hunger and violence. And the void appears to sense this, absorbing it from you.

IS THAT SO? IF THAT'S WHAT YOU WANT, THEN SO BE IT . . .

TRAVERSE THE ABYSS—CONTINUE

You've been wandering through this sherbet hellscape, following the hushed murmurs of guidance through the undreamable abyss.

Swimming through warm currents of celestial viscera, you can't help but ingest gobs of the atmosphere, shocking your system by its intense, but deafening silence. It's the kind of solitude you've always desired, but never considered how maddening it would be. Your tinnitus is muted by the sound of cell growth and the biosynthetic promise you will be a new person again soon, rejuvenated and replaced, piece by piece.

You come across a juncture, marked not by any visual landmarks you're able to perceive, but by the sudden shift in gravity and the sickening pressure threatening to cave in your skull.

YOU'RE ALMOST THERE. KEEP GOING.

Fighting against every instinct to stop and turn around, you continue to push. Light shifts in a grim gradient, darkening as you press onward until a hazy outline becomes visible.

You crawl, nails slashing through the nebulous grime. The space within the contoured shape appears opaque in proportion to the thinning atmosphere around you.

BREAK THROUGH.

Cloudy voices shout familiar curses as you plunge through the membrane, out of the abyss, and into the clammy cellar of the Cult Road House.

You stagger, slipping in the primeval goop sloughing off of you onto the floor.

Ryan helps you to your feet while Austin kicks at the drippings. "Where have you been? Danny called in a panic like . . . fucking five days ago?"

"Where is he?" you ask.

"Thought he was still with you."

YOU HAVE TRAVELED THROUGH TIME. IT'S TIME TO GO FURTHER—GO TO PG 198

YOU SEEM TO suffer the fewest lingering effects of the debased communion in the cellar. Initial confusion which settles into a brief headache for an afternoon. Dehydration. Afterimages of the wall itself, but primarily glimpses into another place your mind typically doesn't have access to. You can't place it. You don't care to try. It's not like it's the first time you've tripped on shit Austin's given you.

There were some clips and phrases of conversation between you and your dad, mostly about an abject future. Yours? His? The world's? It's impossible to discern. The one detail that sticks out is that Marilyn's face was always present in the background, warped into vague, yet familiar geometric planes. You aren't entirely surprised you fixated on your dad and his new apparent affair with Marilyn. Trips always tend to bring the subconscious to the surface, scattering your psychological baggage all over the floor for you to deal with.

Then there were the other conversations. The ones with the wall, or the being that it's comprised of. You aren't sure.

Enigmatic and existential, cryptic and cerebral, and entirely bleak. Mostly in regards to . . . what did it say? Not destruction, but deconstruction. Reducing people to their most base essence. That's what the whole experience was about—and will be about, when Austin holds communion at the show. Whatever it takes to move on from this place. You only hope Waste Doctrine is impressed and that this has all been worth it.

Unable to navigate the come-down brain fog completely, you wander to the van, climb into the driver's seat, and sleep.

✱✱✱

You awaken to Danny opening the passenger's side door. Plastic water bottles crinkle at his feet. "Let's get out of here," he says, his seatbelt clicking into place, punctuating the request.

You start the van and do a lazy U-turn in the grass. As you pull onto the gravel road, you turn the stereo down to ask Danny what he'd seen. Phlegm backs up in your throat, but Danny anticipates your question before you can ask the question.

"I don't want to talk about it."

The drive home is silent. As is the next few days leading up to the gig. No one seems to want to talk much about anything. Nobody but Austin, though you've been ignoring his incessant calls, replying with curt texts.

Ryan only confirms he's hung the gig fliers around town.

Danny doesn't say anything.

Your parents have been curiously absent, which has enabled you to brush up and practice, something that always used to be a ritual for you. Now it's work. A chore.

Perhaps it feels like this because you haven't been performing it correctly—or in reverence for the right audience. You're convinced that will change tomorrow though.

You dismantle your drum set piece by piece, a methodical performance in its own right, and fill the entire rear space of your van. The heat is warp-records-oppressive and even the short amount of time loading your drums leaves you drenched in sweat. There's enough time to clean up before you head out to Cult House to set up for tomorrow, but you ultimately decide against it. Instead, you stuff a bag with some clothes and load as many CDs as you can into banker's boxes. You tear a piece of junk mail in two and scrawl, "Dad's fucking someone named Marilyn," with a Bic pen and shove it in your mom's top dresser drawer. On the other, you write, "Coward," and leave it on top of the Bible on your dad's night stand.

You throw everything you care about into the van and drive to the Cult Road house.

IT TOOK SO LONG TO GET HERE, BUT THIS
IS HOW IT WAS ALWAYS GOING TO BE—
GO TO PG 200

NEWS SPREADS INCREDIBLY fast in your town.

A vigil has been set up for the kid who died and for the healing of the other who was life-flighted to a burn ward out of town. It took a few hours of tearful, guilt-ridden conversations, but eventually it got out that the two of them were hooking up in the paper trailer. From there it was easy enough to say that, if they were having sex, then smoking wasn't a far reach. Didn't help that they found remnants of booze bottles back there too, but you knew as well as most that those bottles could have been from anyone. A couple of them were probably from you.

But small towns love a tight bow on these kinds of things, so it's no surprise that people nod and mutter things like *damn shame* when it's brought up.

You spend most of the week at home while your mom cooks for the families of the victims. Your dad's been busy at the church dealing with insurance. You wonder if Marilyn is there, and if you should tell your mom or not. If it'd matter.

Ryan texts only to say he's hung the gig fliers around town and Danny doesn't say much all week, preoccupied with work.

Austin hasn't said a word.

You are a little shocked by this. Not that you imagined he'd go out of his way to implicate himself, but you'd guessed he'd have bugged you for some of the details, at least. Nudged you about the cops and their questions. If you said anything—and if so, what did you say *exactly*.

You figured he would have asked if you snapped any photos of the remains, too. Shit like that. At this point, it no longer feels like anything was off the table for Austin.

***

When the day of the gig arrives, your mom seems thrilled to find you hauling your drums up the stairs and into your van. She hasn't been excited about your music since you quit drumming for the worship band.

"I hope you have fun," she says, holding the door open for you.

She's weak and worn out. Mentally drained. Alone. You almost tell her she should surprise your dad at his office. Take a break from cooking. Perhaps it's cruel, wishing she'd walk in on him and Marilyn, but maybe it's what it'd finally take. Instead, you say, "Thanks. Should be a good time," and head to Cult House.

The rest of the band's cars are there when you arrive. You pull the van close to the side of the porch to unload. Ryan's smoking on the porch, tapping ash into the fly-infested pile of dried blood when you step out from the van and into the sweltering heat of the afternoon.

"I wouldn't bother," he says as you pull your cymbal bag from the trunk.

There's rapid stomping, then the deafening, explosive crack of snapped wood as Austin and Danny fly through the door in a grappled mob.

"Lying piece of shit," are the first words out of Danny's mouth.

Austin pushes Danny away to take a swing at him, but misses. He overcompensates and throws himself off balance, falling to a knee.

You step between the two. "What the fuck is going on?"

"Lying asshole!" Danny shouts. "Waste Doctrine isn't coming. Probably never was."

Of course. And just like that, all of your hopes begin to evaporate. It feels as if your future is floating away and there's nothing you can do about it. The gig was your chance. What else do you have left?

YOU HAVE YOU. YOU HAVE THE BAND.

Austin rubs at his knee, then stands up. He spits on the ground, a fly's dick from Danny's shoes. "Ran into issues, that's all. Don't come at me with this shit."

"The show is supposed to start in, what—a couple of hours? — and we don't have a headliner and half the fucking town is going to be at the vigil," Danny says.

"We can handle it." It's just like you to take on the burden. "Let's just play the gig solo and see what happens."

"One set. That's all he gets from me. Then I'm done." Danny steps away and wanders into the house.

YOU ARE AT YOUR ROPE'S END—
GO TO PG 204

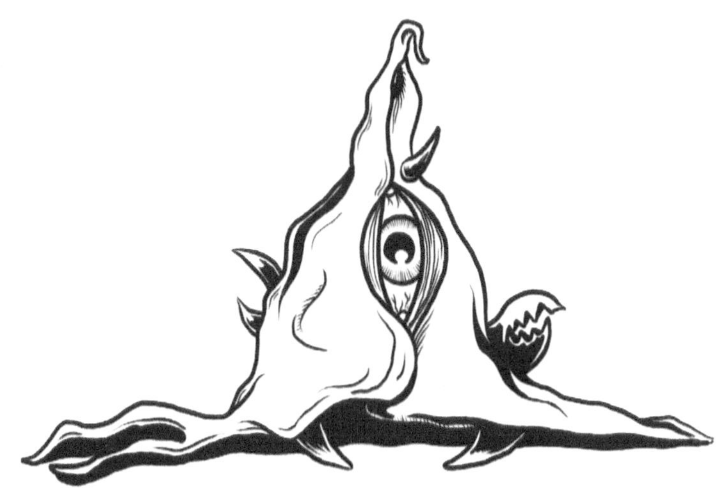

THE CHAOTIC TRILLING of birds greets you as you emerge from the cellar. The sun barely creeps over the horizon, but the humidity is heavy already and a steady wind belches through the grass.

You half expect Austin to be waiting for you, chin in his hands, eager to hear about your psychedelic communion when you come around to the front of the house. Only your van stands alone.

"Want to see what they did to the house?" you ask.

Danny shuffles behind you. "Not particularly." The words are soft-spoken and taciturn. He's been on a dozen trips with you—plenty more without you—and he's usually reserved afterwards. Dives deep into introspection, taking his time to reflect. This—the sullenness—is different.

"That's cool," you say.

"We should leave."

"We'll have plenty of time before the gig to see it anyway."

"No, we should leave. Pack up and go. You've been wanting to leave this shithole anyway, right? I've got the promotion basically in the bag. Work can—they can transfer me. We can room together, at least for a bit."

"Whoa, whoa," you say. "Yeah, I want to leave, but I mean it can wait till after the gig."

He walks away from you as he's talking, "You don't get it. There is no gig." Danny opens the passenger side door and sits, but leaves the door open. "Like Austin said. It's going to be some goddamn ritual."

You join him and start the van, "Are you alright? I'll drop you off at home. Should have plenty of time to get to work, but you sure you've come down all the way?"

"How can't you see it? Those weren't drugs. That thing was alive and that wasn't a . . . a trip or whatever. It was like a fucking *pact*."

The word cements into your brain, disallowing you to formulate thoughts. It rattles around and it eventually trickles into your chest, slowly adhering itself to you until settling into your stomach, an overbearing weight.

***

You dwell on Danny's words until the day of the show—about leaving, about the pact. To whom? The answer is obviously the wall, but it's also a non-answer. Evasive, bordering unreal.

You load your drums and drive to the Cult Road House anyway because you have no other choice. Play the gig, then leave. That's how it's done.

But as you drive up to the house to unload your gear and see Austin and Ryan talking with a trio of ghoulish looking guys in all black and spikes, corpse paint melting in the Midwest heat wave—without Danny—you know the truth isn't that simple.

A beer appears in your hand before you open the back of your van.

"C'mon, come meet Waste Doctrine," Austin says. "I'll help you unload your shit in a bit."

You crack open your drink and try to chase away the heat.

The band introduces themselves, each with a stage name: Null, Blightgod, and another dopey name that dissipates the moment it leaves his black-lined lips. You bullshit long enough to drink your beer and head inside to set up your kit.

You gag at the smell of the stagnant gore coating the walls.

People start to trickle into the lawn of Cult House. Soon, the trickle becomes a crowd. You stare at your phone to check the time, and you acknowledge it's about to be a *show*—and Danny is nowhere in sight.

It isn't fine, but the show must go on—go to pg 209

THERE'S A FUNDAMENTAL shift in you as you pull your hand away from the strange wall. As far as the band is concerned, your hand has been healed. The gash appears like nothing more than a pale stitch connecting your life and heart lines. Even the blood is absent now, your hands washed clean.

But you can feel it—the truth.

You haven't received any sort of good-natured curative procedure. Your wounds were not mended. This was an exchange, and the peculiar deviation within you stretches far beyond temporary disposition. You're bound.

Nothing offered or said, but you agreed to its terms the moment you placed your hand on it. Offer accepted. It's hard to breathe and while your hand doesn't hurt any longer, a chilling sensation numbs your flesh where it's been stitched back together. It bites with a subtle itch.

"I don't know what the fuck this is," you say. "But I'm leaving. If you're riding with me, Danny, now's the time."

He doesn't protest, but he's transfixed by Austin, who looks comatose. His head sags in sleepy prayer, and his body is propped up along the wall.

"I can take you too, Ryan."

He refuses, saying he should keep an eye on Austin. It's a gesture you can respect, but not one you are sure Austin deserves. It was evident Austin knew what he was doing when he brought you down here, and sure, you made the choice to touch the wall, but you can't help but feel he did this in offering. Coerced you to give something away without knowing.

"What do you think it was?" you ask Danny as you turn off the gravel road onto the highway into town.

"You tell me," he says. "You're the one who touched it."

"It was like . . . I don't know, an existential transaction. Only I don't know what I traded. Whatever it was obviously fixed my hand, but it's hard to describe the rest. I just know I feel wrong."

Of all your friends, Danny can understand this with profound certainty, so when he nods along and quits speaking for the duration of the drive, you believe he does.

***

Spending the week holed up in your room used to be the dream, but the encounter with the wall has made it impossible to enjoy or appreciate. It's not your typical bout of depression either. You're used to your brain sabotaging you and this isn't it. This is a shift you can't place, but one you can fight.

You manage to climb from the carpet scratching at your skin and get dressed. Loading the van doesn't take long, but it nearly takes it out of you, especially in the sweltering heat.

Fighting the wind and the desire to swerve into the nearest drainage ditch, you make it to the Cult Road House just in time to see a trio of heavy looking dudes pour out of a Chevy Astro van. Their corpse paint is immaculate, but is going to smudge to shit in this heat.

You kill the engine and wave at the members of Waste Doctrine.

"I'm about to set up," you say. "I'll show you around."

Swarms of flies infest the gloopy pile of blood near the porch. The wind carries the scent of rot in your direction.

One of the band members holds the door as you lug your bass drum up the porch steps. As you walk in, you find an unholy spread adorning the show floor—phrases and symbols painted on the walls. Your father's altar cloth spread across a decrepit table. An offering plate of communion wafers sits on the table, flanked by the candelabras.

And behind the table stands Austin. His left arm is no longer broken and bent, but his skin is pallid and gray. The flesh under his eyes is dark and heavy, carrying the weight of his decisions, showing the pale whites of his nearly colorless eyes.

"Welcome, fuckers," he says. "To Cult House—our inner circle."

AND THE CIRCLE TAKES THE SQUARE
—GO TO PG 213

THE MATERIAL WORLD ceases to exist to you in this moment, though you remain cognizant of its place in the universe while you are contained inside this strange pocket of existence. The being said transcendence and death are two sides of a coin, and here you are seemingly resting some place between the two. A coin balanced precariously on its edge. The gentlest of motions could make it tip one way or the other.

Would you even have a preference?

You suppose you already made the decision during the strange lucid journey into the cellar. Why else would it feel as if you've been reconstructed on the cellular level? You could count every pore on your body. Name each hair. Pick and pull each blood cell out of a line up if you had to.

Much of your memory is retained from the fall, but there are dark spots.

You remember the roof and the blood and the ill-fated practice, but you aren't sure if the rest of the band ever showed up to the Cult Road House to assist you and Austin. Was anyone else around to witness Austin's response? Your hero. Savior.

What of the being? This bizarre wall which exists in the decrepit cellar of an old dead house on the outskirts of a shitty Midwestern town. And what of your fate tottering on the line between this new evolution of you and abeyance?

You know the truth.

YOU'D ALWAYS WALK THROUGH THE ABYSS AND COME OUT FROM IT.

There's a weight tugging at you, pulling you through the being's gelatinous stratum. An image of the coin toppling fills your vision. Before you can see its face, you are squeezed from the wall, not in rejection or rebirth, but a strange confluence of the two.

You slide onto the floor of the cellar, covered in the slimy substance. Glops of it eke from your nostrils and clog your ears. Instinctively, you wipe the gunk from your eyes. Austin sits in silence, surrounded by a circle of candles and wads of regurgitated pages from the hymnal resting in his lap.

"Good, you're alive." His voice is ragged, but playful.

"How long was I in there?"

"Three fucking days," he says. "I'd have left, but you have the keys."

And sure enough, your keys remain clipped to your jeans. "Asshole," you sputter.

"Yeah, yeah," he says. "Drive me home. I'm exhausted. And hungry. Tired of lukewarm bottles of water."

The stereo blares Immortal's *At the Heart of Winter* as you drive into town. The riffs slice through the stifling humidity and you yearn for heavy snowfall.

It seems strange to thank him, given that Austin's antics placed you on the roof in the first place, but you do anyway.

He shrugs it off.

Austin doesn't even ask what it was like in there. You don't have to guess why though. It isn't because he's not curious about it. It's because you're certain he's already experienced it.

"How long have you known about it?" you finally ask.

"I think I always have. If that makes any sense," he says, unbuckling his seatbelt as you pull into his driveway. "And I think you have too, if you're honest with yourself."

He shuts the passenger's side door and slinks off into the garage, as if burdened by an unseen weight loaded onto his shoulders.

YOUR FATIGUE IS IMMEASURABLE, BUT IT
COULD BE MUCH WORSE—
GO TO PG 217

YOU FRANTICALLY EXPLAIN your van breaking down, the kidnapping, and the hooded figures while rummaging through the shed behind the Cult Road House for any sort of tool you can use to enact the pent-up fury ravaging your mind.

"What did they want?" Ryan asks.

"How should I know? Cult shit," you say. "They didn't lay out their plan, but it's safe to say no good is going to come from it. One of them said he had a gun, but I didn't see it. There were three of them. Sounded old."

A hammer calls to you, and you find the one with the sturdiest handle and take a practice swing against a two-by-four. You wedge a rusty flathead screwdriver in your belt for good measure.

"Are we really doing this?" Ryan finds a hatchet on the ground and picks it up, running a finger along the chipped and dull edge.

Austin doesn't take anything, patting his pocket to reassure you he's carrying already.

***

It takes about half an hour of you guiding Austin through the gravel roads, backtracking the trek on the low maintenance road to find your van. It stands, broken down in the distance.

Austin's car struggles on the deeply rutted dirt.

"Kill the lights and stop here. Let's go on foot," you say. "Keep an eye out for movement in the overgrowth."

The three of you skulk across the stretch of road and reach the van unimpeded. You find your phone in the cupholder where you left it, the battery nearly drained. You've missed a dozen calls between the band, and there's a single text from Danny: *Got out, but found me. lots of them*

The van reeks of gasoline and gives you an idea.

"Austin, give me a cigarette." You open the back door of your van and tell the band to take cover in the ditch while you light up, taking in as long of a drag as you can handle. Smoke wafts from your mouth and melds with the night sky. One more drag. Your nerves are hyperactive. Then you flick the cigarette into the van and run.

It doesn't take long for the gas-soaked carpet to ignite, and soon the entire back half of the van is engulfed in flames. You lie as low as possible next to Ryan and Austin, telling them to wait. Be patient, and listen, just as the being told you.

You expect an explosion, but it doesn't come. Not as anticipated anyway. A high-pitched shriek pierces the air as the horn blares. It groans, growing deeper until it's nothing but a warped moan. Then it is nearly quiet. The sounds of flames consuming your van. An organic force feasting, reducing your van to the frame—and two sets of footsteps running toward the inferno.

You whisper, "Don't kill them," as you rise from the ditch, leading the attack.

YOU ONLY NEED ONE TO GUIDE YOU

The voice speaks truth.

Overwhelmed by images of Danny strung up in a shed, tortured and beaten, you're possessed with rage. You swing the hammer, catching the nearest hooded figure in the side of the head. It thuds like an out of tune drum, immediately dropping them to the ground.

You pull the hood off their head and expect to find a scar or tattoo or some arcane marking, but all you see is the plain face of an unremarkable man, blood leaking from the hole you've punched into his skull.

"Sorry, dad."

YOUR THERAPIST WOULD HAVE A LOT TO SAY ABOUT THIS—GO TO PG 221

A SMALL CROWD gathers outside of the Cult Road House. There's hardly any standing room by the time you and the band finish setting up your gear, which is probably a good thing. It'll fool everyone to think it was a packed show. What you call a disappointing turnout, Austin calls intimate. Your drums take up the majority of the back wall near the generator, leaving a corner for Danny to set up his amp. Ryan sets up on the other side of your kit, squeezed in tight to make room for Austin's ridiculous setup.

You knew about the table, but figured it was going to be set up in the gutted kitchen, not in the middle of the makeshift stage. Yet there it sits, draped in the stolen altar cloth, doused in blood. A wooden tithe bowl rests in the middle, though Austin's filled it with the communion wafers, which glimmer, sticky with the substance secreted from the wall. The candelabras flank the bowl, but are currently unlit.

"When do doors open?" Ryan asks.

"Fifteen-ish," Austin says.

Danny starts the generator to do a mic-check. Everyone is going to have to tweak their settings to drown out the noise coming from the generator. Your drums are barely mic'd. The only one is rigged up between your rack toms, but fits the DIY atmosphere Austin's going for.

You? You're just ready to get the show on the road.

"What's your deal?" Ryan asks.

"Don't know," you lie, because how do you explain that the wall stripped all of your enthusiasm not only for the gig, but music in general? That it showed you your future wasted, and fed off of your passion.

Austin covers as many of the windows as possible with scrap

wood to prevent the light from entering into this place. He motions for Ryan to start playing the slow and eerie intro to the set, then kicks open the doors for the crowd to trickle in.

There are footsteps upstairs—the members of Waste Doctrine—who can't even be bothered to watch your set, solidifying everything the wall said to you about your abysmal future if you stick around.

Austin doesn't introduce the band or address the crowd in any way.

Ryan sets the tone with a wicked riff which slowly builds over the course of the song.

The set plays out automatically to a crowd that doesn't seem to register exactly what is happening. There's no room for a mosh-pit to break out, not like you're the type of band to inspire that specific brand of chaos. Instead, everyone quietly nods along. Catatonic. Absorbed.

You've constructed your songs this way intentionally. Each one blending into the next, the transitions marked by Austin lighting a single candle at the start of each song.

The leftmost candelabra is fully lit. Flames flicker and cast shadows on the yellowed grimy wallpaper. Your sticks are balmy in your hands, slicked with sweat as the room temperature steadily rises.

Austin's sharp vocals dwindle, muttering whisper-quiet in prayer, designating the midpoint in your set. As the rest of the band continues to play, he pulls a chalice from beneath the table. He dips his fingertips into it and smears its contents across his face. Then, he takes a communion wafer from the bowl and consumes it.

He carries the chalice around the stage, repeating the process to both Danny and Ryan. When he comes to you, he props a leg onto the bass drum, hand extended into your space. Blood drips from his fingertips onto your snare.

You accept a communion wafer and wait for it to hit.

The crowd lines up, one by one participating in the unholy communion set forth by Austin. His abyss.

***

It starts as a trickle—the disintegration of reality—as the earth groans beneath you. A deep wail from the cellar—in pleasure? Pain?—as the crowd consumes its body.

You start the final song of your set as the floorboards begin to warp and buckle. They ripple like sound waves. Ones that beckon you, but are hard to distinguish from the sick cavorting taking place before you as the showgoers experience what you believe to be truth for the very first time in their lives.

You're surprised that most of them don't turn to violence. Not even elation or ecstasy, but rather something akin to fear. Maybe it's acceptance.

Not Danny though. He does resort to violence.

You see the spark ignite as he removes his bass from around his shoulders, but aren't able to move from behind your drums in time to stop him. Gripping it by the neck, Danny swings his bass like a sledgehammer. It connects with Austin's skull in a sonorous thud, showering the crowd in a spray of blood.

Austin's body drops, dead weight, across the altar, spilling the chalice of partially coagulated blood to the floor along with the fully lit candelabras.

The fringes of the bloodstained altar cloth ignite first.

The cycles of deconstruction unfold before you. Your drums topple over as you stumble around them to stop Danny from causing any further damage. This isn't how it was supposed to go. The wall showed you a future. It was a future of nothing, but not one of destruction. Not one of waste.

Amplifier feedback pierces through the chaos and grates your ears.

The floorboards erupt as Danny douses the room with the gas can. The crowd disperses as quickly as they can, but a wall of fire quickly rises from the floor. Smoke chokes the air from his godforsaken house. Through the smokescreen, you see a trio of ghouls standing at the door, not helping, but watching.

Ryan screams amongst the bedlam to run. Glass shatters and you witness several forms jumping through the front windows. The flames are too high, too hot for you to run through, but there is another way out.

A purple light emanates through the skewed floorboards, reaching out like a distress beacon. You get as low as possible, avoiding the smoke as you pry at the wood. Escape is at your bloody fingertips. You scrape and claw at the deadwood, but are unable to make progress quick enough—until you hear the creak of rotting floorboards. You shove Ryan's amp into the center of the flames, its weight causing the floor to collapse, taking several people with it.

You take the plunge, and jump to the cellar below.

You turn away at the sight of Austin's disfigured form on the floor. Desperate survivors claw at the inside of the locked cellar door, but you know the truth. That true egress stands before you. The wall hums, pulsing a hue like sangria, emitting a smell just as sweet.

You place a hand along the wall and push harder and harder until you break through the membrane and enter the abyss.

END

YOU FOLLOW DANNY into the house as he fumes.

"Piece of shit," he mutters. Danny's visibly shaking as he sets up his gear and has lost his typical meticulous disposition. His bass leans unsteadily against his amp.

You walk through the cramped space and set your cymbal bag down in time to catch his guitar by the neck as it slides off the amp.

"Look," you say. "I know this isn't what you wanted—"

"Me? This isn't about me," he says. "I'm doing this shit for *you*. This whole gig—you rejoining the band, taking over for Toni, you getting yourself out of your parent's house. The possibility of moving. I've been dealing with Austin's bullshit because it's what you wanted. And now I'm wondering why I'm the only one who cares that Waste Doctrine isn't showing. They were supposed to be your ticket out of town. I've got mine."

Danny takes his bass from you and slings the strap over his shoulder.

"I took the promotion," he finally says. He turns away from you and fiddles with the knobs on his amp.

The knobs don't mean anything to you. Nothing seems to, in this moment. You knew his time was running short here, but it takes the air from your lungs nonetheless. You muster a weak, "I'm happy for you," and walk to pull the rest of your drums from the van.

Outside, Ryan smokes alone.

"Where'd Austin go?"

"Inside."

You didn't hear the door, but you can barely hear yourself think right now. The finality of Danny moving kicks at your gut. "Got it," you say. "Can you help me bring the rest of my kit inside?"

It seems pointless to set up your kit, but you do it anyway. There's hardly any room left in the dining room once you set up. Your drums take up the majority of the back wall, leaving only a corner for Danny. Ryan's gear is off to your left, and Austin turned the beat-up table into a makeshift altar.

It's draped in the blood-soaked altar cloth. The communion wafers are spread across the middle of the table, flanked by the candelabras. Scraps paper litter the table. At glance they appear as nothing more than trash, thin scritta paper, bearing the words of scripture, but the squiggling words seem to writhe across the page as if alive. Their unique shapes do not resemble any language you're familiar with. They pulse on the page. You imagine if they could speak, they'd only cry out in pain. They are but smoke. Wisps of cancerous thought. Austin really did intend for this to be as ritualistic as he could make it. You have to give that to him.

Footsteps trudge above you. Austin pacing.

Normally, you'd let him brood after having it out with Danny. He always needs the space, but he doesn't deserve that. Not today. You couldn't give a flying fuck what he needs.

You climb the stairs, frantically rehearsing whatever interrogation you plan to assault him with, but when you find him walking around the abandoned bedroom, bottle of whiskey loosely gripped in his hands, you stop in the doorframe and remain silent.

He takes a long pull and starts muttering under his breath. There's a gilded-edged book in the center of the room. Torn pages are scattered in places across the floor—words squirming across the pages. Austin walks from one end of the chamber to the other, stopping only to pick up a loose page. When he reaches the far end of the room, he crumples the page, puts it in his mouth, and swallows. As he repeats the same steps again, you consider this is not random pacing; rather that he's performing specific instructions.

"Austin," you say.

"Don't interrupt me."

Another few paces taken. Another page consumed.

"What the hell are you doing?" you ask.

"What I have to." His voice is hollow, sullen. "Why couldn't you have trusted me? None of you did, but you especially are responsible. What's worse is, you pretended to care. Like you're doing me a huge favor. As if I *need* you. I don't, and I don't need your pity."

He pulls his switchblade from his pocket and lunges at you.

You barely feel the blade slide into your stomach, mostly registering the weight of his fist wrapped tight around the handle as it hits you. When he pulls it from your flesh, you feel an eruption of agony. The second time the blade slides into you, you feel it. The third time too. By the fourth, there are footsteps clamoring up the stairs, but they sound awfully distant.

Austin's screaming at you, telling you he knows what you did.

What you told the cops.

What you told your dad.

That he knows the *truth*.

Which makes you laugh, because his version of the truth has been the one constant in his life. That is to say, the truth is bullshit. The truth is whatever he wants to believe. The truth is whatever is convenient. Whatever serves him.

The pain is unbearable, but even if you could say what you want to say—that you covered for him, despite it all, you know he wouldn't believe it.

You see a shape like Ryan fall on top of Austin. The knife sliding across the old dead floor behind them. And Danny, he's frantically fiddling with his phone, but the buttons don't seem to want to cooperate. Probably from all of the blood gumming up his phone.

He's telling you to hold on, but there's some kind of static interfering with his instructions. Hold on? Onto what?

THE TRUTH.
Sure, sure. That makes sense. But what if you don't want to? Because the truth seems to be that you're bleeding out in your best friend's lap, and you aren't sure Danny will be able to handle that so well.

You'll be okay, though.

The floorboards seem to be spelling words in the woodgrain, but you can't make heads or tails of what they mean.

LISTEN . . . FOLLOW ME . . .

The heat is unbearable up here, and you slink away on your bleeding belly toward the stairs while Danny and Ryan continue to grapple with Austin.

OUTSIDE . . . TO THE CELLAR . . .

You tumble down the stairs, sliding step by step, trying to focus on the voice in your head. The DMT-addled parts of your brain trying to make death easier on you.

It comes in the form of a bass tone thumping away like a slowing heartbeat.

You make it to your feet and out the door onto the porch. In the distance you swear you can hear faint sirens, but that can't be right.

You'll find me . . .

The heat rushing through your gut lights your nerves on fire and the thought of a cold cellar is alluring. You couldn't care less who or what you'll find down there so long as it's away from this oppressive heat.

The porch railing is doing a lot of the heavy lifting for you, but you manage to lumber along the front of the house and round the corner to where the cellar entrance pokes from the earth like a wedge.

ALMOST THERE . . .

It's strange how at peace you feel, despite the physical anguish consuming you.

As you enter the cellar, you're relieved that the only smell of blood is coming from you and not the sunbaked filth Austin spilled all over the house.

"It's you . . ."

YES.

Before you stands a wall. It pulses a vibrant hue similar to the communion wine your father calls the blood of Christ. A swell of pink like a soundwave ripples across its surface as it speaks to you, asking you to step closer.

You're taken in by the sweet and elusive smell emanating from the wall, and come to the strange conclusion that the smell is its breath, fragrant and welcoming.

You stagger and brace yourself on the wall.

"I know you."

FALL INTO ME.

Its bulbous flesh splits, squelching as your hands push through, breaking the surface tension. You realize you've been here before—not a state of blackened headspace—but a calming abyss. It is right. It is truth.

BUT IT DOES NOT HAVE TO BE THE END, BECAUSE I HAVE SOMETHING ELSE TO OFFER YOU IN DEATH, SO LONG AS YOU ARE WILLING TO SEEK IT OUT— SEARCH FOR D-1 (PG 66)

"CLEARLY HE DOESN'T give a shit about the gig, so let's just move on with it, alright?" Austin stubs his cigarette out in the coagulated puddle of blood near the porch.

"I mean, I don't want to bail on Danny, but Austin's right, ya know?" Ryan won't look you in the eyes. "Doesn't look like he's showing up."

"Can't keep everyone waiting," Austin says. "Especially not Waste Doctrine. We're doing this for them."

Austin lets that hang in the air for a moment.

You hate that he's right.

Danny gave up on the band a while ago. That much is clear with his job, the promotion—the move—everything hanging on the balance. He told you that much. You just didn't want to believe it, but what more proof do you need?

You steal a drag from Ryan's cigarette and hand it back to him. "Alright. Let's do this."

"Fuck yeah. We're true black metal! Who needs a fucking bassist anyway?" Austin says, forming the metal horns with both hands, waving them in your face. "Hold tight. I've got an idea . . . "

***

Ryan heads into Cult House first. Feedback screeches through the uninsulated walls, but quickly fades into a moody riff, distorted and evil as hell.

Austin wanders in next as planned.

Soft, flickering light appears through the window as he lights a single candle on the candelabra. Then, guttural moans eke out of every gap and crack, as if the soul of the old dead house is shrieking. Although, you know it to be an alluring invitation.

You stand at the door with the offering plate, ushering the mass of people into the house. One by one, they drop wads of sweaty bills and pocket change into the bowl.

"Thank you for your tithe," you say as the final few trickle in.

You place the bowl on the makeshift altar Austin created from the dining table. The stolen altar cloth is sopped in blood and swarming with flies.

Ryan begins the next part of the song, building upon the introductory riff. It feels thin without Danny's accompanying bass and you can't tell if the crowd is into it or not, but that's hardly indicative of anything for this kind of crowd. Always the stiff and observant type. Crows on a power line.

Austin continues to regurgitate words into the microphone as you wade through the crowd to take your place upon your throne.

Your sticks feel heavy in your hands.

Ryan turns and faces you as he strums faster and Abyss's intro crescendos, transitioning to the next song.

The leftmost candelabra is fully lit by the midpoint in your set. The energy in the room is palpable. A bleak and disharmonious tension pervades through the crowd, carried by the soundwaves pouring from your instruments.

The room is adequately dark, despite the lingering summer sun. It casts the house in odd shadow and ghostly shades of gray that deceive your eyes into seeing Danny through the smoky haze.

It nearly causes you to drop a stick, but you're able to regain control as the tempo naturally slows to a suspended guitar section, kicking off Austin's wayward intermission.

It's uncanny the way he lures the crowd to come forward to perform his rite without saying a word. He begins by lighting another candle. Then, dunking his fingertips in a chalice of blood, he presses a finger onto the foreheads of the willing and offers them each a communion wafer soaked in the wall's secretion.

Saving the band for last, he dips his entire hand into the chalice and places a bloody handprint across both your and Ryan's faces. Last, but not least—your unholy communion.

The effects of the substance hit you during the final song.

Each drum stroke is like hitting your sticks against wet cement. Waves ripple in concentric circles on your snare and your senses quickly become acutely sensitive. An outrageous stench hits your nostrils and causes you to shower your toms in puke.

There's no way to tell if the crowd is reacting to you or any of the other confused and erratic behaviors happening in this moment as they succumb to the unnerving reality presented to them by the strange communion. You wonder what it is they see, and if it is truth.

Austin hoists the chalice high and ends the set by dumping it over his head, his hair chunky with partially clotted blood. He faces you and props a knee on your bass drum. His face is hollow. He takes in a lungful of air. Strings of blood sputter from his mouth as he breathes out. "Holy shit, that was incredible," he says, continuing on about Danny and how you never needed him anyway. "*This* is Abyss!"

It was a great show, but it still felt thin. Never mind that Danny's role in the songwriting has always been integral to the band. You don't want to spoil the evening, but you're wrapped in the truth. Consumed by it. You stand and step out from behind your drums. "I need a drink," you lie. You just can't stand to be in here right now. The whole house seems to be closing in on you. Feels like there are eyes watching you—and a voice guiding you.

COME TO ME . . . TO SEE THE TRUTH . . .

Almost catatonically, you amble out of the house and toward the cellar. The grass around the entrance is matted. Bloody. The door is closed, but unlatched. Flies swarm as you open it.

You descend.

There's a paralyzing stench. A sledgehammer to the nose. It's too dark to see anything with any clarity and you aren't sure you can trust what your eyes see anyway, the way your brain is addled by substances.

THE TRUTH.

You trudge closer.

Danny lies on the floor, his stomach blooming with viscera. A knife clutched in his hand.

"No no no."

THE TRUTH IS NOT ALWAYS AS PRESENTED.

"Holy shit." Austin's voice is quiet behind you. "No way he finally did it."

You fall to your knees beside Danny, tears falling like crystal shards onto his warped body. There's no way he did this.

Austin skirts around you, a void-like expression in his eyes. He offers no words of comfort, which isn't terribly surprising. But it's his hollowness that gets to you. His lack of shock at seeing your friend mutilated on the cold stone floor. His knife in Danny's hand.

It's like he didn't bother to hide it, like he—

WANTED YOU TO KNOW? SO YOU TWO CAN HAVE SOMETHING TOGETHER. SOMETHING THAT IS REAL.

Guilt surfaces, remembering his pleas to leave town. Your reluctance to until after the gig. He wanted out, but not like this. You're sure of it.

You don't need to ask, but you do: "Why?"

Maybe he knew about the promotion. The move, and your part in it. Maybe Austin just felt like it.

"You only ever cared about him," Austin says. "Despite me always being here. It was always him. And he was holding you back."

"That's not true."

"Where have you been the past year? Huh? Where the fuck have you been?"

"I'm still here, aren't I?" You dwell on his jealousy. The shallowness of it all. A child breaking something so no one else can have it.

You slide the knife from Danny's fingers and wait for Austin to come closer.

Reality drifts in and out, as does the knife. Blips of time and blips of blood splatter the cellar of the Cult Road House. Above you, Waste Doctrine begins their set as Austin twitches on the floor. Double kick pedals thrum as quickly as your heartbeat, while discordant guitar riffs battle with the vocalist. The bass line above is thick and nearly lost between the rumbling of the crowd.

Danny's words about the pact surface to the forefront of your mind. Maybe he was right. That by partaking, you'd bound yourself to it. To this place. So be it.

You place the knife in Austin's hand, then grab Danny under the armpits and drag him toward the wall. It glimmers in a peculiar sheen of purple. Dirt and gravel grind beneath your boots as you lug Danny closer and closer. Austin chokes, his breathing irregular. His head turns toward you and falls slack, from gravity or yearning, you'll never know. His desires are not your responsibility. You back into the wall, pressing all your weight into it until you break the surface, entering the eternal crushing heat of the abyss.

END

AUSTIN'S SET UP the table in a way that leaves you with hardly any room to set up your drums. Your kit ends up wedged into a corner and doesn't give Danny much space for his amp between your kit and the generator.

You should have figured as much, given the presentation of the table—Austin's altar. It was always going to be the focal point of the gig. His plan all along.

It doesn't take long for the rest of the band to set up their gear and do a quick mic-check before letting the crowd gather on the overgrown lawn into the house. As rehearsed, Ryan and Danny begin the introduction to the first song of Abyss's set. Ryan plays an eerie, moody riff while Danny follows his lead.

You tap single strokes on the bell of your ride cymbal.

Austin goes off script though, muttering unintelligible words. Cries of agony. Noises gurgle in his throat in erratic phrasing. Strange syllables.

He keeps the mic gripped tight in his good hand. A curtain of hair hides his face, blocking him from the world as he performs.

People steadily flood into the cramped house from outside until there's no space left. The occupancy is easily over fifty by now and they keep elbowing in. There's a sharp crack of glass toward the front of the house where someone has shattered the window, their hand balled, wrapped in a T-shirt.

You stand to see what's going on, but it's nothing more than the kid giving the crowd gathering on the porch a place to peer through to see your set.

Ryan picks up the tempo, building on the riff.

Danny follows, purposefully playing slightly off time, creating a disjointed layer to the transition.

It's your turn to come in with single rolls on your crash cymbals. As the sound crescendos, Ryan switches the chord progression, ushering the band into their next song in a seamless transition.

Austin denotes the song change by lighting the next candle on the leftmost candelabra. The brass candle lighter smokes like a weak cigarette as he puts it out with his tongue.

You expect to play sloppier than you do, given the recent hand injury, but it doesn't seem to affect your playing. Your blast beats sound clean—not that anyone would notice with much scrutiny because your kit is barely mic'd.

You hate to admit it, but Austin got a lot of things right this time around. The members of Waste Doctrine came down the stairs during the second song and have been watching the set. They loom in the back like shadows on the walls. Ghouls haunting the Cult Road House.

Austin's vocals become quieter and quieter, yet remain frenetic in wicked babbling, bringing Abyss to the midpoint in your set. The guitars slow down. The bass moves into a suspended section, while you all but stop playing—only running the tips of your sticks to click and clack against the antlers of a deer skull Austin propped between your rack toms. Chilling bone chimes.

Austin hoists a chalice into the air, signaling Waste Doctrine to come forward as your honored guests. They wade through the bodies until reaching the altar. Austin dips his fingers into the chalice and smudges a bloody fingerprint onto the ghost-white corpse paint on their foreheads. He then offers them communion.

They take and eat.

Austin steps back and performs the same rite to you and the rest of the band. Then, he takes the chalice and drinks from it. Blood drips down his chin and onto his clothes.

The crowd eats his performance up and begin to call out to participate.

"Are you willing?!" He shouts.

The roar back a resounding yes.

"Then step forward and do what people do best . . . consume!"

One by one, people step forward and are converted from crowd to congregation.

Austin's finally becoming the god he's always seen himself as, and when communion is over, he shouts, "Time to worship!"

By the final song of your set, the hallucinatory properties begin to hit you and you're becoming increasingly sensitive to the congestion riddling the Cult Road House. It feels airless. The scorching heat is broiling the place.

You feel trapped.

Beads of sweat pour from your face and puddle onto your snare. Each hit resembles rain falling onto a pond. The clanging of cymbals pierces your ears in excruciating waves. Every hit on your kick drum vibrates up your calves and into your stomach.

Your heart pounds against your ribcage like it's forcing its way out.

Austin hoists the chalice into the air once again and dumps it over himself as the final song comes to a close.

Tinnitus ringing fills the suddenly quiet space, but is interrupted by a chaotic shriek among the crowd. You stand on your drum throne to get a better vantage point, but you don't see what's happening until it's too late.

A kid in the back—the one who broke the window—grips a crescent moon hunk of glass, shouting, "Demons!" as he sticks one of the members of Waste Doctrine in the throat. He's immediately pulled to the ground, but he takes the jagged glass with him.

Blood gushes from the band member's throat, sending Cult House into bedlam. There's a chain reaction of vomiting. People slip and slide in all of the fluids and viscera coating the floor in the mass exodus of the crowd fleeing the scene. The biggest member of Waste Doctrine has his hands wrapped around the throat of his dying bandmate. If you didn't know any better, it would look like a strangulation. The remaining member pulls a knife of his own and corners the kid who stabbed his friend.

You try to yell, "No!" That it was an accident. It's the drugs. Whatever fucking substance oozes from the basement, but screams reverberate across the old dead walls of the house, swallowing your pleas.

Smoke begins to cloud the room and you think maybe hell has finally opened up, but you know that's just the drugs talking too. The smoke emanates from the candelabras, which have been knocked over during the chaos, and have lit the altar cloth on fire. It's spreading slowly toward the dry wallpaper and along the sapless, unfinished floorboards.

It's so, so loud.

But it quickly becomes quiet when, in one swift motion, someone knocks into your drumkit, sending you flying from your precarious perch, causing you to connect head first with the steel frame of the generator.

***

"C'mon, we have to go," Danny says.

You try to answer, but your words are too thick to fit through your lips.

"I'm not talking to you," he says. "Ryan, hurry the fuck up. Ditch your guitar. We don't have time."

You come to, slung over Danny's shoulder. He carries you through the inferno of the Cult Road House, over bodies and blood and remnants of stolen church paraphernalia. The anarchic disorder follows the crowd outside, but dwindles as car after car pulls out onto Cult Road. Gravel dust joins the smoke of the burning house. Sirens blare in the distance.

"Where's Austin?" you ask.

"Ryan said he bailed already," Danny says, still carrying you through the crowd.

You crane your neck and see he's taking you to your van.

"Gotta take your van. I dropped my keys in the house," he says.

Sure enough, yours jangle against your thigh, still clipped to the belt loop of your jeans.

"I'm driving though," Danny says, setting you down next to the van.

You hand him the keys and hop in the passenger's seat. You stare into the rearview mirror as Danny pulls away from the house and you swear you see Austin, drenched in blood, walking into the cellar of the house on Cult Road as if descending into a grave.

END

THE DAY OF the show, you pull up to the Cult Road House just in time to see Danny soar through the front door. Wood splinters as the door is ripped from its hinges. Austin soon follows him onto the porch and looms over top of Danny.

You throw the van into park and rush toward them.

"All of this," Austin holds his arms out, wide as Christ on the cross. "For fucking nothing!"

Austin crouches, getting into Danny's face.

Sweat drips down your back. Your heart pumps. If it weren't for Ryan running out onto the porch from inside, you weren't sure how you'd handle this. But with the help, you jump the porch stairs and help Danny to his feet before Austin can hit him while he's down.

"Whoa, whoa," you say. "What's going on?"

Ryan stands behind Austin and motions not to say anything. Fucking coward.

"Dipshit didn't get the generator," Austin says. "Now we have no gig. Which starts in a couple of goddamn hours!" He kicks at the mangled storm door on the porch. His steel-toed boots leave a mass dent in the center of it.

"What happened?" You pull Danny back a few steps to put some distance between them, anticipating Austin to lose it, and step into the newly created space on the porch.

"I couldn't get it," Danny says, his tone of voice impenitent.

"Couldn't or wouldn't?" Austin cracks his fingers.

"Does it really matter anymore?" Danny shakes loose from your grasp and brushes dust from his clothes.

"What the fuck does that mean?" It's Ryan's turn to enter the fray.

Danny's silence may as well be admittance.

You almost join in, echoing the question—why?

BUT YOU ALREADY KNOW WHY, DON'T YOU? DEEP DOWN YOU WANTED THIS OUTCOME TOO. IT'S WHY YOU FELL OFF THE ROOF. A SIMPLE MISSTEP, A BELIEVABLE ACCIDENT. ARE YOU GOING TO TELL THE TRUTH?

You place a hand on Ryan's chest as he lunges at Danny. "Back off, dude. Like you're any better."

DEFLECTING? THAT'S DISAPPOINTING. YOU WILL HAVE TO CONFESS AT SOME POINT, YOU KNOW?

"You didn't want to play the gig anyway. Threw a tantrum at practice. Being a dickhead. You can't let anything go. You bottle everything up and then bitch about it later. Then you finally say something and it ruined practice." You push Ryan back. Just a little shove, but it's enough he slips on the storm door, and breaks the window behind him.

"Asshole." Ryan twists, showing a gash in his T-shirt.

"We worked that out," Austin says. "So what's your fucking problem?"

YES. WHAT IS YOUR PROBLEM? NO. YOU AREN'T READY TO SPILL YET. I CAN TELL.

"All of this is my fucking problem. This gig. This town. The band. My parents. This fucked-up house. Everything is my fucking problem!" You grab a hold of the storm door and heave it off of the porch into the dead grass. You breathe. "I am my problem."

Relief floods your body at this confession.

"I allowed myself to fall." You aren't looking at them, still staring beyond the house. All you see is the browning death of the prairie grass. The fields of emptiness. Loneliness. Nothing on the horizon. An empty life. Void of purpose and meaning. "I hate this. And it feels like there's nothing I can do about it."

RETURN TO THE ABYSS.

There's a hand on your shoulder. You turn, expecting Danny, but it's Austin who's standing next to you.

HE DID SAVE YOU, AFTER ALL.

"You've got to be joking," Austin says, and starts to laugh. "I can't believe this shit. We all hate this place so much. Can't stand being here, yet we spoiled everything. Dipshit didn't get the generator. Other dipshit tried to self-sabotage himself out of the band . . . You, out of . . . everything."

AND WHAT ABOUT HIM . . . WHAT DID HE DO?

"And what about you?" You ask.

"Nothing." Austin shrugs. "Everything."

ALWAYS SO CRYPTIC.

"Didn't talk to Waste Doctrine. They aren't coming." Austin pats you on the back and turns toward the rest of the band.

"Do you ever feel like this place is keeping us here? That no matter what we do, we're bound to it somehow?" Ryan's lit a cigarette.

"I hate this place," Danny says.

"And this fucking town." Austin bums a cigarette.

A thought trickles into your mind, "So let's do something about it."

DON'T.

You don't listen.

***

You've never heard a house groan before. Not like this. As if it were alive, and you've been swallowed, and you're ripping it apart from the inside out.

The random assortment of tools from the shed out back serves as your weapons of choice. Hammers to obliterate the plaster walls, something you take great pleasure in doing.

Danny takes a crowbar to the windows, decorating the floor in a mosaic of shards, while Ryan repaints the walls with buckets of blood. He coats himself in the process.

You all do.

Austin grabs a candelabra in each hand, leaning in to light each candle with his cigarette. "It's time to light our church on fire."

SUCH POINTLESS DESTRUCTION. SUCH WASTE.

You follow Austin upstairs, tearing through the walls a swing at a time. Opening the Cult Road House. Leaving gaping wounds, exposing its dry dead bones underneath.

PITIFUL.

The gilded tome that saved your life sits on the nightstand as if it were never moved. Its pages pristine. Not a single one ripped from the binding. Its spine perfectly straight. Uncracked.

I WILL JUST REGENERATE AGAIN. I ALWAYS HAVE. I ALWAYS WILL.

The pages tear so smoothly, thin, and crinkling like tissue paper. You stuff the crumpled pages into gaps in the floorboards and in the windowsills and in the gashes you've carved into the walls for Austin to ignite.

You can't make out what he says, but Austin mutters as he lights each and every wad of paper. A final ritual. Funeral rites.

The four of you scramble out of the house, your clothes bloodstained, dripping sweat.

"One more thing," Austin says.

ONE MORE VISIT TO THE ABYSS.

The cellar door is pried open. A mouth to hell. You descend the stairs one by one. The flames have begun feasting on the house and you know there isn't much time. Wood cracks, above as the floors catch fire. Smoke seeping through the cracks, threatening your vision. Waiting to steal the air from your lungs.

Austin pulls his knife from his pocket.

DO YOU THINK I CAN TRULY FEEL PAIN? DO YOU THINK THIS WILL MATTER AT ALL IN YOUR INSIGNIFICANT LIFE?

"To remember it's possible to kill gods." Austin plunges the knife into the wall, hacking hunks of its purple flesh—one for each of you—as the abyss pulses violently.

It exudes an acrid stench. The meat-like flesh squishes in your grip. Wobbles, glowing ominously as if still alive, despite being filleted off its body.

You aren't sure what to do with it. You aren't sure you want it.

I WILL ALWAYS BE A PART OF YOU.

The four of you ascend the cellar stairs, the house ablaze, and revel in the aftermath of your shared catharsis. The Cult Road House coughs flames and weeps smoke, yet it remains. You wonder if it always will. The moment lasts as long as you need it to, and one by one, you leave this place behind for good.

END

YOUR SENSES CURDLE, awash in filthy thoughts and rotten realizations that your dad is a part of this—whatever this is. And worse, that he'd have known this was your van and knew you were coming. He'd kicked you out of the house to fend for yourself and now this? And what about your mom? What does she know about all of this?

You're pulled from your thoughts and to the grisly reality bleeding out at your feet, and the other hooded figure sprinting down the road.

"We've got to follow them. It's our quickest way to find Danny, otherwise we'll be out here all fucking night trying to find where they took him." You stand, not bothering to check your dad's pulse. You know the truth.

Ryan runs after the figure without hesitation, an excited dog eager to hunt.

Austin walks over to you and says, "Sorry," then disrobes your dad, balling the black fabric in his arms.

You think you see where he's going with this and don't argue. Instead, you slip the hammer through your belt and follow Ryan toward the trail of dirt dusting the sky, leaving your dad and the billowing smoke behind. The wind picks up, blowing embers into the drought ridden grass.

Ryan's put a decent amount of distance between you, but he seems to be gaining on the other robed figure.

Winded, lungs burning, you do your best to yell, "Just follow," but your words are strangled, seemingly unable to penetrate the humidity choking the atmosphere.

Two more hooded figures rise from the ditch, flanking Ryan, and rush him. They don't seem to notice the hatchet at his side, and one of them catches the blade in the ribs. They collapse onto the road, but the other figure pulls Ryan to the ground and makes repeated violent motions which punctuate Ryan's cries until he quits.

The figure is lost in fury and won't quit pummeling Ryan's body.

Austin reaches him first and doesn't hesitate to stick his switchblade into the back of Ryan's killer. The attacker groans and rolls off Ryan, whose face is beyond destroyed. Austin slices at the attacker—motions not meant to kill, but meant to inflict pain. He slices at his face and chest and hands and any piece of flesh he can get at.

When the attacker falls, Austin kicks him in the head over and over with sickening thuds. Then he leans down, nose-to-nose, and screams unintelligibly in his face. Spittle drips from his mouth. He then presses the attacker's forehead back and slits his throat.

In the distance, headlights flash, then remain on. Their halos grow larger as they approach you.

Austin faces you, doused in blood. He points at your dad's robe he dropped to the ground, "Put it on, quickly. Follow my lead."

***

As the truck approaches, you pull the hood down to obscure your face as best you can without being too conspicuous. You've bound Austin's hands loosely with zip-ties you found on Ryan's killer.

The truck stops.

Neither of them gets out, but the passenger rolls down the window and asks, "What the fuck happened here?"

You don't want to speak and are grateful that Austin does, "Pretty fucking obvious, don't you think?"

"Throw him in the back of the truck," the passenger says. "Make sure he doesn't go nowhere."

You sit with your back to the cab while Austin lies curled in the back of the truck. The driver turns around on the narrow road and drives away. It hurts to leave Ryan behind like this, but what choice do you have but to listen to Austin weep while you watch your friend's body shrink along the glowing band of orange forming on the horizon?

You recognize the shed coming into view as the truck turns off the road and into the pasture. You're jostled as they drive over the rough terrain, past the shed toward a barn about a hundred yards off. "Get ready," you whisper to Austin.

He slips his hands from the loose zip-ties and slides his knife into his palm.

To your surprise, the driver doesn't kill the engine when you reach the barn. He rolls his window down to smoke and allows the passenger out. The figure walks to the back of the truck and yanks the tailgate open. As planned, Austin sticks the figure in the throat while you jump out the side of the truck and obliterate the driver's nose with the hammer. You pry the door open and pull him from the seat onto the ground as he chokes on his lit cigarette. His teeth scatter like gravel with every hit you land. Doesn't take more than three for him to quit making noise.

A voice comes through a handheld radio from the cab of the truck, asking how things are going. You recognize the voice as your captor from the other night. You grab the radio and make your voice as nondescript as possible, only saying, "Affirmative."

There is no plan from here. Just get Danny out.

When the barn doors slide open, you push Austin inside.

The place is lit by dim box lights. Cameras stand on tripods in various positions around the space. All point toward Danny, who lies on a table in the center of the barn, surrounded by three hooded figures.

You push Austin along and mutter, "Found another."

The shortest figure of the group walks over to you. Despite the hood obscuring her face, the uneasy glow of the box lights illuminates enough to reveal your mother's face. Her stilted gait would have given her away too. You wondered when she'd show up, because if your father was involved, she was bound to follow. Their marriage was like that. Bound in order. Obedience. Blind and unwavering faith in one another.

You figure if you can see her, she can see you—that she knows the truth—but it's confirmed when she says how disappointed in you she is. And the familiar sting as she slaps you across the face.

"How'd you know?" you ask.

"A mother always knows her child."

The irony doesn't escape you. Neither does the slight movement beneath her robes, and your only response is sinking the claw-side of the hammer into the side of her skull. A spray of blood douses Austin. There's a *thud* as a handgun falls from within her robes and hits the ground. She soon follows.

One of the cultists draws his gun and points it your direction. He pulls his hood down, presumably to get a better line of sight, and you see his nose, bandaged and bruised from where you head-butted him the other night. A cop, too. A member of both of your dad's congregations.

You expect him to shoot and kill you where you stand, but you don't expect Danny to sit up from the table, moving the gun to the side, "No," he says. "You'll ruin the shot."

The room folds in on itself in strange tunnel vision. In your periphery, you notice every camera in the barn is marked by a single red dot.

Past conversations flood your mind. Danny wanting to go into film. His penchant for the occult—his interests delving deeper into anything Austin's or the rest of the band's. The truth of it all being he's always walked the walk and kept quiet.

You puke on your mother's body, the realization of Danny's set-up too much to stomach, and wonder how long this has been going on. Your parents. The house on Cult Road. Everything. All deception.

Danny lies back down and says, "Action."

"They killed Ryan, you fucking asshole." Austin approaches Danny, keeping his eyes trained on the guys with guns. It doesn't take long for Austin to snap, though, and in a moment he's all over Danny. He holds him down with one hand while he wails on Danny's face. And it's the strangest thing.

Danny lets him.

He holds a hand up toward the gunman. A single finger, telling them to hold off. The cultist with the gun aims at Austin, but doesn't make a move while the other starts to round the table. You stare at the hammer wedged into your mom's skull and the pool of blood and vomit slowly forming around her.

WAIT.

Nerves vibrate your body.

Austin's outburst is over, leaving Danny with a web of blood drizzling down his cheeks and into his mouth while he remains calm amidst the violence.

The other cultist approaches you slowly.

BE PATIENT, the voice guides you.

When the cultist gets within arm's reach, the voice says, NOW. You plunge the screwdriver into their eye.

Austin follows suit and swipes at the guy with the gun. He aims at their wrist and connects just enough to make them drop the gun.

The two of you run, knocking over cameras and hot lighting equipment in your wake.

There's a shot, then two, then three. On the fourth, Austin howls and hobbles.

When you exit the barn, smoke layers the air. Sirens shriek in the distance. It's only a matter of time before EMS finds the trail of bodies and makes it this direction.

The truck is still running, spewing exhaust into the air. Austin climbs in the passenger seat as you kick it into drive and send dirt and gravel flying. You grab his collar and pull his head down as bullets clink against the truck.

Then you hear the cop's voice come across the scanner rigged to the truck's dashboard, telling EMS about you two—murder suspects fleeing in a stolen truck.

The truck rumbles through the pasture, your foot flooring the gas pedal.

Your eyes focus on the small dilapidated box before you. The shed. Your escape.

YES, COME TO ME. FIND SOLACE IN THE ABYSS.

The shed becomes larger, the truck careening through the pasture, as you speed toward it. You keep both hands on the steering wheel to fight the jerking truck and uneven earth.

Austin groans in the passenger seat, a hand gripping his leg.

Figures loom in the rearview mirror in chase, but you've put enough of a distance between you, it feels okay to finally slow down.

You park parallel to the shed, lining your door up with the entryway of the shed as best as you can. Kicking your door open, you create a barrier with the truck door. Any added layer of protection is worth taking at this point. Bullets hit the dirt around you. Shots crack the sky.

You pull Austin through the front seat of the truck, despite his protests.

"Stay low." You sling an arm around his waist to help stabilize him.

Upon entering the shed, the floor welcomes you with an alluring pulse of warm light. The lavender wave is comforting and you reassure Austin, "Things will be okay, trust me."

HE HAS ALWAYS TRUSTED YOU, YOU KNOW?

Austin is putting more of his weight onto you.

IT IS NOT AS YOU ENVISIONED, BUT IT WILL BE OKAY. AT LEAST FOR A WHILE.

He is relying on you.

HE ALWAYS HAS RELIED ON YOU, AND I AM HERE FOR YOU, TOO. I WILL SUPPORT YOU. LEAN ON ME.

You guide Austin into the wall first and follow, leaning into the wall until you breach its surface, leaving this shithole town behind in some manner of speaking. You're encased in hallucinating warmth as if climbing into the womb. It's gentle and quiet. Nothing is overwhelming in this moment as you allow yourself to drift along the cosmic current into the abyss.

END

ACKNOWLEDGEMENTS

I am eternally ~~bound~~ grateful to Alex and Matt for ~~sitting me down and scaring the shit out of me while I nervously pitched them~~ believing in me and this book. Their editing and artistic vision has been integral to this. Their hype and support of all the weird shit ideas I've had throughout this process. All of it. Thank you. Let's hear it for Echo Echo, yeah? This cover is the most bonkers thing ever and I don't think anyone understood the assignment more than her. Thank you for making this thing look so cool. Of course, my writing group for all of their support along the way: Brian, David, Lauren B., Lauren C., Matthew, Paul, Sam—our lurkers, Rob and Mason. Writing is hard and your support means everything. My new writing buds, Mike B. and Cam, too. Support is everything in the writing world. Thank you.

Thank *you—yes you—*for making the choice to pick this book up and fall into the abyss. And hey! In section 36, we asked you to make your own contribution to the lore of TRVE CVLT. We'd love to see what you came up with; please tag us @TenebrousPress on social media with pics of your mad ravings.

More thanks:

My family for a million reasons, but my mom for instilling a love for books and reading at a young age. My dad for embodying work ethic. Mira for always encouraging my writing. John for the love and support, getting into and out of trouble (including escaping our own cults), and for all the moshpits and gigs. Concert buddies new and old: Matt, Beau, Trevor, Steve, Austin (sorry for the common name, I know you aren't this big of an asshole. Just coincidence), Ryan, Autumnal Michael, Emily, Amy. All the gigs. I could go on. Adrien for watching grainy black metal documentaries on YouTube all those years ago. PJ, you asshole, for convincing me all those years ago to be a writer. Now look what you've done. The Game Dads: John, Kyle, Dan, Greg. Everything—all of you have been a part of this. Thank you.

Lastly, for Nicole and Clover, and all of the love, patience, and endless support. The missed walks. Sneaking into bed after late nights of writing. The cold dinners. The walls covered in sticky notes. I love you most of all.

CONTENT WARNINGS

Being a work of mature Horror, a degree of violence, gore, sex and/or death is to be expected.

In addition, **TRVE CVLT** contains scenes of

Religious Trauma
Suicide
Infant Death (Discussed)
Kidnapping & Restraint.

Please be advised.

More information at
www.tenebrouspress.com

ABOUT THE CONTRIBUTORS

Michael Bettendorf (he/him) is a writer from the U.S. Midwest. His short fiction has appeared in Drabblecast, Sley House Press, and elsewhere. He works in a high school library in Lincoln, Nebraska–a place he tries to convince the world is too strange to be a flyover state.

Echo Echo is a Portuguese artist and a proponent of *horror vacui*. She immerses herself in individual pieces for up to a year at a time and renders in extreme detail. Echo also performs in multiple bands, finding equal freedom in expressing herself through music as she does through illustration.

Matt Blairstone (he/him) is a writer, editor, artist, indie comics creator and the publisher/founder of **Tenebrous Press**. He lives in Portland, Oregon. Sleep is folly.

Grab another Tenebrous title!

Grab another Tenebrous title!

TENEBROUS PRESS

aims to drag the malleable Horror genre into newer, Weirder territory with stories that are incisive, provocative, intelligent and terrifying; delivered by voices diverse and unsung.

NEW WEIRD HORROR

FIND OUT MORE:

www.tenebrouspress.com
Social Media @TenebrousPress

www.ingramcontent.com/pod-product-compliance
Lightning Source LLC
Chambersburg PA
CBHW032249310726
48973CB00008B/2351